A DETECTIVE MAIER NOVEL

"The narrative is fast-paced and the frequent action scenes are convincingly written. The smells and sounds of Cambodia are vividly brought to life. Maier is a bold and brave hero."

Crime Fiction Lover

"This is noir at its grittiest, most graphic best. There is a lush complexity in the narrative that Mr Vater has brought us readers. To say this was a historically laden story is to sell it short. We are transported into the world of Cambodia, and quite possibly one that most of us will never see in real life. The magic, the awe, the mystique and mystery all accompany the depth of characterization."

Fresh Fiction

"*The Cambodian Book of the Dead* is an enigmatic, unsettling thriller that never lets you get your balance."

CheffoJeffo

Also by Tom Vater

The Cambodian Book of the Dead
The Devil's Road to Kathmandu
Sacred Skin

TOM VATER

THE MAN WITH THE GOLDEN MIND

EXHIBIT A
An Angry Robot imprint
and a member of the Osprey Group

Lace Market House,   Angry Robot/Osprey Publishing,
54-56 High Pavement,   PO Box 3985,
Nottingham   New York,
NG1 1HW   NY 10185-3985,
UK   USA

www.angryrobotbooks.com
A is for Attaché

An Angry Robot paperback original 2014

Cover design by Argh! Oxford

Distributed in the United States by Random House, Inc., New York.

ISBN 978 1 90922 322 6
Ebook ISBN 978 0 85766 320 2

Printed in the United States of America

9 8 7 6 5 4 3 2 1

To my father…
… and to Welt Meister

THE HONEY TRAP

The two men crossed the river road as the sun set on the other side of the Mekong, over Thailand. Hammers and sickles set against blood-red backgrounds fluttered from a row of sorry-looking poles by the water. This was the Laotian way to remind the Thais who'd won the war.

It was early November. The rains had stopped, but the river remained swollen and muddy. The revolution, a long time in coming, had come. And gone. Vientiane looked less like a national capital than a run-down suburb of Dresden with better weather. The sun, a misty, dull red fireball, sunk into the turgid current in slow motion.

Once the American infrastructure – a few office blocks and residential areas, the CIA compound at Kilometer 14, a handful of churches, bars, brothels, clinics and aid agencies – had been removed, closed down or reassigned, there was nothing left to do but to enjoy socialism. More than fifteen years of intense US involvement, political and military, overt and covert, ambitious and disastrous, had left few traces in the city. The locals lingered in hammocks

7

or went about their business in culturally prescribed lethargy as they'd done for centuries.

Once it got dark, Laotians disenchanted with the revolution would take to modest paddle boats to flee across the water to the free world. The authorities, glad to be rid of these vaguely troublesome citizens, turned a blind eye or two. Laos was that kind of place. Not even the politburo took anything too serious. And if it did, no one ever heard about it. No one worried about the consequences of this or that so long as it didn't make any waves in the here and now. Some workers' utopia.

The two men walked at a healthy but innocuous pace. The German Democratic Republic's newly appointed cultural attaché to Laos, Manfred Rendel, strode purposefully ahead, a harried expression on his face. He was the younger though hardly the fitter of the two, and sweated profusely in his polyester suit. No one would have called him handsome, not even from across the river and the free world. Rendel needed to lose weight both in body and mind. For now, it was the mind that was in the process of unburdening itself.

"I tell you, it's serious. Thought it better we meet in the street than in my office, where half the world is likely to listen in. Especially our friends, the Viets."

The second man, broad-shouldered and in his early fifties, his blond hair cropped short, cautiously brought up the rear. He had just arrived in town and wore an innocuous short-sleeved white shirt and gray slacks, black shoes, no tie. He kept his eyes locked to the ground and took care not to look directly at passers-by. He walked the way a predator might move through dense jungle, purposefully, quietly and acutely aware of every movement. Elegant in a way it was hard to put a finger on. A casual onlooker might have assumed him to be a rather superfluous character, a slightly ruffled subordinate of the more dynamic man up front. A very careful observer would have noted that this man achieved near invisibility without a great deal of effort.

"She asked for me, specifically?"

Rendel nodded. "Asked for your codename. Loud and clear. Was a bit of a shock. I mean, no one knows *that* name. Mentioned Long Cheng as well. And gold. American gold. Lots of American gold."

Rendel's eyes flashed greedily.

The man codenamed Weltmeister ignored the attaché's predilection for vice and profiteering and carefully scanned both sides of the potholed river road ahead of them. Everything looked as it always did. The courtyard of the *Lane Xang*, the riverside's best hotel, lay deserted but for the usual half dozen party limos that parked there for the weekend, their drivers lounging under a rickety wooden stand to the left of the building, plucking hair from their chins with steel tweezers, and playing cards.

It was Saturday evening and the country's decision makers were most likely lying half dead in their suites, nursing their foreign liqueur hangovers, fawned over by taxi girls, exhausted from celebrating the revolution the night before or getting ready to do it all over again. Unlimited supplies of Russian vodka, local sex slaves and an entrenched feudal mindset that was immune to both the benefits and strictures of communism could do terrible things to a government, even one that had partaken in beating the world's mightiest superpower.

For the have-nots, it was business as usual. Prior to the revolution, the same drivers had sat in the same spot, waiting for their American employers to emerge from the same kind of weekend carnage.

The traffic was light. A group of female students, dressed in white blouses and dark sarongs, cycled past and threatened to distract the attaché from the clandestine nature of his walk. But the passing girls didn't manage to stop Manfred Rendel grinning with all the severity of a man who'd spent his entire life steadfastly refusing to develop a sense of humor, "Must have practiced pronouncing it. It rolled right off her tongue. Wouldn't tell me anything else. Good-looking little number, too. Pale skin, Chinese features. Nice tits. Bad teeth. Savage basically. She calls herself Mona. And she said the magic word. Weltmeister."

The older man shook his head and hung back, as if trying to distance himself from his old friend who reveled in the loss of his moral compass. But it was just a reaction on his side to hearing his code name spoken by someone else. Weltmeister didn't suffer common afflictions such as moral dilemmas or sentimentality. He was free. Long-term unaccountability in a high-risk profession could do that to a man. He couldn't care less what the attaché was up to so long as it didn't interfere with his program.

"A Hmong girl perhaps. But hardly anyone knows my codename. A few Viets, maybe. And they'd never blab. Even at our embassy here, no one knows."

His cover had been blown. Someone was on to him. Somebody knew he'd been to Long Cheng. Someone was on to the fact that he had been to the secret American base not just as a Vietnamese agent, but that he'd lived and worked there for the CIA. And whoever had made him, they were organized and they were close. But it never occurred to Weltmeister to tell his old friend the truth. The truth hadn't propelled him to the top of his profession.

Right now, he needed more information. If the cat was out of the spook sack, he was finished. As were all those others, who had sponged off his genius years ago. If the U48 surfaced, people would be soiling their government-issue suits from Washington to Moscow, from Hanoi to Bangkok. Retirees across several continents would scramble to hide ill-gotten gains and fear for the retraction of past honors, or worse. No one would be happy. Heads would roll in the White House and the Kremlin. A small but vital aspect of twentieth-century history would have to be rewritten. The man codenamed Weltmeister shrugged. Who cared about *Realpolitik*? His life was on the line. The trenches he'd dug, the palisades he had carefully erected around himself were about to be overrun. He would have to check out of the program, batten down the hatches, close the loopholes and sink into the dust of history, never to reemerge. His war was coming to an end. And he would have fun ending it on his terms.

"No one knows except you, Manfred."

Rendel stopped in his tracks on the crumbling pavement and turned back to his friend, his face flushed with anger and, deeper down, beneath the layers of fat, slothdom and greed, a little fear.

"Well, I didn't shop you. And I resent that remark. How long have we known each other? Didn't I help you get laid at college in Leipzig all those years ago? When you acted like an introvert spy who'd come in from the cold? Semester after semester, I talked you up with the girls without ever hinting at what a truly twisted individual you really were. Didn't I help facilitate your current position? You have changed sides more often than the oldest whore in Vientiane, and the first thing I do when your name comes up is call you. Isn't that what trust is made of?"

The older man smiled sardonically, "You know how it is in our line of work. Take no prisoners."

But Weltmeister chuckled disarmingly, and Rendel let the threat pass. The cultural attaché was a sentimental man.

As daylight faded, the Mekong receded into the almost-silent tropical night, filled only with mosquitoes and military patrols who would have the streets cleared in a couple of hours. Only the cicadas would be singing in Vientiane tonight. Across the river in Si Chiang Mai, the nearest town on the far shore, primitive rock music throbbed from unseen speakers. This was the Thai way to remind the Laotians that the forces of evil had been beaten but not vanquished, and that the river served as one of the most important Cold War fault lines in the world.

The clandestine meeting was coming to an end.

"I mean it, Manfred. Let's play the old game. A little subterfuge. You meet her. Tell her you are Weltmeister. See what she has got for us."

It was the younger man's turn to laugh.

"First, I'll see what she's got for me. This girl is a honey trap if ever I've seen one. I might as well taste the honey before I pry the trap open."

Weltmeister shrugged. "Just get the intel. Find out what she wants. But don't scare her with your cock. Just be me. And if she's Hmong, remind her that the war is over and that the good guys won. The Americans won't be back for some time."

THE MOST SECRET PLACE ON EARTH

Two nights and a day later, Rendel and Maier hid Mona under a tarpaulin in the back of the attaché's jeep and left town. The Hmong girl was desperate to get into the mountains and reunite with her brother, the man who knew where the gold was stashed. The man who'd given his sister one of the most secret codes of the American war in Asia. The man who'd sent her to the city. She'd spent the night with Rendel, only to intone the same mantra over and over again.

"We meet brother Léon. Léon meets Weltmeister. Very good."

And that was all he could lure out of her.

Outside the capital, the roads turned into muddy tracks lined with impenetrable walls of bamboo forest interspersed with tiny settlements and their adjacent fields. Children dressed in rags waved at them from the roadside. Neither man waved back.

The Laotian military stopped them at several roadblocks: Rendel's embassy credentials and a few cartons of American cigarettes provided smooth transitions. They spent the first night in a paddy field hut just north of Ban Houay Pamon. Rendel kept pestering the girl about the gold she'd shown him in Vientiane.

"Are you sure there is more of this gold up there?"

"You see, I tell the truth. Long Cheng, big American airport, many boxes gold. My brother, Léon, he show you. We meet in Long Cheng. You help me and Léon go America. We all rich. I help you."

Weltmeister didn't have any interest in gold, nor did he care about the escape plans of a few CIA-trained Hmong rebels. Thousands of these hill tribe people had been caught up in the almost twenty-year-long war. Some had fled to refugee camps in Thailand, from where they had moved on to France and the US, while others lingered in the Laotian jungles, their futures blighted by their erstwhile alliance with the Americans.

Mona was probably leading them into a trap. But he felt reasonably safe as long as Rendel kept up the charade of pretending to be his alter ego, the elusive superspy. The three travelers all had their private agendas. Loyalty, greed and the need for anonymity would be battling it out soon enough. Weltmeister relished the fact. He didn't like loose ends.

They entered Xaisomboun District. Beyond the small town of the same name, a trader's outpost mired in mud and the deprived locals' long faces, traffic petered out. Wild animals so little known they'd never been on television occasionally ran, scuttled, slithered or jumped across the road in front of the vehicle. The district, until recently the heart of the US Secret War in Laos, was off limits to everyone except Laotian military and local farmers. Even comrades, be they Soviet or German, weren't welcome. It was probably a different story for the Vietnamese. They went everywhere and de facto ruled parts of the country. Victors' justice.

The road snaked deeper into the hills, wearing down the jeep's suspension and the travelers' patience with every pond-sized hole in their path. Halfway through the second day of automotive torture, Mona told them to stop.

"Many army post before we reach Long Cheng. We walk from here."

They pushed the jeep into thick brush. As Rendel pulled the key from the ignition, only the faint tick of the hot engine was audible.

Weltmeister inhaled the forest. He loved silence. Silence, he'd long decided, was his hobby.

Rendel unloaded several backpacks and a couple of shovels and pulled a gun from under the passenger seat.

"Manfred, how much gear did you bring? Are you planning to tunnel through to Vietnam?"

The attaché grinned. "Need something to carry at least some of that gold away with us. Once we figure the situation down there, we take what we can and try and work out a way to come back with a larger vehicle. Was thinking of burying some of it."

Weltmeister held out his hand. "Give me the gun then. I'm a better shot than you."

"In your dreams. This is my *Dienstpistole* from back home, the gun I was issued at the Ministry of State Security, on my very first day at work."

Weltmeister stood waiting, his hand out, an easy smile on his face, waiting for his friend to hand over his duty pistol. Rendel snorted and laughed. The older man didn't move. Rendel stood in doubt for a long moment, then his sentimental side got the better of him.

"Well, you are my old friend. Look after it."

He handed the Makarov and two boxes of cartridges to his partner.

They dropped away from the track into the jungle. Mona walked ahead, barefoot, resolute and sensuous. If she was concerned about the gun, she didn't show it.

"Stay on the path. Maybe land mine around."

Rendel was right behind her, hypnotized by the swing of her narrow hips while Weltmeister cautiously followed. The narrow trail led upwards. The tree cover started to thin. Two hours later, they reached Skyline Ridge, the Americans' last defense. The view was breathtaking.

The gigantic former US air base of Long Cheng, codename Lima Site 20A, lay in a wide, verdant valley beneath them. A couple of years earlier, this unlikely location had been the world's busiest airport. And no one had ever heard of it.

Weltmeister pulled a pair of binoculars out of his pack.

The runway, long enough to take large transport planes, was intact and stretched towards high karst stone formations. The American field agents who had lived here for almost two decades had likened them to a pair of pointed breasts. Dense jungle punctuated by bomb craters spread across the hills beyond the valley.

Everything looked familiar to him. He knew this valley as intimately as any place on Earth.

A ramshackle collection of wooden shacks spread on both sides of the runway, augmented here and there by small clusters of more ambitious concrete structures, the former CIA offices. Long Cheng had been the nerve center of the agency's clandestine war in Laos, a covert slice of a larger conflict fought to contain communism in Indochina. A conflict that had cost more than four million lives and had taken some twenty years to grind itself and the region into dust.

A US-financed secret army, a mercenary force of hill tribe soldiers and their families, some fifty thousand people, had lived in Long Cheng for more than a decade. Most of the fighters had died. Even their children, sent into battle by the CIA, had been lost to the final years of the war.

Weltmeister could see a couple of Laotian patrols on the cracked tarmac. A cow, a long rope dragging behind the animal, meandered towards the mountains, following a faded white line. There were no other signs of life.

The communists had overrun the base a year or so earlier, and since then the secret city, the second largest in the country, had simply died. Weltmeister, in the service of the Vietnamese at the time, had helped oversee the end of the airfield.

Now the jungle, spurred on by the recent rains and the almost complete absence of human activity, was on the move, determined to wrestle Long Cheng back under its control.

Weltmeister laughed inwardly at the sacrosanct absurdities his various paymasters engaged in and the lengths they were prepared to go to, to see their demented visions through. Only the jungle really knew what it was doing.

The thrill of having returned to the scene of his crimes was weighed down by bitterness and misgivings. The devil always ruled both sides.

But Weltmeister wasn't a religious man. And he wasn't driven by ideology either. Rather, he was motivated by a lifelong desire for anonymity. His existence as a nobody kept him focused and interested. He had felt no need for family or friends. For security reasons, he had almost completely denied himself the affections of others and avoided confessions. Almost.

His lack of preference for a particular life had made him an excellent spy in Nazi Germany, and after the war, in East Germany, in the US and finally in Southeast Asia. And now, despite being the best in the business, one of his former selves had been found out. The great cloak-and-dagger game, which until a year or so ago he had thought to be the true love of his life, hung in the balance.

It was time for a purge.

FINGERPRINT FILE

"So the gold is down there, near the runway?"

Mona nodded distractedly and pulled a small mirror from her shirt.

"What time now?" she asked, her voice a monotone of defiance.

"Three o'clock."

"We wait one hour. Before sun goes down, I send signal, my brother. Then we go meet."

Rendel grinned at her, watching a thin rivulet of sweat run from her neck into her cheap polyester shirt.

"No," she said, a flash of anger in her eyes that Weltmeister had not seen before.

He liked her righteous indignation. After all, she'd slept with creepy Rendel to get them here. Now that they were here, there was no more need for pretense. The honey trap had withdrawn its sticky content. They were close. The trap was about to snap shut.

They descended towards the base just before sunset. Mona, dead sure her brother had seen her signal, walked with a renewed spring in her step. They quickly dropped down from their vantage point, carefully keeping low brush between themselves and the lazily patrolling troops on the runway. Fifteen minutes later, they'd reached the first shacks. Whatever trap had been set for them, they were about to walk right into it.

The formerly bustling city was in a state of rapid decline. The roads and trails between the shacks were rutted. The detritus of war lay scattered everywhere – sheet metal, rusting tins of American foodstuff, shreds of clothing, torn and frayed Stars and Stripes, shell casings of every imaginable caliber. The girl led the two men into the heart of the decaying jumble of buildings, towards the concrete structures they'd seen from the ridge.

Weltmeister remembered the way perfectly well. He'd walked along the narrow alleys hundreds of times. But there was no need to let his companions know just how deep his connection with Long Cheng was.

The girl stopped in her tracks quite suddenly and tried to orient herself.

"Guten Abend."

They stood surrounded by armed men. The Hmong militia fighters, some of them teenagers, dressed in rags and carrying heavy weapons, had popped up like ghosts. The youngest couldn't be more than twelve years old. Mona fell into the arms of a handsome boy and whispered rapidly. No one else spoke. Everyone stared at the white men.

As the girl recounted their journey in her own language, the boy, no more than sixteen, watched the two Germans like a hawk. He was tall and pale, with thick black hair and a wispy goatee, and very familiar. Léon Sangster had grown from child to man in three short years. The war had sped things up. His bloodshot eyes burned like black pools of burning coal and he smelt of *lao khao*, the local rice wine. Growing up as an American in this wilderness had freed the young man from some of the constraints of one culture and trapped him within those of another.

Weltmeister had recognized him immediately. There had always been something feral about Léon. And, he noticed, the girl had it as well. But unlike her half-caste brother, Mona was all Asian. The other men looked battle-scarred and resigned to the routine boredom and brutality of war. He would have to play this very carefully. Whatever she was telling her brother, who'd failed to recognize him so far, did not enamor them to the young man. Léon was more *Sturm und Drang* than Weltmeister liked. A sensitive boy, driven by righteous and rightful anger.

Léon looked at him more closely then. "You look familiar. I have seen you somewhere before."

Weltmeister smiled affably and shook his head in mock confusion.

"That seems unlikely, young man."

The young Hmong waved the thought away, led them to a two-story house and entered. His fighters spread around the building and melted away into the shadows to keep an eye out for passing Laotian patrols. The siblings sat down on wooden bed frames without mattresses, the only pieces of furniture in the dilapidated room, facing their visitors. Shovels and sledgehammers leant in an untidy row in the far corner. Otherwise, the room was empty.

Weltmeister noticed that they sat on the old frames in deliberate poses, stiff and tense. One of Léon's soldiers stayed in the room, casually leaning against the back wall, a Kalashnikov strapped across his shoulder. The gold had to be close.

The two Germans remained standing.

"You speak my language?" Rendel barked across the room.

The boy shook his head, skipped the small talk and got straight down to business, in fluent American English, "You'll help us move the gold. We give you twenty percent when we reach Vientiane. Then you help us cross the Mekong into Thailand."

Rendel nodded, wearing his best expression of integrity.

"You are Weltmeister?"

"Yes," Rendel lied.

The boy smiled for the first time. It wasn't a friendly smile. There was too much doubt in it.

"I was here when Long Cheng fell last year. My father was one of the last remaining case officers, Jimmy Sangster. My mother was a Hmong princess. Mona is my only surviving sister. This isn't about politics. It's about us. We want out."

Léon fell silent. Outside, darkness came quickly, the subtropical night descending on the spy city, which was without electricity. Mona stared at her brother in the fading half light, her eyes full of admiration.

For a moment, Weltmeister felt a little sick. This was war, or its immediate aftermath, he told himself. Things were messy. He'd seen all this before. Humanity. Hope. Suffering. Disappointment. And this time, Long Cheng wasn't safe. The beautiful teenage girl, the daughter of legendary CIA case officer Jimmy Sangster who'd given his life for the country, had led them into a heart of darkness he felt no desire to linger in. Familiar and highly dangerous. He was taking a huge risk. To find out what this boy knew about him. What he remembered.

• • •

"The Americans left thousands of us on the runway. Women and children. Old people. We didn't know anything about when the last plane flew out. Our leader, General Vang Pao, escaped in a CIA helicopter and went to America. When the communists closed in on the runway, we fled into the jungle. Some of us wanted to keep fighting. We thought the Americans would come back to save us. We'd given them everything."

Léon looked emotional, the desperate last days of the American war at the forefront of his mind.

"Surely you could have been on a plane? You had great connections," Rendel wondered with his usual lack of tact.

"Our parents loved both their children and their countries."

Léon continued slowly, his voice filled with resentment, "Mona is all I have in this world. And now she has brought me Weltmeister."

"Why me? How do you know this name?"

"The file, it's in the file."

"What file?" Rendel demanded.

"The file my father was responsible for. The file you put together for the Vietnamese. The U48. The file that killed my father. The file you came looking for."

Rendel stared at the young man with his best neutral expression.

The man with the codename Weltmeister knew he was coming to the end of his journey and silently got ready to enter the next phase of his life. He discreetly clicked the safety off his friend's gun.

THE END

"The U48?" Rendel asked.

"Come on, Weltmeister. The secret Vietnamese file? All the names of all the double agents the Viet Cong ran in Vietnam, Laos, Cambodia and Thailand? Even yours. Weltmeister? Can you imagine what we will get if we sell you to the Americans? Or the Vietnamese?"

"Have you read the file?" the real Weltmeister asked, careful to weigh his question with as little urgency as possible.

Léon shook his head but kept his eyes on Rendel. "No, only glanced at it, at some names, at your name, but we knew you would come back to Laos for it."

"Where is the file?" Rendel kept pushing.

The boy broke into his troubling smile again.

"With my father and my mother."

"You said they were killed?" the attaché, exasperated by the young man's monosyllabic answers, asked with a hint of annoyance in his voice.

"I buried them. You see, they never planned to escape without the file and my mother refused to leave her family. The agency left us stranded. Perhaps they had planned to sacrifice us."

Weltmeister got up, walked to the only window in the room and stared out into the night.

Rendel did his best to sound unconvinced. "If the file is still here, the Vietnamese will also be looking for it."

The boy answered, "The Vietnamese dogs shot my mother and father. I buried them with the gold, our last batch of heroin, and the file. My father couldn't leave. He was too attached to this place, this situation. When the Vietnamese and the Pathet Lao attacked, I ran away. I thought the war would continue. That we would get our revenge. Our justice. But our fight is finished. We are finished. Now I'm back to take the file and some of the gold with me to a new life in the West. With Mona."

The attaché did his best not to look out of his depth. "So how did you guess I was Weltmeister and why did you send your sister?"

"My father told me there was a superspy on the list, a German who worked for the US. A lone wolf and a double agent. The man who betrayed Long Cheng. He told me that this man would come because the cover for his identity depended on getting the list. Some of our supporters in Vientiane have been watching the German embassy. And then you arrived. I knew it was my only shot to find closure. And to get the gold out."

"Where is the file?" Weltmeister repeated with more urgency.

The young Hmong looked at him with renewed interest. Weltmeister looked away, nothing more than a casual move of the head. For a split second, a thought seemed to pass through Léon's mind, then it was gone.

Mona got up and pushed the bed frames aside as her brother handed the two men a shovel and a hammer.

"Right here," he said, pointing at the floor. "Start digging."

"Shit," Rendel screamed and fell through the floor as it collapsed around him. Their breakthrough shattered the near silence of their work. They had found their treasure. The trap had opened and closed.

Dust swirled around the room and Weltmeister edged his way to the door. He could hear feet rushing around the house. Probably Léon's men. He carefully opened the door and slipped outside. Far off, from somewhere on the runway, he could hear shouting. The Laotian military was up and running. Time was up. They'd been made. He slunk back inside and shone his torch into the hole in the center of the room.

Rendel was making a lot of noise.

"Get me out of here. I've broken my bloody leg."

Weltmeister shivered uncomfortably. He hadn't felt this nervous since escaping the Gestapo in Berlin more than thirty years earlier. His cover was blown. Timing was everything now.

Léon suddenly loomed in front of him.

"Now I know you. I saw you in Long Cheng. A long time ago, when I was a kid. Now I remember your eyes."

The Hmong sucked in his breath as more unpleasant realizations appeared to flood his mind. He shook his head in disbelief.

"You are the devil who…"

The man codenamed Weltmeister shot the boy. Léon fell beside Rendel into his parents' grave. His next shot killed the Hmong soldier before he had time to move his weapon. Mona screamed and made for her brother, but the third bullet caught her in the neck a split second later. For a moment Weltmeister stood still, listening into the night. None of the other Hmong rebels around the building seemed to have heard the shots. Rendel's *Dienstpistole*, with a silencer, was a reliable tool.

"I'll get you out, Manfred; don't worry."

He climbed down into the chamber below the building's floor. His torch flicked across Rendel who had suffered an open break in his left leg and looked like he was about to pass out. This place wasn't made for cultural attachés with shattered femurs.

To his right, the low-ceilinged chamber was filled with boxes and metal ammunition cases, rusty but intact. The first one he pried open contained gold bars. The second one was packed with sealed bags of Double Uoglobe heroin. He took one of each and stashed them in his pack. But the file was nowhere to be seen.

Léon was still alive.

"Where is my sister?"

"She went outside to get help." Weltmeister answered in a kind tone.

"You save my sister, I tell you about the file. Promise?"

He made eye contact with the young man and nodded solemnly. Léon had not seen his sister die.

The Hmong pointed to the far side of the chamber.

"In the bag under my father's head. Promise."

The young man passed out, a pool of blood spreading under his prone figure. He'd be dead soon enough.

The remains of Léon's parents lay in a crumpled embrace in the far corner of the chamber. Weltmeister assumed that Léon had dragged them there after they'd been killed and arranged their affectionate still life. He found the bag and pried it from under the decomposed head of Jimmy Sangster, his former colleague.

Inside he found his grail.

The man who'd sat at tables with beggars and kings, who'd deceived the Gestapo, the CIA, the TC2 and the Stasi, allowed himself a vague smile as he peeled a bundle of papers from an oilcloth bag. His handwriting was still legible. A neat list of names, codenames, ages, birthplaces, and photographs, including, most importantly, his own, covered page after page. Memos and reports followed.

The U48. The file that had eluded him the last time he'd been in Long Cheng.

The trail to Weltmeister ended here. For a second, he contemplated burning the document. This was the only copy, the only clear evidence of who he was. Of what they'd done. But he couldn't do it. The U48 was too valuable. And he knew he was too vain. He had created this file as much as he had created his persona. The file, he knew, was one of the great masterpieces of the western world. You could hold it up to a Picasso or a Gauguin. It had to live on in some shape or form. Who would be mad enough to burn the Mona Lisa, even if she were to harbor uncomfortable truths?

Rendel regained consciousness and moaned, "We

must leave. The Laotians will be here any minute. I can walk if you hold me. Don't leave an old friend behind."

"Sorry, Manfred, you know how it is in our line of work. Take no prisoners. Silence is everything."

Weltmeister turned to his old friend, raised the other man's *Dienstpistole* and pulled the trigger.

Without losing another second, he wiped the Makarov and pressed it into Rendel's limp right hand, climbed out of the chamber and pushed Mona down into what was becoming a mass grave. Then he moved the bed frames over the hole. Pushed together they completely covered the collapsed floor. There was nothing to be done about the terrible stink that would soon lead anyone within a mile to the gold and heroin. Outside, gunshots began to sound across the valley. The Laotians had noticed the activity and were on their feet. It was time to leave the most secret place on Earth. His eyes drifted across the room one last time. All this money. All this bad karma. He sighed. The list was all that mattered.

A few minutes later, he had cleared the huts and was climbing out of the valley. The Laotian troops guarding the airstrip would finish off the rest of the Hmong.

PART 1

MAIER

A HELL OF A CLIENT

"In 1976, for a few short months, my father was the German Democratic Republic's cultural attaché in Laos. He was an old Asia hand. He knew the region. But he was killed shortly after he arrived and his body was never repatriated. In fact, we know almost nothing about his death. I want you to find out why and how it happened. Who killed him? And I'd like you to find him, if possible."

Julia Rendel didn't waste time. The assignment was on the table before she'd given herself a chance to sip her coffee – black, very strong, no sugar. Nor did Maier's elegant client appear to be perturbed by the fact that half the customers and all the staff in the rather bourgeois but frighteningly trendy Herr Max were twisting their heads to get a better look at her. The detective guessed her to be in her mid-thirties. She had the gift and the money.

Her dark hair was piled high in an unruly and, at least to Maier, pleasing creation. Unruly hair did not come cheap in Germany. Her chunky jade earrings, probably from Burma, accentuated her long, pale neck. Her face was narrow, with high cheekbones and full lips. The stuff of movies and broken hearts. Her eyes shone with this knowledge like black stars. Her pale skin and slim nose somehow accentuated the fact that she was half-Asian. Her wardrobe said dressed-to-kill detectives in the most subtle way. Julia Rendel's silk blouse was low-key but made no attempt to close over her modest but alluring cleavage. The jeans she wore looked like they had been molded around her.

Maier could see why Ms Rendel might have sought his services. She spoke German with a slight Saxony accent and, like himself, had probably grown up in the East. Her father must have been one of the top dogs at what Maier assumed had been a reasonably important embassy in Vientiane. Following the defeat of US forces across Southeast Asia in the mid-Seventies, the GDR, along with other Soviet-aligned countries, had quickly built up a strong presence in Laos.

"I know this is an unusual case, Maier. My father was killed a long time ago in what was then still a war zone. In fact, I made my peace with his murder when I was a teenager. I was ten when he died and I barely remember him. My mother is half-Cambodian, half-French. They met in Phnom Penh in the early Sixties, but my father never married her. He left her and took me to Laos. After he was killed, the GDR authorities told me next to nothing, took me back to Germany and placed me in a foster home."

She took a sip of coffee and continued. "You see, without a bit of family background, this story is not going to make any sense. When the Khmer Rouge took over in Cambodia in 1975, my mother disappeared. For a long time, I thought she'd been killed but she eventually showed up in a refugee camp on the Thai border in the Eighties. I managed to get her back to Germany in '89. I hadn't seen her for almost fifteen years."

She stopped short of another revelation and shot Maier a searching glance. He could feel she was surprised when he made eye contact. Most people didn't notice his piercing green eyes until he wanted them to.

"My father was not a good man. Not much of a family man at all. Until very recently, I had pretty much stopped thinking about my family history. One grows out of trying to come to terms with these things."

Maier had ordered a mineral water and was toying with the metal lid of the three-Euro bottle, keeping his counsel. In Europe, it was near impossible to uncover the motives for a man's murder twenty-five years after the fact. Finding the actual killer was even more unlikely. In Southeast Asia, no one kept records. People were conditioned to forget, not to remember. Especially in a war zone. But all this was immaterial. The woman intrigued Maier more than the case of her deceased father.

Julia Rendel was the most attractive client he'd ever been hired by. He liked her instantly, though he was careful not to show it. In fact, she was so likeable that Maier, for a fleeting moment, thought her a Trojan horse. But he quickly dismissed his hunch. Ms Rendel was paying top rate to Maier's agency.

Julia Rendel casually waved for the waiter. She had an easy way with people, authoritative without being demanding, ever so slightly manipulative while projecting quite the opposite. In the overcrowded afternoon rush hour in Herr Max, everything appeared to revolve around her. Maier enjoyed the show. One of the café's pumped-up and stressed-out employees rushed to their table and almost stood to attention in a way that most Germans had long abandoned. With practiced nonchalance, Ms Rendel ordered another coffee strong enough to make a dead man laugh and waited until they were alone again.

"I had an identity crisis a few years back. But let me take you there in a roundabout way that is pertinent to your job. I finished high school in the GDR, late because I'd been in Asia. In the early Nineties, a friend of my father's adopted me. I was already grown up, of course, but I had no money or prospects. He was a painter and another terrible egomaniac, though a more successful one than my father. He paid for my education. Only the very best. We moved to London. I read political science at Oxford, then went to the States and did a PhD in Asian studies and international relations at Princeton, and finally a stint as an intern at the Bundestag in Berlin so that I'd get reacquainted with the machinations of the fatherland. You know, champagne debates and cocaine in the parliamentary toilets. My step-daddy had also been a GDR diplomat in the old days and had even served in Southeast Asia during the Seventies. If he hadn't come into my life, I would have become a kindergarten teacher or a clerk. So you see, I am set for great things. In fact, I felt like my stepfather had me groomed for great things. I still do."

Something unhealthy crossed her face then, but it was so subtle and potentially scary that Maier refused to acknowledge it.

"Great things being, Ms Rendel?"

She looked at him sharply, perhaps trying to figure out whether to take offence from his interruption. She decided not to.

"Well, this is the odd thing. Despite my father and my stepfather having been part of the old communist regime, I was told that all doors were open for me in the new, reunited Germany. Politics, foreign affairs, lobby groups, think tanks, you name it. Once I finished my studies, all these different bodies were virtually battling each other to pull me in. OK, I'd been to Oxford and Princeton, but I wasn't sure I deserved all that attention. I had done nothing to prove myself in any way."

Maier experienced a strange moment of déjà vu. Hadn't his own career, albeit years earlier and in a different political system, started in a similar vein? He'd been one of the best journalism graduates in his class. But his meteoric rise to foreign correspondent, both an honor and a calculated risk usually bestowed only on the most reliable party members, had come off without a hitch, at a time when East Germany was keen not to deal with the loss of face that defectors caused.

Whatever doubts she was mulling over, Julia Rendel shrugged them off and continued. "I decided to push my luck and change track completely. I joined an NGO called TreeLine. Heard of it?"

Maier was familiar with the organization. TreeLine monitored forest cover in developing nations and released reports on illegal logging and government corruption, most notably in Asia. Its critics, including a plethora of corrupt politicians in said parts of the world, claimed that TreeLine was a Eurocentric outfit, a political tool to push European environmental agendas with little understanding of or sympathy for the situation on the ground in poor countries. Whatever their sins, the more moderate of these unlikely commentators had a point. NGOs rarely prioritized circumstances on the ground. It was a game of donors and budgets.

He kept his thoughts to himself and said nothing.

"Ah, you are a careful man, Maier. I like it. We will get on."

"Get on, Ms Rendel?"

"Oh, yes, I'll be in Laos when you start your investigation. And please call me Julia."

"Please call me Maier."

Maier shot her a quick glance, encouraging his client to continue.

"I am TreeLine's senior analyst for Southeast Asia. I'm based in Bangkok but we're most active in Laos and Cambodia."

This time, Maier could not help himself and quipped, "Because trees do not need saving in Thailand?"

Julia laughed, "No, Maier, because the people who finance TreeLine view Laos and Cambodia at best as uncooperative, at worst as hostile countries. And, if we did report on Thailand, we would not be able to run our office there. Did I tell you my job was sleazy? But it puts me where I want to be right now, and I can still strive for a more worthy existence later. Everything a person does is preparation for something else, right?"

Maier laughed politely.

She snapped, "And don't patronize me, Mr Detective. You appear to see the world in equally jaded terms as I do; you are an expert on Asia and a charming if slightly detached man, which I'd say is almost interesting, though somehow also unhealthy, given that I've hired you. I am impressed. Our mutually complementary abilities of deduction will make our professional relationship that much easier, I am sure. As long as you remember that I am your employer."

Maier shrugged and tried to guide his client back to the case.

"So what about these new developments?"

She shot him a look that made his stomach flutter. For a

split second, he could detect a razor-sharp, dangerous mind, as well as an unhealthy degree of admiration he felt he hardly deserved but was happy to entertain anyhow.

"As I said, interesting. I have a suite at the Atlantic. After a couple of months of shitting in the woods, I feel I deserve a few days of unbridled luxury."

Maier grinned, "Bumped into the Atlantic's resident rock star yet?"

"The really very gracious Udo Lindenberg and I had a long evening of absolutely divine champagne together last week. He's an absolute sweetie. He sat down at his piano and sang *'Sonderzug nach Pankow'* for me, and I've had red roses from him every day since. But don't get jealous, Maier; he wasn't interested in me. He's seen too much in this life. More than you, perhaps."

"What was that about keeping it professional?"

"Oh yes, Maier, we will. Don't worry. Anyway, you're hired and I expect you to put your heart as well as your very sharp mind into the job at hand. I will send out a couple of emails this afternoon, warning Laos of our imminent arrival. I trust you'll also be available to dine with me in my suite at 8pm sharp. You and I being good Germans, no matter how wayward, I'm sure we'll both manage to be on time. I will fill you in on the rest of the case then. Room 172. See you."

Her piece said, Julia Rendel was gone in an instant, leaving Maier with a barely touched second cup of coffee and an inappropriately large banknote to pay the bill. Maier pocketed some of the change, thinking of it as a modest advance on his expenses.

I'LL BE YOUR SISTER

Detective Maier stood naked in front of the full-sized mirror. At 190 cm, his reflection barely fitted into the solid teak frame, courtesy of Hamburg's prestigious Hotel Atlantic Kempinski, that he drunkenly leant against. He studied his lived-in face, the deepening lines that spread around his eyes and along his cheeks. One day, it would all be gone to hell. But his shoulders were broad and he was in good shape at forty-five, all things considered. He still had hair on his head. He didn't need glasses. He enjoyed his vanity and made no bones about it. Old age held off for another day.

He looked deeper into the mirror and could just make out the vague outline of Julia, who lay asleep across the huge bed in the shadows behind him.

His boss, Sundermann, had told him to go on holiday, take it easy, to digest and reflect on the horrors he'd encountered on his last case. Cambodia had been a hard slog, physically and emotionally demanding.

Since returning to Hamburg, he'd been making the effort. He got rid of his moustache – a woman who'd left him, one he had really liked, had ridiculed him for it. And now that she had gone, he had followed her advice and shaved it off. That kind of action – too little, too late – appeared to be symptomatic for the way he failed in his relationships.

He ran near his apartment in Altona. On days he felt particularly energetic, he went and exercised amongst the flower displays at *Planten un Blomen*, a mile or so east of his apartment. He refrained from drink, drugs, sex and even *Bratkartoffeln*, roast potatoes, a German standard he was partial to.

He saw a psychiatrist who did his best to detect symptoms of post-traumatic stress disorder. He watched television. He bought clothes. He polished up his French while forgetting whatever Russian he'd learned in school. He tried to be ordinary. He tried to live down his last job. He tried to accept that the women who fell into his arms fled them just as quickly when they took a closer look.

He was infatuated with his current job, just as he'd been a hundred percent committed when he'd been a war correspondent. Being a relatively successful detective was one hell of a journey.

Born in Leipzig in 1954, to his sweet mother Ruth and a father he'd never met, Maier had done exceedingly well. Following his studies in Dresden and Berlin he worked as a journalist for the East German state organ, *Neues Deutschland*, and covered foreign affairs in Poland, the Czech Republic, Hungary, and Yugoslavia. He had no idea why he'd been awarded such an entrusted and sensitive position amidst the surreal and politically labyrinthine media realities of East Germany. He wasn't a party member, and he avoided the right people as best as he could.

Maier always suspected that his father had something to do with his meteoric trajectory. This father, who'd apparently passed nothing more to his son than his piercing green eyes and natural restlessness, had attended a few lectures at Universität Leipzig, bedded down with his mother for eleven months and simply vanished without a trace one day to leave her with nothing but a broken heart and a child. Scandalous behavior in the former East Germany. The neighbors never talked to Ruth again. But Maier knew she was secretly proud of her affair. She had hinted that the old man had had some role in anti-Nazi intelligence during World War II. His mother had told him that her mysterious lover had never let her take his photograph. Maier Sr was an unknown entity that moved through his system like a ghost and stalked him in his dreams. Maier hoped and imagined that the old man was somewhere out there, keeping an eye on his son, following his path into adulthood and middle age.

He let go of the mirror and almost tumbled to the floor. Good times would do that to a man. It was easy to slide back into the drinking routine. He was so ready for work. In fact, Maier was already at work. His new mission demanded he let himself go immediately. He would grow his hair, adopt mock slothdom, and return to the Far East. He'd look like one of those old hippies who wouldn't hurt a fly, had made a fortune in stocks and greenhouses, and had come back to Asia to relive the dream, man. He'd reinvent himself as a boutique bohemian.

We have a chance to save the world.

Or at least have a drink and let the old times roll before the mornings got so familiar that they'd enter his bones and make him feel his years.

• • •

There was an unearthly quiet in the suite of the Atlantic, which Julia Rendel had occupied for at least three days. That's how long Maier had had his mobile phone switched off, had not been at home nor in the street. Not that anyone was likely to call him. The detective didn't have close friends.

The job had been cleared with his boss. And he could hear his client's gentle breathing, intermittently punctuated by vodka-filled snorts.

He looked down at his flaccid cock and grinned to himself. How much better could life get? The Atlantic was one of the city's swankiest watering holes. The century-old pile offered almost two hundred fifty sumptuous rooms and suites, overlooked the *Außenalster* and hosted the annual media ball for more than twelve hundred guests. The chandeliers, the gallons of vodka diluted with freshly squeezed orange juice, the drunken sex and his client's story of a lifetime, which, told from one inebriated person to another, had quickly taken on epic proportions in his addled mind. They'd even filmed a Bond movie in the Atlantic. High times.

It had been some journey getting here for Maier. When the satellite states of the great Soviet experiment started to crumble, Maier absconded to West Germany. He seamlessly integrated into the capitalist media apparatus.

His new employers in Hamburg sent him on the road, just as his old employers in East Berlin had. For some years, he covered German interests around the world, until he maneuvered himself into the most extreme corner of his profession, graduating from roving German reporter to international conflict journalist.

Maier covered many of the dirty little wars at the close of the twentieth century. But he found himself to be too restless even for this most intense and reactive employment. He got sick of describing truths prescribed by his employers.

After eight years on the front lines, Maier quit his career as a high-testosterone reporter and slunk back to Hamburg. At age forty, tired but not finished, he retrained and joined Sundermann, the city's most renowned detective agency. Four years later, he was the agency's Asia expert and one of its top operatives.

And now he was on his way to Laos. A beautiful woman had hired a jaded detective to find her father's killer in one of the world's least-understood nations. With a treasure of American war loot thrown into the mix. Gold!

The quickest way to Laos was via Bangkok. He would be on a plane to Thailand in a couple of days. A Hmong hill tribe man, a member of one of the communist nation's countless ethnic minorities, had appeared with new information as to her father's demise. That's all she'd told him. About the job.

Maier had visited Laos several times as a journalist. Following the collapse of the Soviet Union, the country's main source of cash since the revolution, he had covered the slow opening of this sleepy backwater in a handful of feature articles. He had traveled widely around this ancient, landlocked empire, which was covered in dense, primordial forests stretching across uncountable mountain ridges, interspersed with reassuringly insignificant villages, and dotted with otherworldly temples, their curved roofs shining like medieval receivers attracting distant starships.

He sucked in his stomach, then let himself go slack again. The Atlantic was not the place to start a weight-loss program. It was also a long way from Laos, a country many Germans would be hard-pushed to find on a map.

"Come to bed, Mr Detective," Julia whispered from the four-poster. He staggered back to her and sat heavily on the edge of the bed. She looked at him with eyes full of pleasure.

"When you get to Vientiane, go to the Red Bar or the Insomniacs Club and ask for Léon. The young Hmong. That's our man. Kanitha is his girl. Meet them. I'll join you there once you have made some headway with him."

Maier grinned down at her. He liked the way she weaved the mission and the night together into a heady mix of mystery and, well, more mystery. He was sure Julia had so much more to tell.

In the suite's living room, a doorbell rang with the urgency of a wind chime.

"That must be room service," he said, and stumbled into a pair of shorts. Julia had passed out again. Maier thought about ignoring the door. They hadn't called for anything. The bell tinkled a second time.

He couldn't find his shirt. Well, if they were happy to put up with rock stars, they would be able to cope with his opening the door in nothing much at all.

He left the bedroom and crossed the immaculately lit teak-floored hallway to the living room. The Chet Baker CD Julia had put on at his request had finished.

He pulled the security chain off the hook and opened the door.

The fist came at him at an unlikely velocity. Maier swayed out of the way and instinctively threw a right hook at his assailant. He could hear a man's nose crack before he could see anything. His satisfaction lasted less than a second. The hand of a second attacker came wrapped in a knuckleduster. Professionals never arrived alone. A flash of brass, and Maier blacked out faster than Chet.

And it had all started so well.

ENTER THE DRAGON

Maier had always liked the shallow easiness of Bangkok. The Thai capital was a mind-your-own-business-unless-you-would-like-us-to-mind-it-for-you kind of place. A city where the unchangeable was not tampered with and everything else mutated as quickly as possible. Sometimes even quicker. A metropolis of ten million people who never talked to each other but smiled and smiled and smiled. Every now and then, the Thais' inability to communicate with one another erupted in wild cataclysms of political violence and military coups, both sponsored by aspiring demagogues. The streets would run red with blood, and the violence triggered by temporary dissatisfaction was almost always manipulated or paid for and soon petered out. The very same people who'd been killing each other a few days earlier would now clean up the mess they'd made, so that both rich and poor could get back to their assigned places in this world and smile until the next cataclysm. Buddhism, a

47

rigid social hierarchy and a widely held belief amongst the country's elite that knowledge of almost any kind was dangerous kept people in their places.

But this time, Maier worried and the famous Thai smile, multifaceted and ambiguous, failed to touch him. His client had been kidnapped, had been virtually pulled from his arms. His eye hurt. Maier knew he'd never catch up with the two men who had knocked him out. They'd been anonymous, faceless messengers of doom.

Shortly after he'd returned home from the Atlantic, following a long interview with the police and Kreuzwieser, the hotel detective, he'd received an email from a 1000 Elephant Trading Company. He quickly established that no such entity existed.

He could have Ms Rendel back in exchange for a spot of professional consultancy, the message assured him. Further instructions were to follow by email once he'd reached the Laotian capital Vientiane. The IP address pinpointed an internet café in the city.

His case was going Fu Manchu before it had started. His client had touched him. He had the weird and completely inexplicable feeling that she was a soulmate. As if they had shared more than a night together, as if she had given him more than just another mission. Irrationally, he also sensed that she would come out of it just as fine and dandy as when he'd last seen her lying in her four-poster bed in the Atlantic, drunk and full of sex. But he could not rely on an emotional hunch. Men of violence connected to the pursuit of the gold had taken her. After conferring with Sundermann, his boss, he'd jumped the first plane east.

• • •

He took a small room in Chinatown and lost himself in the city's back streets for a day until he was sure that no one had noticed his arrival. He visited Wat Traimit and queued with camera-toting tourists to catch a glimpse of the temple's enormous solid-gold Buddha, the world's largest. It seemed like an auspicious thing to do, given that he was on a gold hunt. He talked to no one but the roadside noodle sellers.

Reasonably sure his anonymity was intact, he took the overnight train to the Thai-Laotian border. He entered Laos quietly, cloaked in the tribal conformity of an ageing hippie. He wore gleaming leather chapals, khaki cotton pants, a white shirt with too many buttons undone and one of those sleeveless vests with countless pockets favoured by photojournalists and would-be adventurers. Sunglasses covered his black eye, which remained dark as night, with the colours of the rainbow mixed in hourly in unearthly patterns. He looked fit enough not to be mistaken for a sex tourist. He didn't sleep and kept an eye on who was coming and going in his second class carriage.

At the crack of a pale, cool dawn, he disembarked at the Nong Khai railhead and grabbed a taxi for the Thai-Lao Friendship Bridge that spanned the Mekong and connected one vaguely cruel world to another. The Thai immigration officers wore brown uniforms so tight they looked like they'd been sewn into them. They were surly and disinterested. Their Laotian counterparts wore ill-fitting bright green outfits and caps that were too large. They smiled with faux embarrassment as they demanded additional fees for their dedicated work. The bribes were modest, mere fractions of a dollar.

"Welcome to Laos." They turned up their smiles to genuine happiness once he'd paid up.

Maier cleared immigration and emerged onto a dusty road.

Arriving in Laos was a bit like being released from prison. Freedom and loss rolled in equal waves. A feeling of *what now?* welcomed visitors.

The road into Vientiane was barely paved, and lined with fenced-in fallow plots, interspersed with minor ministries, shops selling farming equipment and national pharmaceutical factories that looked like they'd not produced a pill in years. International NGO offices with fat cars parked outside looked more with it than the destitute government buildings. Advertising billboards and consumer goods were noticeably absent. Laos was one of the poorest countries in the world.

Hunter-gatherers had been living in the region as far back as forty thousand years ago. In the fifteenth century, the Lan Xang Empire, ambitiously named the Land of a Million Elephants and the White Parasol, though a rather modest kingdom by regional standards, established itself as a nation-state of sorts. A couple of hundred years later, the fledgling affair was virtually crushed between larger neighbors and almost went out of business. The French showed up in the nineteenth century and saved Laos for its Indochina experiment, though this protectorate never made the colonizers a great deal of cash.

During World War II, the Japanese briefly ran the show, allowed the Laotians to declare independence, which was quickly denied by a vociferously resurgent France, smarting from its collaboration with the Nazis. Only in 1953, following France's total defeat at the hands of the Vietnamese in Dien Bien Phu, did Laos achieve independence. A monarchy, a right-wing dictatorship, a dysfunctional democracy, almost three decades of US sponsored war, and four years of secret carpet-bombing paved the way into the current and slowly declining revolutionary paradise.

Essentially Laos remained what it always had been, a sparsely populated land of mountain ridges, few roads and an atrophied political system dependent on foreign donors and neighboring states. Even now, a significant number of the six million Laotians had little or no contact with their government. There was no economy to speak of. People did the same now as they had then; they grew rice and took it easy. Hammocks were more important than cars, rice wine more ubiquitous than beer.

An hour of avoiding sleeping dogs, pedestrian monks, and cycling Jehovah's Witnesses later, a rickety Toyota Camry dropped Maier off by the Mekong in the heart of the Laotian capital. Vientiane. Population one hundred sixty thousand. He paid the modest cab fare and decided to walk around town to catch his bearings before checking into a hotel.

Lao national flags fluttered next to Hammers and Sickles along the river, tattered cloth flapping above modest outdoor restaurants overlooking the uncertain embankment. As on previous visits, Maier felt like he had re-entered a dream world, a land where everything had slowed down to the bare necessities, the opposite of exuberant, decadent and hedonistic Bangkok. Laotians had modest aspirations – one had to live with a stagnant economy and a government that ruled, just barely, as if it had experienced a bad spell of taxidermy. It was quiet. No one was watching, because there was nothing to do. This was a brand of communism so very different from the former East Germany's heavy-handed, cruel realities he had experienced as a young man.

Maier had learned that barbarity was a universal currency, spent freely by the left and right, by the powerful always, and sometimes by the meek. Laos too could be a dark place.

For a while he criss-crossed streets aimlessly and passed temples, carrying a modest, stylishly tattered backpack, making sure that no one followed him.

The attack at the Atlantic had made him über-cautious. The men who'd knocked him out in Julia Rendel's suite had been Asian. Someone had sent two able messengers to Hamburg. They'd managed to enter one of the city's most salubrious hotels and stolen away with one of its guests. The snatch had been so audacious, there had to be more to it than a simple case of kidnapping. This notion had established itself firmly in Maier's head and kept him on the right side of despair over his client's disappearance.

The dream of a luxury holiday with his Poirot-style deductions on the side had evaporated. Laos wasn't going to be as easy or glamorous as he'd first assumed. He worried about Julia Rendel. Others were on the same trail as him, and they were somewhere ahead.

Maier checked into a modest hotel off Samsenthai, took a shower and fell asleep.

As night fell, the detective headed for the river. Open-air food stalls offered salted fish baked over open coals, accompanied by papaya salad laced with chili and crabs. On a small square, the decidedly un-communist sounds of the Village People pumped out of a portable stereo with maximum distortion, loud enough to banish any thoughts of revolution. Disciplined citizens, almost all of them women, moved in unison, dancing through aerobics routines.

The buildings that lined Fa Ngum Quai Road, the long avenue that ran through the capital along the Mekong, made up an eclectic mixture of traditional wooden homes, Chinese shop houses, colonial piles, modern US-financed structures and cheerless Soviet-built concrete boxes, offering visitors a quick run-down of the country's recent history by way of its architecture. He passed cheap restaurants geared towards young backpackers and stalls selling pirate video CDs of the newest Hollywood blockbusters – one of the world's last Stalinist regimes was not immune to the tepid cultural temptations of the decadent West.

No further messages waited in his email account. No news on Julia Rendel. No lead on his client.

Maier had to double back a couple of times before he found the rather innocuous entrance to the Red Bar, a three-story affair trapped in a hundred year-old shop house, and the only happening night spot on the riverfront. Even so, the receptionist in his hotel had assured him that the Red Bar, along with every other watering hole, would close at midnight. Vientiane had never been a dynamic metropolis.

In the Sixties, the Americans had pumped more money into Laos than into any other country in the world, with predictable results – widespread corruption, a burgeoning sex industry and heavily manipulated elections undertaken by a populace accustomed to centuries of feudal rule. As a result, the city had come to life as something of a modest party place, though it had never been a refuge of debauchery and ruin comparable to Bangkok or Saigon. But this was history. The revolution in 1975 had put an end to the good times. Socialism had stamped out the evils of decadence, whether of Western or Eastern origin. And while Laotians knew where to go and have a moderately good time behind closed doors, foreign visitors were herded to the Red Bar.

Maier headed upstairs. The first floor gave way to a large, barely lit room with several pool tables, occupied by a smattering of bored bar girls who, in the absence of cash-flashing Western visitors, played desultory games amongst themselves. A Britney Spears song leaked from invisible speakers, putting a further downer on the scene. Modernity could be frightening. As he passed, a collective cry of professionally enthusiastic delight emanated from the tables, but Maier didn't stop.

The second floor was more amenable to his tastes. A round bar of heavy teak stood in the center of a large, well-lit room. Huge windows opened onto the river with views across to Thailand and the free world. Punters sat at low wooden tables, roughly hewn from illegally logged teak, knocking back the country's most coveted product, Beerlao. More bar girls toyed with the umbrellas in their cocktails, appraising each new arrival with the seasoned eye of a quality checker on an assembly line. The Who threatened to escape from the speakers. Old music for old people. Not quite Babylon, but better than Britney Spears. Maier cruised past the girls with a smile suspended in neutral.

The barkeep was a squat, careful-looking guy. He was decidedly not Laotian and combed his white hair like a Fifties newspaperman, strands of silver brushed across his slowly balding head. He wore thick, horn-rimmed glasses. Around fifty years old. He was on the brink of getting heavy, but Maier supposed that he had enough discipline to not let himself go to seed. There was something in his eyes that gave him the appearance of a man toying with going downhill, but he still teetered at the top of the crest, and any uncertainties in his movements might have been for show. He was clean-shaven and plucked the hair from his nostrils. He looked more like a history teacher than a bar manager in his plain white shirt tucked carefully into his neatly pressed blue jeans. A man who probably cared too much about what others thought of him.

Maier broke all the local rules and ordered a vodka orange, his preferred poison.

"Hey, I'm looking for the Insomniacs Club."

The little man pushed the glass across the gleaming teak counter and eyed him without great interest.

"Who's asking?"

"My name is Maier. I am a friend of Julia Rendel. Of TreeLine."

"She's not here."

"I know she is not in town. But she asked me to drop by the Red Bar and find her friend Léon. Or ask for the Insomniacs Club. But you are not Léon?"

The barman registered Maier properly for the first time. The joint might have been red but its manager was decidedly North American.

"Can't place your fucking accent, dude. You German as well?"

The detective nodded, keeping his eyes to himself.

"Maier, from Hamburg. Professional traveler. Mostly harmless."

"Vincent Laughton. Pleased to fucking meet you, Maier. You don't look harmless. But you do look German. You had a fight with a water buffalo?"

Maier shrugged, trying to place the man's accent.

"I ran into a beauty on a moonless night, Vincent."

The bar man smiled with as little sympathy as he could muster.

"Must have been some gal. Not Julia, I presume."

"No, it was her cousin Arthur."

Something prickled between the two men. Maier wondered whether Vincent knew Julia was missing. The barman snorted and pushed another vodka orange across the counter.

"I haven't seen Julia in a while. I'd like to think she's out in the sticks somewhere. As a matter of fact, Léon was looking for her, too. So I'll give you the benefit of the doubt, being the generous kind of guy that I am."

"Where does one acquire an accent like yours, Vincent?" Maier asked carefully.

"Smalltown, Ontario. Canada. Nothing like Laos. We got fucking roads there. Fuck, I never walked more than three hundred yards in my life until I arrived in Laos, unless it was into absolute wilderness. Some irony ending up in this dump, ha?"

Maier laughed politely. He'd rarely heard a man swear so much. Vincent had a slow and deliberate way of expressing himself, and a lazy melodic drawl in his voice that Maier associated more with the southern United States than with Canada. He also had an air of noisy resignation about him, a need to let the world know that he hadn't been treated fairly. Perhaps that had something to do with his diminutive size and unattractive shape.

Some men were like that.

"Back home, we drive cars, ride horses and shoot bears from pickups. No need for fancy footwork. Arriving here was a bit of a shock – there are few rides in the Lao PDR. It's a pedestrian kind of place."

"You own a great bar."

The Canadian shrugged, marginally more friendly, "Just filling in for a friend. I'm a freelance journalist based out of Bangkok. I got stuck here somehow. There just isn't enough writing work around anymore. Fucking Internet is killing the profession."

Vincent scanned the bar to see if anyone was listening into the conversation. Maier assumed that the level of privacy they enjoyed would determine the amount of bragging his new friend would come up with.

"But you came to the right place. I'm the founder of the Insomniacs Club. And I keep a tight check on who gets to join and who doesn't. We're the only exclusive after-hours speakeasy in town. In the country. The only cool fucking place to go to in the Lao PDR."

The Canadian, surely the most laconic man east of the Mekong, wasn't finished. He leaned across the bar with all the authority his short frame could supply him with and grinned at Maier with a conspiring air of self-importance.

"We're totally under the radar. Even the government pretends we don't exist, because it enjoys a drink here. And we like to keep it that way. Otherwise, we get closed down. Like all good things in Laos."

"What does the Insomniacs Club offer that the Red Bar cannot provide?"

Vincent shrugged, lit a cigarette and stepped out from behind the bar.

"Man, you can't compare the two. It's like day and night. Anyone and his fucking uncle can sit in the Red Bar. The club is a different proposition. It has an eclectic members list. The backpackers aren't allowed in. And as I said, the government snoops come to drink, not to give us trouble. Fuck the closing time. Fuck the drug laws. An escape from the tawdry communist bullshit. Unheard of in the region, man. You really a friend of Julia's?"

Maier nodded as earnestly as he could. The Canadian looked appeased.

"Follow me. You'll be the second German to be admitted. And you're a bit early. The Insomniacs Club doesn't get started properly until everyone in the Red Bar starts going the fuck home."

The Canadian didn't reach to Maier's shoulder but he probably weighed as much as the detective. He exuded all the charm of an overfed spider. He led Maier to the exit and back down the stairs. They crossed the pool hall on the first floor, meriting barely a glance from the bored young women around the tables. Three doors loomed at the back of the room: Ladies, Gents and a third which sported a metal plaque that read *Tired, bored and lonely? Go back upstairs!*

Vincent pulled a pass key from his pocket; the kind usually used on trains, and turned to Maier. "In case she failed to mention it, Julia's my girlfriend. And she's your pass into our exclusive little circle. She told me to look out for you. Otherwise, you'd never be here. You look like a slippery fucker to me. That's why I was testing you. Old journo trick, you know."

Maier was sure the Canadian lied, at least about Julia warning Vincent about his arrival, but he didn't press the point. Perhaps she had emailed him after their first meeting.

The cowboy from small town Ontario flicked his cigarette into a dark corner, opened the door and grinned back at the detective. The relative warmth in his expression surprised Maier almost as much as the fact that he was Julia Rendel's partner. He just couldn't imagine the two in bed together. Nor did he want to.

"Welcome to Vientiane's best-kept secret, Maier. Don't be too fucking bad."

THE INSOMNIACS CLUB

Long couches and low tables spread around the lounge. Black curtains covered walls and ceiling. The Insomniacs Club had no windows. A large fridge with a glass door packed with Beerlao bottles was the main light source, throwing long shadows. The smell of marijuana wafted through the air-conditioned room. Small groups of people mooched around talking in hushed tones. Jazz, not quite insipid, but certainly not free, poured from invisible speakers.

A feisty-looking girl, Thai or Laotian, sat on the felt of the only pool table, nursing a beer, looking distractedly in his direction. The dim glow of the table's overhead lights lent her a wonderfully remote aura.

The fridge was guarded by a dwarf who perched on a low stool like a retired albatross. A small person. A very small person sucking on a joint almost as long as his arm.

"This is No-No. My little fucker. Keeps tabs on what you drink. He is a picture of integrity. Don't fuck with him or you'll be removed from this place, never to return."

Having completed his precise instructions, Vincent turned and made for the door to resume his duties upstairs.

"See you later, Maier. Don't do anything I wouldn't do."

With his wizened sad face and his tiny body strapped into a white shirt and black tie, a waistcoat and black pants, No-No looked like the gatekeeper to undesirable realities. He opened the fridge and, without a word, handed Maier a Beerlao.

"Vodka?" Maier asked gently.

No-No shook his head.

"Beerlao. You want?"

Against his better judgment, Maier took the bottle.

"Who is Léon?"

No-No pointed towards the pool table and resumed his love affair with the joint. Maier passed a group of older white men sitting in a tight circle. They glanced up as he made his way past them, several sets of hard eyes following his steps. Considering the dreamy ambience, there seemed to be an inordinate amount of unhappy types in the Insomniacs Club. These guys would have been more at home in one of Bangkok's nightlife ghettos than in an exclusive filling station on the banks of the Mekong. He heard American accents and kept moving.

"Hi, you Léon?"

The girl on the table smiled and nodded, just a little. Her short black hair was a carefully crafted mess, and she wore her black eyeliner thicker than her purple lipstick.

"Who wants to know?"

"Maier, friend of Julia's."

"Ah yes, she mailed me a few days back, told me you are coming. Didn't tell me you were one-eyed. Nice to meet you, Mr Maier. I'm Kanitha."

"Just Maier, please. The dwarf seems to think you are Léon.

The girl jumped off the table. She wasn't quite a midget herself, but she didn't reach his chest either. Still, she was too tall for No-No. She threw Maier an impish firecracker smile.

"We know so much about you. The famous PI from Hamburg."

Maier was stumped. She had the cutie sheen of a Japanese manga character, with perfect features, light immaculate skin and a figure that suggested she either did yoga all day long or was familiar with tantric sex practices inappropriate for her age group. She wore a critically short skirt and her perfect legs reached down into high black leather boots that wouldn't have looked out of place on a dominatrix. Maier started to warm to the Insomniacs Club.

"What else do you know about me?"

"Julia told me you used to be a journalist. Like a top guy. A great writer. Like me."

Maier felt uneasy. What else had Julia mailed her friends?

"Don't worry; only me and Léon know who you are. Léon knows where the gold is. He also knows where Julia's father died."

"How is that?"

"The man who killed Julia's father also killed Léon's sister. Tried to kill Léon too. Bad guy, definitely. That's what Léon says."

She had a strong American accent with a soft Asian lilt. Maier pushed dark thoughts away. She was very young.

"Where are you from?"

"Bangkok. But my mom's Laotian."

"And how old are you?"

She pulled a face and strained to look like a grown-up.

"That's a loaded question, coming from you, Maier. Old enough to make all the same mistakes you made. In a girl's way, of course."

Maier smiled at her and refrained from commenting.

Her eyes narrowed.

"Twenty-two and counting, if you must know."

He nodded and left her remark standing in the room. He could sense that any comeback would only rile her.

"Is Léon here tonight?"

The girl shook her head. "No, he's out of town. But I can take you to see him. And then he can take you to the gold. I mean us. It's still there, he thinks. So get it into your head right away: You need me."

"So you're a friend of Julia's?"

"I've known her for about six months, Maier. And I plan to be a real journalist, just like you. I graduated from Thammasat with a first-class honors in media studies. You know, the best, like, university in Bangkok. I also spent a year in Texas and did an internship at a local paper there. I've lived in New York. I've been places. I know people."

Maier was intrigued. She might have been bragging but she was probably too young and too earnest to stray too far from the truth. She knew people.

"I am not a journalist."

"But you used to be, I looked it up on the Internet. You're legend, dude."

"Writers are only as good as their last story, and I stopped writing a long time ago."

She shrugged in a dismissive way that befitted her permanent air of youthful discontent and quietly grinned into her beer. Maier had the feeling that his protestations were meaningless.

"It must be journo night tonight. Your smooth-talking friend Vincent is a writer, too."

She shook her head. "No, Vincent is a hack. And he'd sell his mother for a story. He's desperate. I am eager. There's a difference. And he's not my fucking friend."

Maier grinned. "Maybe the twenty years separating you have something to do with it? But you swear almost as much as him."

Kanitha shrugged. "The way he charms people with his linguistic fireworks is way beyond my abilities, Maier. And I reckon he was always like this. Probably not a bad writer at the beginning, but no pride and too much jealousy. As you said, we're only as good as our last story. I'll remember that one."

Maier looked at her more closely. This girl was sharp, free-thinking and independent. Asian hardware, Western software. He noticed that he was patronizing her and changed the subject.

"And how does No-No fit into all this?"

Kanitha laughed, her teeth shining like a priceless pearl necklace.

"I'm just telling you because we will see more of Vincent. He sometimes looks like he can't think his way from here to the toilet, but he has his ear close to the ground. Everything that happens in this country washes through this club sooner or later. And past No-No. He is just the beer clown. A good soul. And Vincent's spider."

"I thought Vincent was just filling in for someone?"

"Is that what he said? Playing the great writer?"

Maier wasn't sure whether the local rivalries had any bearing on his case. He'd cross that bridge when he got to it.

"So, Julia told you I was coming, but omitted to tell her boyfriend?"

"Ah, Maier, you are beginning to get up to speed. Brilliant. Julia and I know each other from TreeLine. I did a short internship with them in Bangkok. And I read your stuff. You're tops."

Maier frowned into his bottle.

"The Beerlao is not bad, but I usually drink vodka orangevodka orange."

"Don't go off subject like that, dude Maier. I read your stories from Palestine, Yugoslavia, Nepal and Cambodia. They were all translated into English, ran in the *Tribune*. All over. You've seen a lot of war, Maier. You've been around. You were at the top of your game. Why'dyou pack it in?"

"My best friend in Cambodia was killed during an attempt on my life, dude Kanitha. After that, it was time for a change. I had enough." Seeing her take a step back, he added, "Slow down a bit. Otherwise, there won't be any mysteries left in the world by the morning."

"Are you making a pass at me, Maier?"

"No, you arc too young."

The girl threw him an ungrateful look. His last quip had slowed her down. But she hardly missed a beat.

"In 1971, the then government created an artificial lake north of Vientiane. Following the revolution, the Pathet Lao, our victorious armed forces, banished all the capital's undesirables to two islands located on this lake. They cleared Vientiane of the good times almost overnight.

One island for all the female sex workers, another for the pimps and the drug dealers. Most of them have either died or gone, of course. The lake is called Ang Nam Ngum."

"Great story, Kanitha, but it is not going to force me out of retirement."

She laughed. "Ah, you're so German. Léon is on the island that once held the female exiles. He has a small house there."

"Hm, that sounds like paradise. How far is it?"

"You'll see tomorrow. I've rented a car. It'll be a bumpy ride; the road up there is no good. Meet me outside the Red Bar at 8. And don't get your hopes up too high. The female subversives that are left are of retirement age. Even older than you, Maier. So old."

The tiny dance floor at the back was almost deserted, and it was so dark Maier could barely make out the other customers. Just as well. A middle-aged foreigner with a tired bar girl attempted a Lao-style dance. It looked sad.

"As old as Mr Mookie," she added.

The man she pointed at discreetly looked around sixty. He had short white hair and was decked out unfashionably in gray pants and a blue anorak. He sat next to the dance floor, surrounded by younger men in leather jackets. Perhaps he was a government official. He looked like a war criminal. He had the best table and the youngest girl. As he rose slowly from his couch, the chicken song blasted from the speakers. Clearly, Mr Mookie was in a dancing mood.

Maier assumed that the Insomniacs Club had seen this before and that the chicken song was the old man's favorite tune. Why else would one want to make the rest of the punters in Vientiane's only speakeasy squirm? Wealthy and influential men in Southeast Asia appreciated small torrid gestures that appeared to reaffirm their usually undeserved status and helped them, for a few blissful moments, to forget about who they were going to screw next.

Mr Mookie grabbed the girl and hit the center of the dance floor. Some of his companions drifted around the edges, but the old man had the limelight all to himself. The girl, dressed in tight jeans, equipped with WTC-sized platforms and a mobile tied to her belt, a rarity in Laos, pirouetted around the old man and giggled as if scared to death. Mr Mookie broke into a sweat. The song mutated into another "Agadoo" style party number, and the old swinger changed his step into a backwards-forwards penguin shuffle, accentuated by the anorak's relentless shimmer under the mirror ball. It was all too much. The music finished and the girl led the blue anorak back to his table. Minutes later he got up, slowly, ever so slowly, and with the help of his lady friend and his bodyguards, headed for the exit.

"Latioan Intelligence, that guy." The young siren to Maier's right grinned.

"Welcome to Laos."

A handful of Beerlao down the line, Maier began to appreciate the people's utopia brew, but he'd had enough for the day and arranged to meet the young reporter the next morning. The evening had been more productive than he'd expected. Léon knew who'd killed Manfred Rendel. Perhaps the twenty-five year-old murder would be resolved after all. He touched her shoulder as he waved her farewell. That did make him feel old, older than Mr Mookie.

As he crossed the dark room for the exit, a huge, broad shadow, a bear of a man, moved into his path.

"Well, evening. Don't think we've had the pleasure. And I usually make everybody who drops by the Insomniacs Club. You new in town?"

Maier took a step back to gauge the unwanted human obstacle. The man was nearly as tall as the detective but twice as wide. American. His pockmarked face was pale and leery. A moustache fit for a walrus divided it neatly into up – mottled cheeks, red veined nose and tiny, curious eyes – and down – numerous chins, covered in dirty stubble. Since Maier had lost his own moustache to his slowly improving taste, he looked with pity upon others who wore them. He had come to think of moustaches as an affliction, like a terrible skin rash.

While the man had no shortage of facial hair, his head was polished like a slippery bowling ball. His breath wasn't good. Maier guessed him in his early sixties. Once upon a time, he'd been in very good shape. Perhaps even handsome. That time had passed and it had left few traces. Life could be cruel.

"Maier, professional traveler. Who are you?"

The American with the oversized whiskers shot him a searching look. Maier sensed that his name had preceded him to this unfortunate encounter. This guy knew who he was, what he was. But the older man caught himself instantly and smiled without passion.

"A devil in his own right, Maier, a devil in his own right. Name's Charlie Bryson. I'm an American, and a veteran. Back in the Seventies, I worked in Laos as a pilot for Air America. More than twenty thousand hours' flight time. Now I'm running some MIA ops north of here. We're looking for our buddies who gave their lives for the agency. Some of them were lost up around Long Cheng. Heard of it?"

Maier shrugged a fake smile onto his face and shook his head. This guy was more dangerous than the faded military tattoos on his hairy arms suggested. He was a smooth liar.

"Well, I saw you talking to young Kanitha there; I assumed you were a journo like her, looking for that mega-scoop, snooping around. I keep telling her it ain't gonna happen. Not in Laos. And now that I look at you, you don't really look like a hack. So what's your game, Maier: just looking for girls?"

Bryson was trying to provoke the detective. Did the old American refer to his client or was he making an innocuous comment about Kanitha? Maier was right in the middle of his case. Perhaps Bryson knew of the gold. Perhaps he had Julia. Maier abandoned his strategy of verbal non-aggression to see if he could make the old guy blow his top.

"Ah, you don't think me very classy, Charlie. Try shooting closer to the mark. In time you might hit something. We all have our dark sides. Yours is bad attitude, friend."

The old American gripped Maier's wrist, hard. For a split second, the detective thought of freeing himself and decking the insolent, drunken soldier. But he checked himself. A bar room brawl was the last thing he wanted. Bryson had friends no more than two meters away. Bryson knew things. And Maier didn't want to be barred from the city's most exclusive drinking hole on his first night in town. He wasn't going to get his client back by getting into a punch-up with this hard man. He relaxed and waited for the American to calm down.

"Hear this, Maier. I saw you walking down the street earlier. It didn't look right. You're a know-it-all. Be careful with our circus; otherwise, the tigers might get nervous."

He let go of Maier's wrist.

The detective, sorely tempted to tell Bryson he'd already seen the clown act, smiled with as much naivety as he could muster, "Charlie, so great to meet you. You look nervous already and I have no desire to see your tigers miss one of the hoops you undoubtedly make them jump through."

The American grinned, his expression sour.

"Well, Maier, nice talking in analogies. Now we both know we're clever. One day soon we'll have to have a real conversation. But for the time being, fuck you and the fuckin' horse you rode in on."

"That's what Mr Mookie just said about you, Charlie," Maier replied flippantly, not really sure why. The older American recoiled and stared hard at the detective. But he didn't say anything else. Strange for a man who looked like he always had to have the last word.

THE ISLAND OF LOST DEALS

Kanitha proved to be a highly efficient guide. The jeep's silent driver raced, slid and pushed through eighty hellish kilometers of muddy roads in four hours and deposited Maier and the girl on the shores of Ang Nam Ngum just after midday. In the shadow of a rickety sala, its grass roof torn away by the rains, Kanitha negotiated the hire of an equally unsteady-looking long-tail boat. The boat man took his time filling his plastic fuel tank, and Maier could feel the girl getting restless. But she didn't complain and sat silently in the prow as they pushed off towards Léon's home.

The small island rose from the water like a magical place in a fairy tale. Fields graced the tree-lined hillsides, and small canoes lay on the grassy shore. Old people pottered around between water and sky. There were no roads or towns. Nothing had happened here for years. The island looked like the world's last idyllic hideaway.

Smoke rose from the next cove. They rounded a headland and paradise was gone to hell in an instant.

The boatman switched off his engine and they drifted towards the shore in near silence. Flames rose from a small property close to a jetty. One look at Kanitha, and Maier knew they were too late.

As soon as the boat touched the jetty, Maier jumped off and ran to the burning building. Kanitha followed him with uncertain steps, crying. Her sobs, the crackling of dying flames and the small waves lapping against the shore made for a dismal soundtrack. The small inferno had the atmosphere of a heavy scene in a Peckinpah movie. But there was no movie, only real life, bleeding slowly into the placid water.

An old woman sidled up to Maier as he picked through the charred remains of what had been a modest beach hut. Flames still licked around the blackened stumps that once held the structure upright. The woman wore a tattered, bright red Chinese polyester dress, the kind that was popular all over Southeast Asia during Chinese New Year, and too much make-up. Her mouth, smothered in cheap lipstick, looked like a wound. In the harsh November sunlight, she had all the charm of a starving vampire.

The ground was charred; fences had melted away. Half-burnt garbage lay everywhere. The carcass of a dog had been impaled and roasted on a wooden pole in the center of the inferno. Its head, stuck on a second pole, greeted Maier from the space that must have once been the hut's front porch.

Whoever had taken Léon had made sure he had nothing to return to. The scorched earth reached all the way down to the lake shore. This had not just been a kidnapping. The scene smelled of erasure.

Maier smiled at the woman and took her hand. She was happy to be led. He took her to the water's edge and found a dry piece of wood for her to sit on. He asked her name but she only smiled vaguely and gave the standard Laotian answer to uncomfortable questions.

"*Bo pen yang.*" Never mind.

He turned to Kanitha, who had slowly followed Maier onto solid ground.

"What's her name?"

"I only know her stage name, which she got when the Americans were here. During the war. She was called May Lik then. Fucking sad."

"Ask May Lik what happened."

The woman started talking, more to herself than to the two arrivals.

Kanitha was still struggling to come to grips with the signs of recent violence.

"I met her when I stayed here with Léon. Vincent and others from the Insomniacs Club have also been here, and she always comes down when we sit on the shore, drinking, having a good time. She's been here since the Seventies. She's mad as a box of frogs."

Maier stifled a laugh, listening to the girl's appraisal while observing the carnage. Sometimes, he couldn't stand his own cynicism.

"It does not matter. We will not have a more reliable witness."

Kanitha nodded and swallowed her tears.

"The dog's name was Poe."

"As in the American writer?"

"No, Maier, as in Tony Poe, CIA case officer in Laos in the Sixties."

Maier looked at her blankly.

"Tony Poe, Maier. Where have you been? The wildest, craziest of the Secret War warriors who lived in Long

Cheng. Remember Brando in *Apocalypse Now*? That character was based on Poe. I thought you were the Southeast Asia expert."

"Where is Poe now? Still around?"

The girl shrugged.

"No idea. But Léon met him when he was a kid and named his dog after him. The guy must have left an impression. Léon told me that Poe used to walk around with a necklace made from human ears. His flower bed in Long Cheng was framed by communist skulls. He was the business."

Maier shook his head. The madness of that war was like that of all the other wars. The rules of commonly accepted conduct disappeared as soon as the first shot was fired. The war pig came out. And stayed out. It squealed and ravaged, pillaged and raped, while generals, politicians and the media told the world the beast was extinct and that an honorable creature sat in its place, spreading justice and punishing those who deserved it. Simple stuff. One look at May Lik told him this was not so.

"So what happened here today?"

"She said that a boat arrived very early in the morning. She can't sleep at night because it's so quiet here. So she sits in her cabin, up on the hill. She saw a motorboat. Five or six men got off. They knew exactly which house to go to. They took Léon and burnt his hut and killed his dog. They had a machine that spat fire."

"They were Asians or white men?"

"She says they were Laotian and Vietnamese. With a white man. Very tall and fat and wearing a colorful shirt."

"The white man had a bald head and a moustache?"

May Lik shook her head and stared hopefully at Maier.

Despite the pale sun, high above them now, Maier felt a chill.

Everything had been said.

The story of the old woman had set new wheels in his head in motion, but he couldn't place the man in the colorful shirt. Not unpleasant Charlie Bryson from the Insomniacs Club. But there were other objectionable characters around. And if the Vietnamese were crowding in on his case, there would be more complications. If the kidnappers were government people, they could do anything they wanted in Laos. If they were a private outfit, they would do anything they wanted in Laos. The difference was merely in the language. Vietnam was a powerful neighbor. Still, those were a lot of ifs.

With the air of a funeral procession, a smattering of old women slowly walked down the hill, gathered in a wide circle and stared at what was left of the cabin. No one spoke to the visitors. Everyone kept their eyes on the burnt-out shell of the hut. No one made eye contact. One bunch of strangers in a day was quite enough.

May Lik spoke into the long silence.

"She says they beat Léon until the white man made them stop. They were very angry. That's why they chopped and burned Poe."

Kanitha picked herself up. She was pale but composed. She put her arm around May Lik and asked her to continue.

Maier shook his head. What was a white man doing with a bunch of Vietnamese enforcers?

May Lik brushed the girl off and walked to the lake shore, where she continued to mumble at no one. The old woman in her tattered dress implored unseen friends and enemies, begging for a better deck of cards than the one she'd been dealt. Then she lapsed into a loud silence that stretched as far as the water around them. Maier was moved by her desperation. No winners today.

"She says that Léon was a good man. They should not have taken him."

"Why did Léon choose to stay on the island of the old ladies, rather than the one with the pimps and hustlers?"

Kanitha shrugged, "Where would you have stayed, Maier? He wasn't well. He'd been shot in the war and never really recovered his strength. He thinks the bullet grazed his lung, but with medical facilities in Laos being almost nonexistent and he being a Hmong whose parents had clearly been on the US side…"

"You and Léon are pretty tight, right?

The young woman gestured helplessly, as only a near-teenager could. She wouldn't meet his eye.

"With me and Léon, it's one day at a time, Maier. But that has nothing to do with how I feel about what happened here. We have to find him. We gotta find my buddy, my soulmate. And I want to know which bastard killed and burned Poe."

Maier got up and kicked the pole that supported the dog's head into the dying flames of Léon's inferno. It was time to go.

"I don't suppose May Lik has any idea where they took Léon?"

"Of course she does. She told me immediately. They took him to Muang Khua. It's in the north, near the Vietnamese border and very close to Dien Bien Phu. You know, the last stand of the French in Indochina. Muang Khua is little more than an obscure river outpost. They told May Lik to tell anyone who was coming to look for him. They said they'd be waiting."

Maier mulled the kidnappers' message and made a snap decision.

"Julia already told you that she hired me to find out about her father. Do you know she was kidnapped in Hamburg last week?"

He watched the younger woman pale, stagger to her feet and throw up into the shallow water.

"Maier," she shouted between heaving saliva and air, "why didn't you tell me this when we met?"

He didn't answer. The case was slipping through his hands before he even got started. Both his client and his only local source of information had been kidnapped by at least one opposition he didn't know existed and didn't need. His trail to the gold was quickly wearing thin.

Maier caught a flash of light across the water. The sun was behind them. It was probably the reflection from a piece of glass lying on the distant shore.

"I think we need to go to Muang Khua. Have you been there?"

Kanitha shot him a weary look and nodded. "I went there for a travel magazine. A wild, beautiful stretch of the Nam Ou River. There is some talk of re-education camps in the area that were built for enemies of the state after the revolution. My story was on trekking, though. And I didn't see any camps."

Maier smiled. "So you are a writer after all. Maybe you can show an old dog a few new tricks."

Kanitha smiled into her shirt and said nothing. Maier gave May Lik a fistful of kip, Laotian bank notes, and started towards the boat.

"Great, you'll be my guide, then."

"And we'll find Julia."

Whatever lurked on the far side of the water flashed again. A signal? Maier's hair stood on end. Not a signal. He threw himself onto Kanitha and they both tumbled into the shallow water. The shot rang out a second later, the sound delayed by the distance. A sniper.

"You OK?"

Kanitha tried to get up but Maier pushed her behind the boat and crawled through the shallow water next to her. She nodded, her eyes wide with fear.

"It's OK; they missed."

He turned to scan the shore behind them. They, whoever they were, had not missed. May Lik had collapsed, a hole in her thin chest, her smudged mouth a silent scream. Everyone else had disappeared.

Maier waited thirty seconds and then crawled over to the old woman. She was dead. He slowly crawled back to the boat.

BAD ELEMENTS

They stayed in the water until they couldn't stand the cold any longer. They pushed the boat – a petrified boatman lying motionless in the water-filled bottom of his vessel – around the island until Maier felt it safe enough to get out of the water. Once it got dark, the boatman agreed to return to the shore. There was no sign of the shooter.

Shaking, wet and cold, they rested in an abandoned farm hut before hitching a ride with a tourist group in the morning. The vacationers were somewhat excited at seeing an older Western man and a very young Asian woman, both of them caked in mud, emerge on the side of the road and flag down their four-wheel drive. Maier spun them a story about being a journalist on the trail of illegal loggers with his fixer, having run into trouble in the forest.

Certain that his hotel was being watched, Maier didn't bother returning to his room. He stayed with Kanitha in her cramped two-room apartment above a Chinese goods store set a couple of blocks back from the river. He slept on a tattered sofa covered in cigarette burns and held together by duct tape. The perfumed sheets of the Atlantic in Hamburg were a distant memory. The actual life of the private eye had caught up with him.

No matter how many times the detective turned the events at the lake over in his mind, he couldn't understand why the Vietnamese had shot the old woman. And if May Lik had not been the intended target, then why would anyone have taken a shot at him? The kidnappers' message had been loud and clear: Try to come after us and we'll kill you. It also meant that Léon was of no value to them dead.

There was of course another, more troubling possibility. Maier and Kanitha could have been followed from the capital to the lake. While he and his youthful sidekick had been in pursuit of Léon's kidnappers, others had been in pursuit of them. And where was Julia?

Maier was in the deep end.

He knew next to nothing about the kidnappers, even less about the killers who might have been on their trail. Unpleasant thoughts formed in his mind like heavily laden monsoon clouds. One could imagine enemies everywhere.

"Maier, I'm scared. And we need to talk."

The detective, showered but not shaved, sat on the small terrace of Kanitha's apartment and studied a map of northern Laos. Children played on the unpaved road below. A woman passed, pushing a cart with steaming corn on the cob under a tree, calling for hungry customers. From their vantage point, the world looked non-threatening, pastoral.

"You have information for me that you previously withheld?"

"Of course, Maier. I'm a journalist, remember, not a public information service that spills all its secrets because a tall, handsome German correspondent claiming to be a private eye steps into the picture. And you didn't tell me Julia was kidnapped. You don't trust me."

Maier shrugged. "Get over the celebrity thing, Kanitha. I'm just another Joe making a buck. And my journalist days are long gone. I am no longer interested in investigating truths and then finding out that my employer has an agenda that contradicts my story."

"So you think the truth should not be told at all?" she asked defiantly.

He looked at her in what he thought might be a disarming way. "When you are young, you know that you can change the world. When you're my age, you know it's impossible. Both insights are close to the truth. Does that make sense?"

She thought about it and shook her head.

"So why won't you sleep with me, Maier?"

He looked up from the map and focused on the beautiful girl next to him.

"I am not looking for attachments."

Kanitha rolled her eyes and pushed wayward hair from her face.

"I'm not asking you to marry me, dick."

"You're a beautiful girl, Kanitha…"

She cut him off.

"Blah blah blah…"

"Your boyfriend has been kidnapped."

Her face was a mixture of shame and fury.

"Like I said, Maier, with me and Léon, it's one day at a time."

Maier cut her off with a curt gesture.

"You are my understudy. Perhaps I can help you get a scoop, an important exclusive, if you help me get to the bottom of this gold saga. This case just smells of things larger than the sum of the parts we have seen so far. We have a deal?"

He held his hand out and tried for his most genuine smile.

After a moment's hesitation, she took it and tried for a tight, manly grip. "Old men are such pussies. You're probably right. I'll take a shower and get myself together, don't disturb. And know what you're missing."

With that she got up, turned theatrically, pulled off her T-shirt, flashed her breasts at Maier and walked inside. Her perfectly smooth, pale back swayed away from him, out of reach, and he hoped half-heartedly, out of mind. He wasn't sure how the conversation might have ameliorated any of her fears. He'd avoided all her questions. And she was avoiding most of his while toying with him.

Maier left the apartment and found an Internet café. This time he had a message waiting. From the 1000 Elephant Trading Company.

We offer Julia Rendel in exchange for Léon Sangster. When you find him, get in touch. Refrain from all other investigations or you will be stopped with maximum force.

An hour later, Kanitha was back at his side, wearing a black blouse and a long skirt over her boots. She looked like an Asian rockabilly cat.

"Ready for the wilderness, Maier? Are you?"

Maier held up the maps. "Sure, but how do we get there?"

"Let's go to the Insomniacs Club. Vincent knows a good boatman."

Maier shook his head, "Kanitha, I've been doing some thinking. We met at the Insomniacs Club, and Vincent knows I came looking for Léon. When I left, I was stopped by this MIA guy, Charlie, who wanted to know whether I was interested in Long Cheng. The old US airport? Ring a bell?"

Kanitha thought about it. "I know Charlie. He and his crew work all over the country, especially in the north. Retired Air America, CIA. Long Cheng is not far from here as the crow flies but hard to get to. Bad roads, Hmong rebels, Lao military. Off limits to tourists and snoops like us. Even Charlie and his guys can't go there unless they have prior clearance from the right ministry. But his lot have lobby groups in the US who pressure congressmen who in turn might be talking to the Laotians. There's big money involved in digging up American soldiers. I've tried to go to Long Cheng. But I got stopped at the first army roadblock and was sent back. Definitely a story."

As an afterthought, she added, "And Léon has been there, too. He was there as a kid. He told me that his parents died there. But he was pretty sketchy about it. I mean, he was definitely holding out on me."

"Is there anything else I need to know about before we head north?"

Maier didn't try to keep the hard tone out of his voice. If he was to travel with an unpredictable young woman, he needed to know everything she did.

"He told me that he got shot there. That his sister was killed there. In the Seventies. By a double agent. I dunno, that just sounds mad. But as I said, he was a kid then."

Maier said nothing and looked at her expectantly. There was more.

"Léon's second name is Sangster. His father was American. His mother was Hmong. He told me she was a princess. The whole family lived in Long Cheng."

Maier thought about the information she was spoon-feeding him.

"The gold is in Long Cheng, I think. It must be."

He scanned the maps again. Long Cheng was a long way from where Léon had been taken. "But I don't think his kidnappers know that. And I am sure they are Vietnamese, as May Lik said. They are playing safe, keeping him near the border so they can whisk him away quickly if necessary. And they are not just careful because I am nosing around. There are other players out there. This 1000 Elephant Trading Company and the Vietnamese are hunting for the same prize. One lot have Julia, the other lot have Léon. One lot burned down Léon's house, the other lot shot May Lik. And both parties think I have the key to the gold. That's my theory at present. It comes with a fifty percent error margin."

"So what do we do?" Kanitha asked impatiently.

"We take a trip to Muang Khua. Quietly and carefully."

Maier, marooned on Kanitha's tatty sofa for a second night, was alone in his dream. His world was on fire. Way ahead in the distance, partly obscured by flames, wavering like a mirage, he could see the silhouette of a man, standing on a wide-open plain dotted with villages. Broad shoulders, short-cropped hair, a fierce gait, his arms apparently embracing the world. Every time the figure vibrated slightly, a huge roar sounded across the plain. Maier knew that the ground shook, though he couldn't feel it. The man started walking through the fire towards Maier. The closer he came, the more familiar Maier felt about his lean features and his purposeful, economic movements. Soon he would be able to make out his identity. Just a few more meters. As the man got closer, Maier noticed something else. Wherever this black shadow of a man walked, his outline defined against the inferno around him, villages went up in flames, forests burnt like matchsticks, rivers dried up in seconds and people died and died. Maier moved towards a village that the black shadow, the broad-shouldered man with the short cropped hair had just passed. The second the detective's mind touched the village, he recoiled and woke up, breathing much too quickly. But he felt himself immediately sucked down into the dream again. All the houses were burning. People ran from their homes, their backs and hair in flames. Children watched their skin peel away from their arms as clouds of chemical warfare washed across their community. Mothers and fathers, uncles and aunts, grandparents and neighbors, builders and tailors, idiots and wise men wilted away in an instant. While one village burned, a great silence descended on the next, as another shock wave hit buildings and tore them to pieces, seconds before the noise of the explosion deafened every living being within a mile radius. He looked up into the sky but saw nothing but silence.

"Gods," an old man shouted. "These are gods that spit fire from the sky. We cannot fight them. We must go underground."

The next moment, the old man had gone, had been atomized by the harbinger of sorrows. The black shadow continued walking through a land he emptied with his passing. Every time Maier could almost make out the ogre's face, another huge explosion would light up behind him, leaving his identity obscured.

Dawn came and Maier woke up, grappling with the quickly fading dream, trying to fall back down into it to find out where it might take him.

NEVER GET OFF THE BOAT

The Lao Airlines jet banked dangerously and wobbled towards the Luang Prabang runway. The flight had been short and frightening. The plane was as ancient as the hills it had crossed and in much worse condition. The tourists on board applauded when the pilot touched down and got his machine under control as they rattled towards the ramshackle airport building.

Maier had been to Luang Prabang on an assignment covering German restoration efforts of the historic city center just after Laos had opened its doors to foreign visitors, a cover for his investigative work on the Hmong rebels who continued to fight the Laotian government in the mountain ranges to the south of the city, decades after the CIA, their erstwhile paymaster, had abandoned them.

The city itself had escaped the war unscathed – the Americans and Vietnamese had decided early on that Luang Prabang was too attractive to be destroyed. Perhaps it had been the town's spectacular collection of sixteenth century temples, each one a striking physical poem to form and faith, that had saved the city. More likely, both factions had decided to use the former royal capital as a holiday spot while the rest of the country was being vaporized. Luang Prabang was the Laotians' most magnanimous tourist cash cow, a UNESCO world heritage site with a rapidly expanding infrastructure of hotels, restaurants, bakeries, shops and cybercafés.

Maier and Kanitha carried hand luggage only and caught a taxi straight to the town's ferry pier. They were too late. Their destination, Muang Khua, lay on the banks of the Nam Ou River, a day's journey north on a long-tail. The regular boat had left.

"*Bo pen yang,*" the ticket seller smiled, "Never mind. Another boat tomorrow."

They ambled down to the waterline, where a group of boat captains sat under a tree and played cards. Half an hour of intermittent bargaining later, they sat in the back of a long-tail boat.

The captain, a cheroot-smoking old man with arms as thin as matchsticks, grinned at Maier and asked, "Honeymoon?"

Maier first assumed the boatman to be sarcastic, but when he turned to fix him with a stare, the poor soul, intimidated and embarrassed, simply wilted and squeezed out another *bo pen yang*.

The Laotians were agreeable people, keen to avoid confrontation of any kind.

"Why rock the boat, Maier? Leave him his assumptions," Kanitha said and hooked her arms around his. Maier didn't resist.

A few minutes later, they had left Luang Prabang behind, headed up the Mekong and entered one of its countless tributaries, the Nam Ou. Small villages lined the river banks. Gardens stretched all the way down to the water's edge. Buffalo stood and stared at them as they passed.

Children waved and jumped into the floods while their
mothers showered or beat their washing on flat stones,
clothed only in sarongs that clung tightly to their skins and
shimmered in the afternoon sun. From the passing boat,
the scenes were bucolic, framed by the natural poetry of
the world's honest and hard-working people, the salt of the
Earth. Maier relaxed, knowing he was lucky to enjoy these
glimpses of partial truths and to be able to separate them
from the harsh realities the country's rural population
faced.

Four hours upriver, they approached Nong Khiaw,
the halfway point between Luang Prabang and their
destination. The boat slowed to a crawl as the captain
made ready to pull in and stop. Like other villages they
had passed, Nong Khiaw, a modest collection of homes and
shops, a few guest houses and a jetty cum bus terminal,
clung to a steep embankment. A concrete bridge crossed
the river high above the village. Karst stone cliffs topped by
clusters of bamboo framed the idyllic view. More dollops of
paradise were likely to be around the corner. The pandas
couldn't be far. For a brief moment, Maier had that tourist
feeling that he almost never got. Innocence had its benefits.

"Shit," Kanitha suddenly exclaimed and pointed to the
jetty.

Charlie Bryson, his shining bald plate poking out behind
a jeep, was directing a group of workers to transfer tarpaulin
bags to a long-tail boat. As they neared, he abandoned his
mission and scanned the river.

With a mad hug, Kanitha fell on top of Maier. They
tumbled into the bottom of the boat. For a moment, he
couldn't see a thing as she smothered him. He smelled her
faintly delicious perfume mixed with sweat.

"*Mai yud, baw yud*, don't stop," she shouted to the boatman in both Thai and Laotian. The driver looked at her, confused. Naturally, he'd made no connection between her sudden affection for her partner, the commotion on the river bank and her desire to continue at top speed. Embarrassed, he decelerated to a crawl. Kanitha continued imploring him. They drifted by the jetty in slow motion just as one of the workers dropped a large bundle he was carrying. The American turned and shouted at the man. The boat passed. Maier glanced back. Kanitha continued to berate the boatman. A few seconds later, they had cleared the spot and Kanitha let go of Maier, sat up and returned to her seat. She grinned at him victoriously. They'd been lucky.

Almost.

As they crossed under the bridge, Vincent, Ontario's greatest journalist, appeared on a balcony of a restaurant shack overlooking the river. The Canadian stared straight at Maier. He gave no sign of acknowledgement. But as the boat passed the bridge, Maier saw him get up and hurry away. Then they were gone.

"What is he doing here with Charlie and his gang?" Kanitha wondered aloud, shaking her head in frustration.

Maier had regained his composure and laughed. "Quick thinking, Kanitha. But we have been spotted. How close is that Canadian guy to the MIA program?"

The young Thai shook her head, somewhat dejectedly.

"I didn't even think they had anything to say to each other. Never seen Vincent sit down with Charlie. In fact, Vincent always talks about how he will one day expose the MIA activity in northern Laos having as much to do with recovering loot from the war as with finding the remains of American soldiers."

"He changed sides, perhaps?"

"Anything is possible. He thinks the world owes him. He would naturally see you as a challenge just because you are a new face in town and you appear to be doing something. That can make expats stranded in small-town Asia with not much to do homicidal. You're a man of action, Maier. This is more than what can be said for him. And Charlie is a regular at the Insomniacs Club."

Anything was possible with anyone in this game, Maier thought as he listened to his young companion. How the hell did these guys get on the river here? Did Kanitha have another agenda other than springing her one-day-at-a-time boyfriend and getting her scoop? How innocent was innocent? And why did she have to smell so damn good?

The boat captain started shouting above the noise of the engine. Maier understood a smattering of Laotian, but this man was almost completely unintelligible. The detective experienced a momentary lack of confidence in his beautiful travel companion. But he needed to trust her.

"We need petrol. We don't have enough juice to get all the way to Muang Khua. And it's getting late. Our man does not want to travel in the dark. He says there might be bandits. The closer we get to the Vietnamese and Chinese border, the higher the risk of an ambush at night."

Maier pulled a map from his vest and scanned the river villages. Muang Ngoi, a tourist outpost on a peninsula in the Nam Ou, was close. The captain confirmed the availability of gasoline at the village. They would be able to melt into the tourist population without attracting attention. It was time to get off the boat.

THE GOOD AMERICANS

She lay deep in his arms as if she belonged there. Music drifted from a campfire through the small gaggle of riverside huts occupied by young Western travelers. Someone was strumming a guitar, not too competently, but it hardly mattered. Maier could see fireflies bouncing around in front of the window.

Muang Ngoi was the last frontier for the Lonely Planet set – a laid-back Lao village that had made the necessary concessions to the twenty-first century nomads that scoured the Earth in search of cheap foreign thrills packed with the necessities to keep the comfort zone intact – beer, marijuana, pancakes and fried rice. The Internet wasn't long off. Travelers needed little more than that to continue their consumption-driven lifestyles in front of a more exotic background than the suburbs they came from. Luckily, the young people traveling the Asian pancake trench were not particularly observant. For the most part, they were busy positioning their own narrative in a strange land, posturing with disc players, singing songs that had originated, like themselves, thousands of miles away, falling in love with the Other but sleeping with

acquaintances they met on the road. They talked about
the price of this and that across Asia – where to scuba-
dive cheaply, how to beat the entrance fee to a temple,
which beer had the best flavor at the lowest price with the
smallest headache factor. They were experts in scrimping
and saving but learned little about the land they passed
through or the people that lived in it. And most of them
were alike, even looked alike. A generation entranced by
the conformity of individualism. No one had looked at
Maier and Kanitha as they'd checked into one of the huts.
In the travelers' world, old age made men and women
invisible.

Maier loved being unseen, though he knew the locals
would remember him.

Kanitha, her eyes closed, her breath hot against his
chest, didn't appear to remember anything. The worm had
turned and no one was more surprised than the detective.
He'd been so determined not to fly. She was too young.
She was part of the case. She was the second woman
connected to the case he'd ended up in bed with. Perhaps
he'd entangled himself in more than he could keep track
of. He didn't know whether to feel happy, stupid or a tad
too predatory.

He could tell she wasn't sleeping.

"So, tomorrow we try to spring your boyfriend from
captivity, and tonight we are having a ball? I mean, I like
you. A great deal. You are a wonderful woman, Kanitha.
I have the feeling you have been digging away at me ever
since we met in the Insomniacs Club. But I can't figure
out why. I am sorry, but I don't quite buy the cub-reporter
story. I did a little checking on you myself. You are widely
published in the region in the past six months. You have

a pretty good reputation amongst the NGO set and expat readers in Thailand. You don't need me."

He gently placed her head on the moldy pillow they shared and pushed himself up on the worn-out mattress. She didn't react. Maier slunk out from underneath the mosquito net and reached for his clothes. The girl grumbled but made no move to follow him.

"There must be more to this than what you have told me."

Kanitha opened her eyes and looked at him as he pulled on his faded khaki pants.

"Where you going?"

"Beer run. And when I get back, you better have a story as good as the time we just had in the sack. Otherwise, I may be gone when you wake up tomorrow. We detectives move in silent and mysterious ways, you know."

As he opened the door, she spat angrily after him. "Come back to bed, Maier. We are so drunk, we'll never notice if someone comes and tries to kill us in our sleep. What do you need more alcohol for? And the boatman will not go without me."

Maier laughed. "Oh yes, he will. Money talks, bullshit squawks."

"Marry me, Maier."

He turned back to see her sitting up under the net, laughing, flashing her breasts, acting her age.

"Get that shock off your face, old man. Relax. You're so old-fashioned. We're on the river of dreams. It's a trip. Get some beer and when you get back, if I can figure out which side you are on, I will tell you the rest. And then we make love properly."

Outside, the party had almost finished. Village children

cleared away beer bottles and other debris. A campfire behind the huts was burning down. The flames, the only light source other than the moon, threw long shadows. Maier found the bungalow colony's owner sitting on a plastic stool by the river. When the woman saw him coming she pulled a nylon net filled with Beerlao bottles from the water. He handed her a bundle of kip. The Nam Ou flowed all the way down from southern China into Laos, but its temperature was lukewarm. Maier disliked warm beer more than cold beer. But he understood that the day the first fridge arrived here would be the end of an era and the beginning of times he had no desire to witness.

The woman smiled at Maier in the dim light and said in broken English, "You very old man, monsieur. Tourist in Muang Ngoi always young. Why you come? You not look like tourist. Which country?"

Maier looked her straight in the eye.

"I am German. From Germany."

She didn't flinch.

"Ah, Deutschland," she said, and fell silent.

He guessed her about sixty, though she might have been ten years younger.

"Many visitor from Deutschland, but not look like you."

"What's your name?"

"Bua Kham," she said, smiling.

"You have lived here for a long time?"

"All my life."

"You have family?

She looked at him with eyes long inhabited by sorrow.

"My husband dead. My son dead. My daughter, she cannot walk. Stay in Luang Prabang with auntie, sister. Only me, alone. Make money for family."

She thought about her words and a vague smile passed her lips.

"Every year, more and more tourist coming."

Maier already knew she had something to tell him. But one didn't press the point with older people in Southeast Asia. She would get around to it in her own time.

"I sell beer, rent room. Good job. I too old to work in the field."

She nodded to herself.

"In the war, American planes fly across Muang Ngoi. So much bombing. We live in the cave. Everybody live in the cave. Only at night we come outside and do the farming. I grow rice with my husband. But not enough to eat like this, so sometime we plant in the day. One day the plane come. You hear the sound of the bomb falling, you know in few seconds you maybe die. So much explosion and everything dark. The tree falling, the river like boiling water. My husband die that day. Many people die that day. I never see American people at that time. Only see the plane. I don't know how far away is America and why they come halfway round the world to kill Lao farmer. I not understand."

She lapsed into silence, her face a mask of suffering.

"After the bomb, so many body. We put all dead together and put petrol and burn. No time to take to pagoda. Maybe more planes coming. Sometime we leave the body in the field because too much danger. And then very bad smell. We go back to the cave and hide."

She nodded, to herself more than to Maier.

"After the war finish, my children they go out to play, they find American bomb. Small bomb, like toy. Boom. My son die. My daughter lose one leg."

"Do you hate America?"

She shook her head, got up and walked to her nearby home. Maier sat alone and stared into the silent, dark river. He wondered how often the woman had told her story to visitors. A few minutes later, Bua Kham was back and pressed a tennis-ball-sized object into his hand.

"Bombi," was all she said.

Maier felt the cold metal of the explosive. During the Secret War, American planes had pummeled Laos for almost a decade, dropping off gigantic payloads round the clock, day in, day out. B52s filled the skies and carpet-bombed village after village into oblivion to cut the Ho Chi Minh Trail, the Vietcong's supply line that ran from North Vietnam through Laos and Cambodia into South Vietnam. Pilots who failed to use up their payloads were ordered to return to their Thai bases empty and dropped their remaining munitions indiscriminately over Laos. The country became the Vietnam War's dumping ground. By the time the US exited Southeast Asia, Laos and neighboring Cambodia had earned the sad monikers of being the most heavily bombed countries on Earth.

The bomb he was holding had originated from a large cluster bomb case dropped by a plane. The case was designed to open in mid-air releasing thousands of these bombis, packed with nuts, nails and bolts, and operated with a spring. The small ball-shaped bombs needed to turn several times before exploding. Some malfunctioned and hit the ground in one piece. Children, mistaking them for toys, played with the bombis and completed the final turn necessary to detonate the device.

Bua Kham continued in a more upbeat manner, "Now young American come back. Bring money, buy beer, rent

room, eat fry rice. No problem. Different American. Very
nice."

Maier opened one of the beers and took a swig.

"But Vietnamese very bad. No buy beer, no friend. No
smile. Just make problem."

"But the Vietnamese left a long time ago, didn't they?"

The woman looked at Maier, as if trying to fathom his
reasons for appearing on her doorstep.

"Yes, they go. But they never go. Sometime come
back. Lao government build prison upriver. Near Muang
Khua. But prison not Lao, prison Vietnam."

Maier assumed she meant one of the re-education
camps the victorious communists had established across
the country following the departure of the Americans. In
these tropical jails, bureaucrats and soldiers loyal to the
old regime were indoctrinated and sometimes killed, or
simply kept out of circulation for a decade or more. The
camps were self-defeating, the resultant brain drain on
the country catastrophic. But the communists, like their
imperialist nemesis further west, had long understood
one thing: keeping people stupid, either by depriving
them of stimulation or forcing them to be constantly
stimulated, made them malleable. It kept the number of
rebels to a minimum, made accountability unnecessary,
and when the war pig made its return, no one was likely
to question its appearance.

"Aren't these places all closed?"

The woman shook her head violently. "Not closed.
Only few days ago, Vietnamese stop here for petrol. Very
bad men. They have one prisoner in the boat. I can see he
is prisoner."

"A white man?"

Bua Kham thought about her answer for a while. "I not sure. He have bag over head. But I think maybe Asian, maybe local. They not pay for petrol. Just take and go. But they talk Lao with prisoner. Tell him they wait for his friend, then shoot him dead. You his friend?"

Maier felt sorry for the woman and admired her shrewdness. But he wasn't sure whether he could trust her. He remained silent and concentrated on the river again.

"And some young tourist go upriver. Never come back."

Her expression swung from compassion to indifference and back.

"What do you mean? Never come back? They might go up to Phongsali. And then leave by road. Into China. Or back down to Udomxai. They don't have to come back this way."

She shook her head and brushed a strand of thin hair from her narrow face.

"They never go Phongsali."

"How do you know?"

Bua Kham rose slowly.

"Enough beer? I go sleep."

He sensed he wasn't going to get an answer to his last question and nodded in silent agreement to end the conversation.

She smiled her vague smile once more. "I think you good man, monsieur Deutschland. I think you here because of Vietnamese. You careful in Muang Khua. These men make me very much scare. Very danger. And they travel with big white man, very nice shirt. Very loud man. Your friend?"

Maier shook his head.

May Lik, the woman who'd died because of his visit to the island, had told them the same thing. The Vietnamese were traveling with a Westerner. Not a prisoner. An operator. At least Maier now knew that Léon was alive.

Bua Kham faded into the night. By the time the detective returned to their hut, Kanitha had passed into deep sleep. He sat on the small porch, drinking, watching the fireflies, too lazy to fend off the mosquitoes that devoured him, in too much turmoil to lie next to the young woman whose dreams and stories were waiting for him.

The case was beginning to eat at Maier. The same questions rolled around his head like empty Beerlao bottles, making a vague, undefined sound he didn't care for. Was he being played? Was Kanitha a spy? Or was he just such a smooth, handsome and beautiful guy that twenty-two year-olds latched on to him the way flies were drawn to honey? And what the hell had happened to his client? Where was Julia? Just ahead, the river rushed on, not offering a single answer.

ONE VELVET MORNING

The fried eggs Bua Kham served with strong Lao coffee were only mildly appetizing. Kanitha had dark rings under her eyes that kept pace with Maier's slowly healing injury. Despite her wasted countenance, she looked ravishing, and the detective watched her for a small eternity as she put on and laced up her boots and made sure her spiky black hair rose to disorderly attention. As she stood up and walked down to the shore, she looked like a pygmy warrior queen about to rouse her troops. She didn't have any troops, of course. She just had Maier. Or perhaps it was the other way round.

Mist hung over the Nam Ou. The sun still hid behind the craggy mountains to the west. The first light of dawn caressed the ridges; shadows rippled across tree lines. The movement gave the forested ravines the appearance of a slowly moving reptile. The air was cool, and a thin film of dew covered the world like a glass blanket. A couple of egrets rose from the far shore, drifted across the brown water to find a perch on a nearby hut and proceeded to clean their white plumage. If only it was as easy as that.

Despite the night's excesses, Maier and Kanitha were the first guests to greet the new day. The backpackers were still asleep in their hovels. The silence was waiting to be shattered by the noise of boat engines and transistor radios.

"I'm so hungover," she groaned, obviously enjoying her destitute state as much as the changed energy between them.

Maier felt awful, but he had no urge to report on his physical state.

"I'm so hungover," she announced once more, more forcefully this time.

Maier was not forthcoming with prattle this morning. "Go tell the boatman," he said, and grinned at her.

The detective drank his second coffee and watched a small, almost transparent paddy field crab move through the dust by his feet. The crab moved sideways, stopped and started, scuttled a short distance before coming to a complete halt once more. Maier likened the crustacean's journey to his work. He moved about a little, usually sideways rather than straight ahead, talked to some people and then stopped and took stock, assembling the available information, hypothesizing various realities. He did it automatically, instinctively, like the crab which had now pushed off towards the river.

And what a great moment to take stock it was. He was stuck with a keen child in the middle of the Laotian jungle, about to confront a dangerous mob of Vietnamese assassins accompanied by a fat white man in a loud shirt. He'd set off to spring the child's boyfriend from the clutches of men whose agenda was unknown to him. He remembered that Kanitha had confessed during the night, not in so many words, but in essence, that her stories had been half-truths, selected facts, perhaps even red herrings. Having lured each other into rolling around in the hot night– there was no point, he had decided, to blame either party – made things more difficult, not easier.

But Maier enjoyed the feisty Thai woman's company.

"Never underestimate your charisma, Maier. These eyes of yours know how to melt a girl's heart. Even when one of them is black. That's why I wanted to sleep with you. But it's not a hanging matter. It's not a capital crime. I am twenty-two, you know."

He did not have it in him to remind her that they were together so she would get her big break and they would both get their man. A second later, he realized she was toying with his ego. The girl from Bangkok was still one step ahead.

"Don't be so serious, Mr Detective," she laughed. "You're an amazing guy, Maier. Don't be too humble. I would love to spend more time with you when this is finished."

"And what is *this* exactly?" he countered.

"Good question, Maier. I am confused about it myself. And since you turned up, it all seems to be tightening somehow, racing towards a darker place."

"Come on, journalist, don't give me poetry. We need facts."

A somber voice shattered the peace. Prehistoric tannoys suspended from a pole near Bua Kham's collection of huts coughed to life. As in every village in Laos, the morning propaganda was pumped into the day whether people wanted it or not. The Laotian government demanded its due. Speech was followed by marching music, followed by more sonorous speech. A sleep-deprived tourist complained loudly from his hut, to no avail. The Laotians were reminded daily that they did in fact have a government, that this government had saved them from a fate worse than death – capitalism – and that it would always be there for them, even if it did absolutely nothing to support them. Totalitarian political systems demanded total attention, as Maier knew from his own childhood in Leipzig. Democracies, on the other hand, didn't want you to give any attention to its caretakers at all.

Laos still had some way to go before it would reach an unhappy medium.

The detective turned to the girl. "Tell me what else you know, and tell me all of it. If I get the impression you are holding more stuff back, I will continue the journey upriver by myself."

He realized immediately that this wasn't the way to get the best answers out of his companion. Threats didn't work with all-or-nothing rebels.

"And if you tell me more, I will help you get your scoop."

Kanitha, barely suppressing her anger at his condescending strategy, managed to smile with remarkable sweetness. "As long as you don't take me seriously, you're not getting anything out of me."

Maier stared across the water.

She added, with a modicum of youthful menace in her voice, "But I'll be nice to you. Again. And you can be nice to me. Again."

One of the travelers nearby cranked up his stereo. Bad resort funk drowned out the communist sermon. The egrets rose from their perches. The morning shattered like glass. The village had turned into a noisy bus stop. It was time to go.

Kanitha looked around, perhaps to see if anyone else might be listening. It was a rather theatrical effort. When she turned back to Maier, her face was deadly serious.

"I'll tell you the rest. What I know. You promise you will look after me up there. You won't leave me behind?"

Maier tried to assure her with a stern look.

"Have you ever heard of the U48?"

He shook his head.

"This has to be our secret. This is my story. This is the story. No one gives a damn about gold or drugs. The Vietnamese upriver, the Americans behind us, perhaps even Julia, they are all after the U48."

"What is it?"

She chewed her lower lip, "I am not sure. But Léon does know. And he told me that the U48 would reunite him with the man who tried to kill him. Soon."

Maier had no idea what she was talking about. More subterfuge, perhaps. No answers. Without a word, he got up and went to find Bua Kham. He paid the bill and said goodbye to the old woman. This morning, her face was closed. He was just another transient. Maier was disappointed to see her so cautious, but he said nothing and waved goodbye.

When he returned to the hut, Kanitha had already moved their belongings into the boat. He followed and jumped in. The boatman cranked up the engine and they pushed out into the Nam Ou River. The sun rose quickly and would soon touch the water. A beautiful day was on its way. A day with answers.

Muang Ngoi receded behind them as they pushed north. They rounded a bend in the river and the village disappeared. They had the world to themselves. The trees grew taller. The brush by the river's banks looked impenetrable. The Nam Ou narrowed and the jungle closed in from both sides. All signs of human habitation vanished. The river snaked deeper and deeper into the evergreen forest. Maier leaned back and relaxed. This was an exceptional way to travel. Everything would work out OK. He didn't have anything to offer to the Vietnamese when they got to Muang Khua, but he knew from past experience that a deal of some kind was always possible with them. The Vietnamese were extra-rational and wanted to get things done. He drifted into daydreams and watched the elemental scenery slide past. Strange birdcalls he'd never heard before could be made out over the din of the engine. A clan of monkeys lounged in the trees by the water's edge, only vaguely upset by the passing vessel. Kanitha, who sat in front of him, turned and smiled. They rounded another bend. He watched his young companion scan the forest to their right. He saw her smile fade.

A shot rang out, clearly audible over the engine noise. It was Maier's turn to grab the girl and pull her to the bottom of the boat, with somewhat less affection than she had shown him the day before in Nong Kiaw. This was turning into a killer honeymoon.

He turned, but the boatman had gone. The long-tail's screw ripped out of the water and the boat immediately turned sideways in the swift current. It started to take water. They would capsize in seconds. Maier jumped up and grabbed the tiller. The engine howled. Kanitha lay frozen, a look of terror on her face. He pushed the screw back into the water and tried to turn the boat back into the on-coming current. The girl screamed and pointed to the shore. Maier saw a man rest his rifle on a rock no more than a hundred meters away, its sights pointed straight at the boat. He couldn't make out the shooter's features in the few seconds it took to move past.

"Down! Sniper!" Maier screamed. He turned the boat. Just. He pulled hard on the wire that served as the throttle. They shot away from the riverbank. The narrow vessel shook wildly as Maier fought to control the engine. The river curved again and Maier pushed ahead at full speed. They would make it. Maier lowered himself into the boat as much as he could without abandoning the tiller. He pushed the screw deep into the water and banked hard. The engine roared. The long-tail shot forward. Seconds later, they were out of the gunman's line of sight.

Maier could feel sweat dripping off his brow as he straightened up and looked back. Nothing but forest. The boat was taking water. For a moment he thought he'd gone deaf; then he became aware of the noise of the engine.

Kanitha sat up and scanned the jungle on both sides of the river. Pale and troubled, but on the rebound, her spiky hair wet and screaming in all directions, she looked striking.

"The boatman?" she shouted, her voice breaking up with the adrenaline she was pumping.

He shook his head.

"Do you think there are more?"

Maier had no idea what lay in store for them. He didn't answer but pushed ahead at maximum speed and kept his eye on the water, in shock. He tried to keep the boat in the center of the river, as far as possible from either bank. Every tree, every bush, every blade of grass looked hostile.

The boatman had been the second innocent Laotian who'd been killed because of his investigation. Someone was toying with him. Someone with a sensitive trigger finger and perfect aim. Maier shuddered as he banked another curve in the river. For just a moment, he didn't want the girl to see his face.

THE FREE STATE OF MIND

Maier didn't dare stop the boat to check how badly damaged it was. He wanted get as much distance between themselves and the boatman's killing as possible. If the boat leaked critically, they would still have time to swim ashore and hide from whoever followed them. This time he was pretty sure the shot had been meant for him rather than the boat's captain. Pretty sure. But not completely sure. Perhaps he was being warned or tested. This was the second time a sniper with considerable experience had killed the person closest to himself and Kanitha. Maier had seen snipers at work in Sarajevo, gunning for moving targets. At a hundred meters, the shot had been a routine target for a professional. But the sniper had only pulled the trigger once. The detective knew that a man who didn't go for the double tap would be someone with extreme confidence in his abilities.

The river narrowed further. Ancient evergreen trees, some more than thirty meters tall, leaned out over the water like old drunken men whispering to one another, their canopies almost touching, suggesting a tunnel. Maier thought he could spot a swing hanging from a thick branch above the waterline. The nearest road or village was miles away, but they were not as alone on this stretch of water as he had expected. He slowed the boat, wary of another attack.

"Watch out," Kanitha shouted, and dropped back on all fours.

Several ropes dropped out of nowhere and tightened across the water. Maier cut the engine, but it was too late. As the boat zipped underneath the taut lines he leant back. He was too slow. The detective was ripped overboard.

The shock of the cool, fast-moving water took his breath away. As he surfaced, tree branches rushed towards him, suspended by more ropes. Before he had time to dive, a piece of heavy wood connected with his skull, a rough net closed around him, and Maier went under.

"You have a jungle visa?"

Maier slowly returned to the here and now but he kept his eyes closed and remained motionless. It was best to play dead detective until he could sense in how much trouble they had landed. He could hear the river rushing near-by. His clothes were wet. The day smelled of morning. He hadn't been out long.

"What the fuck is a jungle visa? You guys can't be serious. You sank our fucking boat."

Kanitha was alive.

"No pass without a jungle visa, lady. That's the law in the Free State of Mind."

Kanitha sounded more angry than scared. Maier pretended to come round slowly and blinked into their newfound situation with what he hoped looked like the innocence of a newborn.

"He's coming round. He's coming round," a chorus of voices whispered in unison.

Maier raised his head to confront an incredible sight.

Kanitha sat on the forest floor, a few meters to his right, stripped to her underwear. A gaggle of young men – at least that's what Maier thought they were – stood gathered in a tight knot around her, staring. They wore torn shorts and little else. They were all barefoot. Their expressions were pretty vacant and they looked tired. Perhaps they had all smoked strong marijuana. Perhaps they were opium addicts. A few carried outdated guns. War antiques from the Seventies. The rest carried more traditional weaponry – spears, knives, axes, and machetes – and puffed on cheroots. But the eclectic armory wasn't nearly as strange as what had been done to their bodies – every man's torso was covered in strange swirly patterns. As Maier took a closer look, he realized the men were tattooed, all over their chests and arms, all in a similar way. Some had their foreheads and necks inked. Intricate diagrams and geometric patterns, and a script – familiar, clearly Asian, though he couldn't decipher it – covered almost every inch of bare skin. Tigers, buffaloes, elephants, snakes, crocodiles, dragons and other obscure creatures, hermits, monks, martial arts fighters, and Hindu deities complemented the abstract designs. The writing looked like Khmer but the letters were unfamiliar. Maier had rarely seen a bunch of white boys more flipped out. These kids had been in the jungle a long time.

The young men were mesmerized by Kanitha's state of undress, but there was little sexual tension in the air. Maier wasn't sure what to make of it. He sat up. They shrunk back as one and shifted their focus to the detective.

"Without a jungle visa, you can't pass," they crowed in unison.

Kanitha shouted back at them. "Fuck you and your jungle visa. Boats travel up this river every day and you can't possibly be attacking all of them. Why us? Why? And give me back my clothes, motherfucker!"

The young man who had first spoken to Kanitha moved away from the rest of his gang and turned to Maier. He couldn't be more than twenty years old. A circular diagram had been etched onto his shaved head. Blue lines described a shape somewhere between a bull's-eye and a Ouija board. He didn't look threatening, just ever so slightly mad.

"You! Where is your jungle visa?"

British, judging by his accent.

Maier turned to Kanitha.

"You OK?"

"I am courageous when I have to be. But they took my clothes, these clowns. They are trying to figure out whether we have *sak yant*."

"What's *sak yant*?"

She pointed at the men behind her.

"These tattoos they are covered with. They call them jungle visas. They are sacred tattoos. *Sak yant* in Thai. Lots of people in Thailand and Cambodia wear them. Maybe in Laos, too. The wearers believe they have magic powers."

"These guys do not look like they have magic powers," Maier muttered under his breath, but she had heard him and he could see that she took courage from his quip. He didn't get the feeling that these forest hippies were out for blood. Still, they had sunk the boat. He turned to their captors.

The young man with the head tattoo waved impatiently and two of his minions pulled Maier to his feet. He felt dizzy and wanted to sit back down. They stripped off his shirt and, despite vague efforts to resist, untied and pulled down his pants and looked him over. They had no interest in the bundle of documents and money he wore taped to his right thigh. Disappointed, they let him drop back to the forest floor.

"No jungle visa," their young leader muttered. "You entered the Free State of Mind without valid permission. You infringed on our territorial sovereignty. You will have to come and see the Teacher."

"We didn't enter anything. We were just passing on the river."

The boy didn't answer. His companions pulled Kanitha off the ground, grabbed Maier and marched them off into the forest.

THE TEACHER OF AVERAGES

Within seconds, the rush of the river was swallowed up by the dense vegetation, and they walked submerged in a soundscape of insects and birds, of things moving in the bush, of the jungle inhaling and letting its breath go slowly in a subsonic hum of growth and decay. Maier hadn't been this far from a city in a while.

A narrow trail, almost invisible, led east and upwards. There were no views from which the detective might have been able to orient himself, though he guessed they were walking roughly in the right direction, towards Muang Khua and the Vietnamese. The group's leader was ahead and made no attempt to communicate again. The rest of his gang also remained silent.

The sun stood high in the sky and tried to find its way through the canopy into the jungle twilight below. The leader started a pompous monologue.

"You have to give it to them straight, you see. But when we do that the usual way, when we talk in the straight and hard way and tell them what their problem is, they become defensive. They don't think about what we say, they just think that we aren't nice. And all this being straight will do nothing for us. It won't have any effect. The message is lost. So we're better off telling it straight but with a smile. We're open. We make eye contact. The same way we're making eye contact with you now. And you will take it and not be able to reject it or hate us for giving it to you – straight. And this is the secret of our success. And you, Maier, have beautiful eyes, but not much success. Except with the ladies, perhaps."

The Teacher of the Free State of Mind flashed a semi-pleasant grin at Kanitha and swayed on the edge of drooling. His eyes shone out of his withered face. His receding hairline gave way to a blue ribbon of the same strange alphabet Maier had observed on their captors, snaking across his wrinkled forehead. He was dressed in the white cotton pajamas of a Buddhist layman, had dyed his long hair black and wore his beard like a nineteenth century Chinese warlord, but he was obviously a white man in his early sixties.

"My troops took legitimate action. You were attacked downriver. Your driver was shot. The opposition's boat was faster than yours. Somewhere on the shore, they had a crack shot who can tickle a flea from two hundred yards. We had to intercept. Another half mile upriver and they would have sunk your vessel, anyhow. The Viets don't play around. They would have cut off your cock and tits and stuffed them down your throats. It's a war out there."

The Teacher offered no apologies for his imaginative descriptions but paused for dramatic effect before relaunching into his speech.

"My men pulled the mission off with utmost precision. No injuries besides wounded prides. They take their jungle visas very seriously. But they are well disciplined. No funny stuff, *na*?"

He looked at Kanitha for confirmation. She looked right back, her dark eyes on fire. His faint, unhealthy smile suggested he didn't care either way.

"Our listening posts downriver heard shooting. You were deemed a security risk. Your boat was not steered by a local. That's unusual. All boats must be steered by local people."

The Teacher sat on a throne of sorts, which appeared to have grown from the roots of an enormous strangler fig. Animal skins, perhaps once worn by unlucky leopards, served as cushioning. His seating pad was raised above the forest floor, so that he looked down at them.

He was American, but he looked as if he'd worked hard, and for a very long time, to obscure his origins. He had the slightly uncertain air of a man who'd spent considerable effort to deconstruct the very essence of who and what he'd been in his last life. Every square centimeter on his ageing but very fit body was covered in blue squiggles, shapes, figures, numbers and diagrams. As he leaned forward, Maier detected older, less traditional tattoos on both his arms. This guy had been in the US military once. The Teacher noticed Maier's interest.

"Ah, you are an observant type. You smell a bit like a spook. In some ways you look almost familiar. As if I had met you before. But…Welcome to spook heaven. Who'd you work for? What do you want? What are you doing on my stretch of the river? Are you a threat to the Free State of Mind?"

Maier knew it was pointless to play the tourist. But what to tell this man? He needed more information before he'd be able to voice credible excuses for their presence. He shrugged and tried to turn the tables.

"We did not know that you control this part of the river. We are on our way to Muang Khua. What is the Free State of Mind? What are all these young people doing here?"

The Teacher shifted on his throne but made no attempt to get down.

He cackled at the detective. "Questions and counter-questions. Hm. In the old days, I would have started cutting bits off the lady to get answers. No one likes subterfuge. No one knows you're here. Hardly anyone knows we're here. And I want to keep it that way. Understand?"

"You're MIA?" Kanitha blurted out. "You're one of those guys who disappeared in '75? Huge and wealthy organizations are looking for guys like you. You'd be a massive story if you walked out of the forest."

The Teacher laughed, flashing a row of black teeth. Years of chewing betel could do that to a man. He leaned towards Kanitha and pulled his lower lip down. The word *SILENCE* had been crudely poked into the inside of his mouth.

"OK, so you're a journalist. Good to see your breed hasn't become extinct yet. During the war, our military realized that it was of utmost importance to keep you guys out of the real business and in the show business, on our side of the story. And most of you cooperated and wrote the pap we wanted to you to write. Are you one of those agreeable kinds of writers? Or are you the rare, contrary kind, obsessed with the truth, one of those who contributed to our defeat? Cause you know, the truth is just another story."

He looked her straight in the eye and leaned back, roaring with laughter. The boys around them joined in, guffawing as if it was the law. It probably was. The assembly smelled like a weird cult.

"I don't suppose there's too much about you that is agreeable. You are young and probably stubborn."

He leaned back and began pulling on his fingers. His followers immediately fell quiet. Every now and then one of the joints in his knuckles cracked. In the near silence of the forest clearing, the grinding bones sounded like small explosions.

"Come on, guys, it's good to be here. It's good to be anywhere. We're all survivors. Let's make a deal. I am a reasonable guy. Otherwise, you would be at the bottom of the Nam Ou by now. I tell you a little and you tell me a little. OK? That way, we won't have to kill you. Maybe."

Maier had no choice but to agree. They needed to get moving again soon. They had a mission. He had a case as impenetrable as the jungle around them.

"We were on our way to Muang Khua."

The Teacher smiled benevolently.

"You already told us."

"Our boat man was shot downriver by persons unknown. That would not have been any one of your guys?"

The Teacher snapped upright and craned down towards the detective, "What do you take us for? Savages? The Free State of Mind is a civilized country. The world's smallest and least known nation. An independent entity since 1975. An open society. We have no police and no judges.

No foreign embassies and shopping malls. And certainly no assassins and sharpshooters. There is no executive except me and I am not one for executing. Unless you threaten us directly, I don't mind what you do. I didn't put snipers on the river to engage in a pre-emptive strike. We made that kind of mistake when we came to Indochina in the Sixties. Phoenix Program and all that. And so many of us died. And we killed so many of them. Millions in fact. Millions."

With the disengaged mannerisms of a compulsive obsessive, the old king of the jungle pulled his beard straight.

"But I was lucky. I was reborn. I got a second chance. And I built myself a world where I give the orders, not some incompetent, careerist general looking to pay for his kitchen extension or his wife's new set of tits. I give the orders. To live and let live. To die. My way."

"My way," his disciples bellowed.

"You were with Special Forces in Laos?"

The Teacher laughed. "There were no Special Forces to speak of here after Kennedy and Khrushchev made their neutrality deal for Laos in '62. Only a few hundred guys from the agency. Low-key. We trained local militias. We used Thai border police to do the donkey work. Showing these montagnards, as the French called them, mostly Hmong and Yao hill tribes, how to hold a gun, fly planes and kill commies. Stone age to space age in six weeks for those guys. But we were discreet. We hardly left a footprint."

The Teacher paused and cracked knuckles again. The man was quite mad. But he got his wind back and returned to his story with the enthusiasm of a lonely pensioner who had found an audience for the tales of his glorious youth.

"US aid pumped in money, rice and infrastructure. They built hundreds of airstrips across the country, called them Lima Sites. Those were the key to the Secret War. There were no roads in Laos, like none. All supplies, rice drops for refugees, ammo and troop drops, the constant movement of money, all that could only be achieved with small planes and a network of hardly noticeable landing strips. It worked for a while. But we got what we deserved supporting two parties on opposing sides. Corruption and chaos. The very best weapons to fight communism. It was a childish game, really. If you guys won't let go, we'll destroy everything. That was the way we did things."

Maier looked around at the citizens of the Free State of Mind. He could read nothing but admiration for their leader in the young faces around him. He was touched by their need to belong, to follow. These kids would kill in an instant if this man so much as lifted a finger against his captives. The Teacher had clearly gone rogue.

"You were CIA?"

The Teacher nodded.

"Twelve years in the field. Worked with all the greats in Laos. Bill Lair, Tony Poe, Vint Lawrence. We were on the side of the angels in the early Sixties. We were fighting the good fight. We needed to stop the Reds. So we trained these mountain peoples to fight with us. We paid them. It was an honorable relationship."

A film of sorrow settled over his eyes and he paused, lost in time and space. Maier remained silent. The boys expected more and leaned into their leader. They had heard the story before, in the same way a congregation had been comforted by their religious leader on countless Sundays past.

"But then, in the late Sixties, we lost our way. The Vietnamese started helping the Pathet Lao and killed many of our local troops. The military wanted a look-in on the action and we started to bomb the hell out of this place. That's when I began to have my doubts. Throwing napalm and CBUs on farming communities wasn't my idea of fighting the good fight."

"So you quit?"

The Teacher laughed and looked at Maier with a paternalistic expression. "I left. I had to. There was an incident in Long Cheng in '73. One day, I caught a transport back to Vientiane. When I returned, several case officers with whom I'd shared bunks had been killed. Shot at close range. One had disappeared altogether. No body. It all got blamed on communist infiltrators, but I never bought that idea. I think it was an inside job. They would have done me too if I'd been there. That was the moment when I thought, ah, I better get out if I want to survive the war. I got cold feet."

The Teacher had checked out of the program.

"So what's with the jungle visa?"

The Teacher laughed and ran his tattooed fingers down his equally tattooed left arm.

"So many questions. You're not British, are you?"

"German."

"Never been there, buddy. I gather Germany is doing quite well these days. But why are they sending people into the jungle? You BND or something? German secret service? Ex-Stasi?"

Maier shook his head and threw a quick glance at Kanitha. She had regained her composure.

"How about some clothes, at least for my companion?"

The young Thai woman looked to the ground and smiled.

The Teacher shrugged and snapped his fingers. The boy who had led them through the jungle ran off. The rest of the group, perhaps thirty in all, sat in a wide circle around the captives on the forest floor. Maier felt ridiculous standing in front of these crazies in his underpants like some lost Tarzan. He felt even more ridiculous telling them who he was.

"I am a private eye. I work for a detective agency in Hamburg. I have no government affiliations. I have been sent by a client to find out about her father's murder which took place in Laos in 1976. My client's father was the cultural attaché to the East German Embassy at the time. He probably was Stasi. He was killed by forces unknown."

"So you're not here for the U48?"

Maier looked at the Teacher in surprise.

"What is it?"

The Teacher watched him closely, then shrugged. "I guess you don't know, judging by your expression. But you have heard about it?"

"It's been mentioned. But I don't know what it is."

"Can't help you there, Mr Detective. Your job to find out. But what are you doing here? The German attaché was killed around here? And what was his name?"

Maier tried to weigh up how much he would have to tell this man. They no longer had a boat. Muang Khua was at least three hours away via the river. Walking up there would take a long time.

"His name was Manfred Rendel. I don't think he was killed here. Does the name mean anything to you?"

The Teacher shook his head, his expression unreadable.

"But what, Mr Detective, are you doing here, on my doorstep?"

"My client gave me the name of an informant in Vientiane. A Hmong whose father was an American agent here during the war. One of your colleagues."

This time the Teacher raised both tattooed eyebrows.

"That wouldn't be one young Léon Sangster, son of Jimmy Sangster and his Hmong princess, by any chance?"

Kanitha jumped up. "Wow, you know Léon? You know where they have taken him?"

The apparent leader of the Free State of Mind looked at her with intense concentration.

"This gets more interesting all the time. Let's say that I did know his father."

His eyes flicked back and forth between his captives.

"Perhaps there are higher reasons why you washed up on our jungle doorstep."

"Higher reasons," the young citizens of the Teacher's jungle empire echoed in reverential unison.

The Teacher sat back, letting the sycophantic mutterings of his disciples run their course. He pulled at his long beard and took his time processing the information.

The young man who'd been sent off to fetch their clothes returned.

"Get dressed. You're my interesting guests tonight. Make yourselves at home in the Free State of Mind. But don't try to run; we have mined and laid traps in the forest. You'd lose a limb if you walked five hundred meters by yourselves. Trust me on this. Have dinner with us tonight and we will talk."

The Teacher's disciples rose as one and spoke as one.

"What about the jungle visa?"

The Teacher got off his throne and descended to the forest floor. Only now did Maier notice that the man had a false leg. Not a modern plastic prosthetic but a rather crude wooden stump that had all the charm of an unvarnished chair leg. Even standing amongst his devotees on a single limb, he was a towering figure, an operator who had found his vocation in life. He noticed the detective looking at his defect and grinned at Maier.

"I know all about landmines, Mr Detective. I laid hundreds if not thousands of them in the war. I taught the Hmong how to lay them. And then one day, I stepped on one and in an instant, I became an office slave. Served me right, I suppose. Life-changing experience, trust me. Losing my leg and seeing my best friends killed by one of our own mines caused a seismic shift. I mean, my mind was gone. Once I had left Long Cheng, I decided never to follow an order again. A few are bound to lead. The rest are meant to bleed."

He laughed madly at his inept rhyme, grabbed a crutch one of the young men was holding and moved surprisingly swiftly away from them. His disciples flowed around him like a tide of amoebas, repeating his slogan over and over again, "A few are bound to lead. The rest are meant to bleed."

"In time, children, in time. We all know the rules. No one can pass through the Free State of Mind without the jungle visa."

THE JUNGLE VISA

Seconds after the Teacher had finished speaking, the clearing around the throne lay deserted. The show had simply melted away. Only Kanitha, Maier, and the boy who had returned with their clothes remained. Their captor waved them to follow, away from the river, deeper into the jungle.

"What do you think?" Kanitha whispered. Maier detected no fear in her question, only curiosity. What a girl.

He wasn't quite sure why, but he smiled at her reassuringly and answered, "I think we will be able to make a deal. I suspect it might cost a bit, but we will get out of here alive. If they wanted to kill us they would have done so already. And anyway, this guy is just a stooge."

"He is?" she asked with obvious doubt in her voice.

The detective slowed to create some distance between them and the boy ahead.

"Well, who tattooed the tattooed? He must have learned about these magic diagrams somewhere. We are yet to meet the Teacher's teacher."

They hit a narrow path hemmed in by giant ferns and clusters of bamboo, and marched in single file. When

Maier tapped their young guide on the shoulder to get his attention, the boy snapped around with a solemn expression and shook his head. The kids were either highly disciplined or brainwashed. How had the Teacher gathered them in the forest, tattooed them from top to bottom and kept them here? Didn't these young men miss their creature comforts, girls, technological gadgets, the football scores and the latest episode of their favorite TV series, or were there still romantics left in the world?

Hundreds of thousands of travelers stepped off flights from the developed world into Asia every year. Most came to carry on their lives in the sun with a little soft adventure thrown in – full-moon parties and hill tribe treks, the ubiquitous visit to a sex show, a toke on an opium pipe or a scuba-dive course. Some came because they knew their parents wouldn't follow them into the jungle. A few came looking for more, though they hardly knew what they were so desperate to find out here, other than the loss of the certainties of home. The sacrifices the Free State of Mind demanded from its citizens were considerable. Back in Europe, full-body tattoos weren't exactly the rage amongst employers.

Maier stopped himself judging his younger compatriots. Everyone had to work out their own stuff. He'd never had the opportunity to become part of a tribe. In East Germany, subcultures had been viewed as a direct threat to socialist cohesion.

The trail led into dense forest. Even from a helicopter hovering right over the canopy, all signs of life beneath the trees would likely remain undetected. Several times the boy led them around camouflaged pits peppered with sharpened wooden spikes or alerted them to almost-invisible ropes crossing the path that would presumably trigger a swift demise if pulled or stepped on unwittingly. Maier shook his head at the set-up. This could be going on in the twenty-first century?

A couple of hours into nowhere, the path snaked steeply upwards around a scattered group of large boulders the color of ash and the size of small houses. They crossed a low pass, little more than a hump between two stone cliffs, and for a moment the trees gave way to sheer rock and open skies. From the crest of the pass, they caught the sun dropping towards the Nam Ou behind them. From their vantage point, he couldn't make out any traffic on the short stretch of river visible below. As he turned to Kanitha, he could see the entire scene reflected in her dark eyes. The river, the looming silhouette of the jungle, the quickly sinking red fireball made for an immense, otherworldly view. The panorama danced on her glistening eyeballs. She was clearly moved by the scene. He found the moment strangely touching, standing there, watching her while she was watching it. For a split second, he thought about her the way he'd promised himself not to. As they started moving again, he considered trying to ask her outright what was really driving her to accompany him into this subtropical quagmire. But he had a hunch that this would lead to some kind of schism in their brief communion and remained silent.

Their guide signaled them to push on, and the trio quickly dropped away from the sky back down into the forest without time to catch its collective breath. Maier's thoughts returned to the immediate prospect of facing the Teacher's teacher, the man who ruled this fleck of jungle.

Maier and Kanitha sat with the Teacher and his disciples on straw mats that had been spread in the ragged-toothed mouth of an enormous cave. It was quite a refuge for a group of children who had thrown it all away, who had moved farther from the center of things than most of their compatriots back home could imagine.

Floodlights had been installed along one of the cave walls and on steel poles rammed into the solid stone floor around them, lending the austere space a festive ambience. An orchestra playing Mahler symphonies wouldn't have looked or sounded out of place.

The monk made an impressive entrance. The community fell silent. Two boys led the old man past them to a low wooden bench that had been positioned a little deeper into the cave. The bench was flanked by several low stools and a free-standing shelf that served as a rack for the monk's steel needles and other accessories. Wooden masks of hermits and deities lined the top of the shelf. Clearly, the master had arrived.

The monk sat heavily and slowly crossed his legs while facing his visitors. Every inch of skin that protruded from his robes was covered in sacred diagrams and prayers. Only his lean, deeply lined face was unmarked. Maier guessed the monk to be in his eighties. Kanitha approached the old, wizened man, got down on her knees and bowed three times. The monk showed no reaction and stared into space.

"Luong Pho Mai is very happy to have you and your young journalist friend here, Maier. We hope to get some answers about what is going on north of here in Muang Khua, and your arrival has thrown a new light on the affair."

The Teacher fell silent, deeply touched by the appearance of the monk. His young followers were in awe. Maier relaxed.

"Everything I have learned about *sak yant*, I know from this man. Everything I know about compassion, I have understood because of his teaching. And the teaching of his needle. The teaching of his tattoos. What the disciples call jungle visa. Sacred designs that the Hindus brought to Southeast Asia from India millennia ago and that we apply to the human skin."

"Why are you in the jungle?"

The Teacher smiled broadly.

"I didn't have it in my heart to go back to Minnesota after the war. I needed saving. Jesus was no longer my ticket after what I'd seen in the jungle. But the war saved me. And Luong Pho Mai saved me. And in a way, I saved him. Couldn't save the war, though. And now the venerable Luong Pho Mai will save you too."

Maier looked at the blind man. There would be no shortfall of salvation today.

The Teacher got up remarkably quickly and waved Maier to follow him towards the back of the cave.

"You see, the communists weren't keen on the old animist worlds the Laotians lived in. And still live in. Buddhism was OK; it could be coerced, controlled, organized along revolutionary lines. It was inherently socially conservative, so that fitted in well with the new program. The monasteries had to agree to teach communist propaganda to the novices. I guess whether you learn to read and write with the help of Pali scriptures or *Das Kapital* is academic. Anyway, once the deal with Buddhism had been made, the animist rituals were suppressed. And *sak yant*, a tradition the Sangha – the Buddhist council – never liked anyway, was banned, and its masters, those who did not escape to Thailand, were sent to re-education camps. Luong Pho Mai was incarcerated in Muang Khua. He was tortured and blinded. And I got him out. You can imagine how much he hates the Vietnamese."

Maier said nothing. The old American was on a roll; it was best to let him pour out his story.

"Since the revolution, the tradition has died. Serious adherents go to Thailand to get tattooed. Luong Pho Mai is the last of the great Laotian masters left."

"So you saved all these kids by branding them so badly that they are permanently excluded from the rest of the human race, only in order to spite the local government?"

"I saved them. Of course I did. Don't be so... old, Maier."

Kanitha chuckled next to him. Maier remained calm as the old American continued with his far-out realizations.

"The world isn't a level playing field. It doesn't care to include everyone. One has to make one's own way. Even in Vietnam, the blacks had a much harder time than the white grunts. The war taught me ground realities. In extreme moments of life and death, you can really see what we are made of, what we are. None of these kids would have come to this point of self-realization by themselves. They would have all gone back home, and the more ambitious of them would work in offices, while the lazier ones would either end up slaving in the local fast food joint, join the military or sell drugs and go to jail. So don't judge our little jungle state too harshly. Which brings me to the point. It's not like our modest empire here isn't profitable."

He hobbled a little further into a natural alcove. Maier and Kanitha followed. The smell inside the narrow space was intense. Maier recognized it immediately. Plastic crates were stacked several meters high. A long table stood covered with plants. A group of young women, probably from one of the minorities living in the area, stood separating the buds into different piles of varying quality. They barely acknowledged the Teacher and his guests. The old American waved his arms in a wide sweep across the scene. There was no need to explain just how special a life he and the young disciples led. For most young men, a free state built on dope and sex was about as good as it got. Maier looked at the Teacher, who grinned at the girls.

"Now you understand why the boys are here. You see, no one gets anything for nothing. And that includes you two. So I'll let you in on something else."

Maier wasn't sure he wanted in on any more of this man's secrets. Knowing about the little cottage industry would cost them.

The Teacher brushed a long strand of hair from his leathery face.

"Right now, we have a potential conflict of interest with our neighbors to the north. A situation. The Vietnamese and some old Pathet Laos retirees recently revived the old re education camp in Muang Khua, the very place where Luong Pho Mai was held. Apparently, they're building some kind of debriefing center there. A place where they can hold someone in complete isolation. I don't think it's Léon Sangster they are after. But they have him there."

The Teacher pulled a packet of cigarette papers out of his trouser pocket and handed it to Maier. "Do us a favor,

Mr Detective, and roll us a number. It's a pain with my bad leg, doing the balancing act with the crutch."

The girls were almost done. Maier noticed that they too were tattooed, though they hadn't gone for total alienation. The table was covered with the remnants of a long plant-trimming session. The boxes were packed tight with marijuana, destined, Maier assumed, for Thailand. The dope would be loaded onto boats and shipped downriver, all the way to the Thai border at Huay Xay. This place was making cold, hard cash.

"Why the dope?"

Maier pulled a dry bud from the table, stripped the tiny leaves off their stalks and rolled them into the paper. He passed the sorry-looking joint to the Teacher, who pulled a lighter from his pocket and lit up.

"In an earlier incarnation, Luong Pho Mai used to be an officer in the Royal Laotian Army. We used to haul packages of opium from the Air America flights that rolled into Long Cheng. We ran a narcotics industry in those days. The stuff was packed so tight and there was so much of it that it would leak from the canvas sacks like syrup. We pulled them off the planes and into the lab, right by the runway. And every day, planes would fly junk out of there, number-one-quality heroin. It became too successful. By the late Sixties, we had a third of our buddies in Vietnam hooked on the stuff. And we never saw any of that cash. The agency used it to finance our damn war. A war we were going to lose anyway, one day. But that made me think, Maier. Losing the leg just made things clearer in my head. Loyalty to the agency didn't pay. I went rogue just before Long Cheng fell."

He took a long drag and offered the joint to the detective.

Maier shook his head.

"Does the monk know his following is in the drug business?"

The Teacher laughed gently, "Does the monk know? What a question. I told you we used to haul junk together in Long Cheng. The monk knows everything, Maier. He can see with the needle. The moment he cuts you, he can see."

The Teacher turned to go but stopped in his tracks and grabbed Maier by the shoulder.

"We're showing you our darkest secrets for good reason, Maier. We're not doing it lightly, and if we thought you had impure motivations in this work of yours, we'd kill you without hesitation. But you will understand our dilemma. I will show you tomorrow. And then we'll go and get Léon in Muang Khua and encourage his captors to vacate the area. You see, we have similar interests. We should accept this opportunity by reaching together for a common goal."

"Which is?"

"Anyone who knows anything about tattoos will know who put the *yant* on you and the girl. You will be branded with his needle. That's the price of knowledge, Maier."

The Teacher laughed and limped away, back into the main part of the cave, towards his master, trailing marijuana smoke behind him.

"You see, the re-establishment of the Muang Khua camp is threatening our country. The Laotians know that we exist and leave us to it. We pay them every time we transit with our product. A routine has been established. The Vietnamese hopefully don't know yet. But they are bound to find out if we leave things as they are. They are inquisitive people. If they send troops up here, we're done for. The Laotians who take our money will lose a little face and will no longer deal with us. But Luong Pho Mai suggested we intimidate his erstwhile captors a bit. Do a raid. In fact, he insists."

He sighed and appeared to look inside himself as if he'd misplaced his heart.

"Nothing lasts forever, of course."

NINE PILLARS

In the morning, Luong Pho Mai sat on his bench as if he'd never slept, staring straight ahead. The Teacher sat next to his master on the cave floor. The kids, both girls and boys, gathered in a wide circle as Maier rubbed the sleep from his eyes.

"Jungle visa, jungle visa," they chorused quietly as the old monk got his needles ready.

Maier looked skeptical.

"Tattoos last forever, I am told. Do I really need to have one?"

The old monk gave no indication he understood Maier's protest, and waved for his guests to come closer. The Teacher laughed softly. He turned towards Maier and explained, in a near-whisper, "I wouldn't be happy to watch one of my boys shoot you in front of our modest abode. It's not up to me or Luong Pho Mai. The kids will not let you go without one. Our authority is limited when it comes to laws of faith. They only respect us because we live by the same rules as they do."

Maier shook his head at the collective lunacy. The kids were crowding in, prayers on their lips, caught up in a sway of tribal currents, pushing a common identity it was impossible to fight.

The Teacher rose and addressed the small congregation. "Brothers and sisters, the time has come for each and every one of you to choose. You have ten heartbeats to choose."

The congregation gasped at their leader's poetic eloquence and turned to Maier and Kanitha to repeat their leader's wisdom.

"Ten heartbeats."

The Teacher continued. "Our guests have chosen. They will accompany us north to fight the enemies of the Free State of Mind. They will travel with their jungle visas."

The old monk dipped a long steel needle into a tiny pot of black ink, and intoned a mantra to bless his tool. The Teacher walked across the smooth floor of the cave to Kanitha. She looked up at him with a jaded, unsympathetic expression.

"You think you can make me, you boneless old cripple?"

The congregation took a collective breath and the old blind monk stopped his prayers for a moment. The Teacher smiled and limped through the crowd like a royal emissary, soothing ruffled egos with simple hand movements. The boy who had just collected them from their hammocks walked up behind Maier and pointed a gun at the detective's head.

"Jungle visa, jungle visa," his companions chorused.

Kanitha shrugged, got up and approached the old monk. This time, she did not offer the traditional bows of respect. Two boys peeled away from the crowd and made her sit with her back facing the old tattooist.

"Put the bloody gun down," Maier told the boy behind him, who looked at the detective with glazed eyes.

The two kids flanking Kanitha made her take her shirt off. No one appeared to be interested in the young woman's nakedness. Some of the girls in the gathering looked away. For the devotees, she was just a canvas.

Luong Pho Mai started into another mantra as the two boys next to Kanitha pushed her forward and stretched the skin on her left shoulder. The blind monk did not need guidance. The needle went in. The young men and women gasped and strained to catch the master at work. Kanitha faced Maier head-on, her face without expression, looking straight into his eyes. There was nothing he could do. The boy behind him still had the gun in his hand.

The monk worked quickly. His hand was steady; he knew where to put his needle. Every now and then, one of the boys wiped the blood from Kanitha's back. They'd done this many times before; their communication was nearly silent. The devotees drifted into reverence. The needle played across her skin. The monk mumbled another prayer. It was done.

Kanitha got up slowly and faced the crowd. Her perfect breasts pointed beyond the young men towards the forest and freedom. The two boys who had been assisting the old monk turned her around and a wave of adulation went through the congregation. Five strips of archaic calligraphy stretched down the girl's left shoulder blade, a trickle of blood running from the design down her back.

It was Maier's turn, and the boy pushed the detective to get up.

He walked through the crowd towards the monk. He sensed that the cave's inhabitants were getting excited at the prospect of a fellow white man getting inked. He passed Kanitha, who offered him a crooked grin.

"It's meant to help me make a fortune and protect me from harm, Maier. Let's see if it works."

Maier sat and the two boys to his left and right stretched his skin. He could hear the monk pray behind him. Luong Pho Mai shifted on his bench.

The needle went in just below the neck. Laos was taking more from him than he had bargained for. He watched Kanitha float away, her lithe silhouette in sharp focus against the morning light, giving her the aura of a sacred waif, a picture of great beauty wholly lost on the congregation. As she moved out of his field of vision, he closed his eyes and concentrated on the needle that traced shapes he couldn't guess at across the center of his upper back. There was nothing spiritual about this procedure, he told himself. Maier exhaled and let himself fall into the rhythm of the steel point piercing his skin. Suddenly, there was only the needle playing around his breath.

He had left the cave in the jungle. He stood on a runway surrounded by high karst mountains.

A man walked towards him. Maier could not make out his face. He knew that he needed to make eye contact with this man if he was going to solve his case. The gold, his client, the U48, the men who were hunting him… everything led to the man on the runway. But Maier couldn't move. He stood rooted to the ground, a huge weight tied to his back, pressing him down. The man walked past him, the sun behind him. Maier could not see anything but his squat, well-trained physique, his quiet, sure step, his long breath. The man didn't turn his head as he passed.

He was back. Luong Pho Mai mumbled a last prayer. The tattooed children in front of him stared. Some cried. Others shook their heads in beatific mindlessness. He could see Kanitha at the mouth of the cave, her back turned to the Free State of Mind, watching the forest. Maier lingered in his trance for a moment, watching the world from within, quite unable to speak.

"It's time to go," the Teacher said.

His disciples crowed agreement. "Time to go."

WALK THAT WALK

The Teacher proved to be surprisingly spry for a one-legged man. For almost two days, he had managed to make good speed on his crutches, all the while pontificating across his shoulder. He truly spoke to the jungle. The kids, still dressed in little more than rags, were now heavily armed. The entire group of tattooed warriors marched silently, in single file. Only their leader talked incessantly. They'd obviously had some military training. Their weapons were ancient but in good condition. Perhaps they had stumbled upon a cache from the war. What these tooled-up hippies would do when they reached the prison camp was another matter.

The detective had not seen his tattoo yet. There'd been no mirrors in the cave.

"Don't worry; the image is not important. It's the rules you need to follow if the jungle visa is to work," the Teacher said. He added, "But you should be pleased, you are wearing a *gao yod*, the nine pillars *yant*. The top pillar, the one right in the center of your neck, represents Nirvana, Maier. Remember that. It will protect you from harm."

Maier looked at the Teacher, trying not to appear opinionated.

Far out, man.

His mind wandered back to the hallucinatory journey the tattooing had taken him on. The vision of standing on the runway had shaken him. Who was the man walking towards him every time he closed his eyes? As the intensity of the imagined near-encounter faded, he shrugged into his shirt and tried to push the memory aside. He had more immediate problems at hand.

Both he and Kanitha knew too much.

Many of the plants stood two meters tall and were heavy with buds. The forest was pungent with dope for miles in all directions. During the war, napalm dropped from US planes had gutted patches of jungle. The citizens of the Free State of Mind had cut down the brush. They had left the larger trees that had grown back since the war stand and planted marijuana around them. Lots of it. Maier guessed at an area as large as a football field.

They stopped by the Nam Ou for lunch, hidden from river travelers by dense foliage, but close enough to hear passing boats. Several boys climbed up into surrounding trees to keep a lookout for unwanted guests.

The Teacher bristled with self-confidence. A man with a plan, Maier thought, watching warily.

"My kids will bring a couple of boats upriver that we will sink once we have sprung Léon and scared the Viets. They will think we have gone down with the boats. It'll look like a massacre. It's all about surprise."

Maier couldn't imagine any kind of surprise would faze members of the TS2, the Vietnamese secret service. Those guys were hard.

The Teacher called the boy who had captured them.

"Give our new friend your revolver."

Maier could see that the inclusion of two strangers in this expedition flustered the young man with the tattooed skull, but he obeyed without hesitation.

"Tomorrow is our day, Maier. Are you ready?"

Maier didn't like carrying a weapon but he kept his mouth shut.

He wasn't ready.

Getting Léon out without attacking his captors was unrealistic. With this gang of outlaws, they stood a chance. But what could they do, kill all the Vietnamese secret service men? No one would get away with that. It would mean the end of the Free State of Mind.

Maier had the impression that the Teacher knew this. That he had made a deal with the devil, the old monk, a long time ago and had now been asked to deliver his side of the bargain.

Maier worried while flashing his best smile. The death of his best friend and fixer in Cambodia four years earlier had made him extremely averse to violent confrontations. He knew there was nothing anyone could do to stop people killing each other. They did it for the most trivial reasons. But death was never trivial, and it was ahead of them, somewhere along the trail.

The young citizens of *the Free State of Mind* were tense and spoke little while they ate. Eventually, the Teacher got up and took Maier and Kanitha aside. He wore his long hair piled up like Audrey Hepburn and a bullet belt stretched across his bare, tattooed chest. He looked as mad as Colonel Kurtz, but Maier doubted the American really knew just how far he had drifted from the program. In some ways, the detective admired the former CIA man for taking his chances away from the crowd. The Teacher was the most extroverted drug peddler the detective had ever met. But now, away from his group, he seemed a little worried, paranoid even.

"We go in as a tight group. We will have the advantage of surprise and altitude – the camp is ringed by low hills. We will hit them just as it gets dark. You get your man Léon. We make it look like a bandit shoot-out. Just between you and me, I think it's madness, but Luong Pho Mai insisted. He has bad memories of that place. His anger is considerable, even though he has meditated on his incarceration since he got out. We're making so much dough with the weed that, in my humble opinion, it's worth trying to bribe our way into the future. Just as long as there aren't secret prison camps on our doorstep. Now, to increase our chances of total success, I have a suggestion."

DEATH COMES IN SURPRISES

Maier almost saw the trap before it sprang. Everything just happened a little too quickly. He'd been ground down by the Teacher's incessant talking.

As the long day slowly faded into night, Kanitha, wearing a torn sarong, an old blouse and a faded cap, for once barefoot rather than booted, was the first to go in. Shouting for help in Laotian, she slowly descended from the ridge above the camp. The prettiest Trojan horse Maier could imagine was on its way.

The compound looked like the stage set for an action B-movie, a square space dotted with simple huts and ringed by a bamboo palisade three meters high, topped by barbed wire. A couple of makeshift watchtowers, little more than wooden platforms with grass roofs looming above the bamboo walls, stood unguarded. Jungle LEGO.

As soon as the girl reached the camp, its guards switched on a couple of flood lights. The bamboo gate remained closed.

Maier could see several armed soldiers in the harsh glare of their lamps.

This didn't look like they would have to fight the entire Vietnamese army. With a little negotiation, a bloodbath might be avoided. The kids far outnumbered the camp guards.

One of the soldiers climbed the watchtower closest to the front gate and shone his light at the girl. Maier could not hear the words the man and Kanitha exchanged. But she had her story down pat. She was from Vientiane on a trekking tour. Her boyfriend had broken his leg upriver and she was desperately looking for help. Any fear she betrayed would only be natural under the circumstances, the Teacher had suggested.

The soldier in the tower signaled back to his companions and the gate opened. Sometimes, the simplest plans worked.

Then the boy next to Maier pulled the trigger on his rifle.

The soldier in the tower fell.

The citizens of the Free State of Mind broke into a mad run, howling like banshees all the way down the hill. It hadn't been much of a feint, but it worked. They rolled towards the camp like a primitive wave of doom. Seconds later, they broke through the gate, Maier swept along in their midst. The solar lights died. Shots rang out. Men screamed into the darkness. Maier found Kanitha and they scrambled for the protection of one of the compound's huts. In the strobe lights of a few weak torches, the kids let themselves go and butchered two more soldiers. By the time the Teacher limped into the camp, an older man in military fatigues was the only opposition alive. The Teacher stood facing the prisoner, looking unhappy. Maier understood that this was not a victory. One could win a battle against the Vietnamese, but never a war.

"You have a prisoner here?"

The older man knelt on the ground, blinded by two portable floodlights that the kids held just inches from his face. He didn't answer. Maier doubted he spoke English. The man looked up at the Teacher with undisguised hostility and spat on the ground. This guy was not going to talk.

The Teacher waved to his kids and they swarmed out into the night. Then he called Maier and Kanitha into the circle of light and addressed everyone, breathing heavily like an overworked devil.

"You see, Mr Detective, it's hard to guess how much you are with me on this. I'm assuming you are a shrewd fella and know that you will be dead in a few minutes. As soon as we find that Hmong rat Sangster, we can pack up and go home. And you and your teenage monster here will be blamed for the deed."

He laughed and added, "The Free State of Mind has prevailed, Maier. You get Léon. We get peace."

The boy who had sunk their boat days earlier came up behind Maier and took his gun.

The detective turned to Kanitha who looked at him expectantly and whispered, "You better have an ace up your sleeve, Sherlock; otherwise, we're screwed."

Maier had been called Sherlock before, under less strenuous circumstances. He couldn't think of a flippant reply But he did not show her his fear, either. He'd been tricked by a cripple who hadn't seen a road in twenty-five years. And he would find a way out.

Maier stepped into the light to look at the Vietnamese.

The old man raised his head and stared. The boy handed the Teacher the gun Maier had been carrying.

Time took a deep breath and the night, what was left of it, crowded in. He thought of looking at Kanitha. He tried to think of ways of how they could still be some use to this crazed renegade. But the intense stare of the intelligence officer kneeling in front of him pulled him back into the vortex of the mess they were in. The man was looking at Maier like someone who was struggling to accept the existence of ghosts. There was nothing desperate or hopeful about his intense gaze. All his men were dead and he knew he was next. Yet the Vietnamese soldier pointed calmly at the detective and started talking, quietly, succinctly. The kids, their weapons now slung casually across their shoulders, drunk on blood and victory, gathered around the small group.

"Who speaks Vietnamese?" the Teacher demanded, but Maier knew his heart wasn't in it. There was nothing to be gained here for the one-legged soldier, no matter what the Vietnamese had to offer. The Teacher had written the script for this scene long before the attack. He needed everyone dead, and he needed Maier's corpse to get away with his ruse.

"Weltmeister," the Vietnamese said.

Maier clearly heard the man speak German. The soldier pointed at the detective and repeated the word.

"What's he saying?" the Teacher demanded.

Maier answered quickly, "No idea; he's speaking Vietnamese. I don't understand a word."

"Can't be that important," the Teacher said, and shot the soldier in the head.

"Can't be that important," the kids huffed as one, and shrank away from the executioner.

A commotion behind them prevented Maier from going into shock. He turned just as two of the kids led a middle-aged man into the light.

"You must be Léon Sangster?" The Teacher smiled at the new arrival. He had the killing fever in his eyes; everything about him was dangerous.

Léon looked tired but unharmed. His hair came down to his shoulders. His handsome face, darkened to an attractive copper hue by years spent in the sun, was on the verge of going to seed. The white, flowing beard he tried to grow made him look a little more imposing than he might have been otherwise. He wore a thin cotton shirt and a ripped pair of jeans. He looked from Kanitha to Maier, expressionless and silent. The detective could see how quickly this man was assessing the situation. As Léon made eye contact with the detective, he jerked back, an expression of deep bewilderment on his face. For an instant, nothing and nobody existed except the two men and an undefined space between them. Léon, Maier thought, looked at him as if he'd recognized a long-lost cousin or someone he had met before and never expected to meet again. The dead Vietnamese officer on the ground in front of them had looked at Maier the same way. Maier had never met either of them. Not in this life.

"Impossible," the prisoner muttered under his breath.

The Teacher hadn't noticed. His script was still playing. And Maier was about to be written out of it.

The Teacher beckoned his disciples closer to Maier, Kanitha and Léon. Thirty guns pointed at three heads.

"We have been waiting for this opportunity for months. I remember you, Léon, when you were just a kid. I liked your dad. He was a good agent. Shame he perished when

the shit came down. But he was always stubborn. He
valued his wife and children more than the duty to his
country. Admirable, really."

The Teacher laughed a laugh that looked like the mouth
of his cave, and brought his warriors into the conversation.

"We've been trying to figure out how to get rid of this
camp before it ate our business. We even thought we could
arrange a shoot-out between you, Léon, and the guards
which would have left everyone dead. But five against one
wasn't going to stick. Then these guys actually come to free
you. With a little help from us, you will create the perfect
finale and allow the Free State of Mind to remain a rumor,
a dumb tale that tourists tell around camp fires."

Maier doubted the Vietnamese were as dense as the
Teacher hoped them to be. The one-legged dope dealer had
fought for more than a decade in the jungle and seemed
none the wiser for it. That's what happened to people who
spent all the time in their own heads or with sycophants.

Léon continued to stare at him. Kanitha, who hadn't
said a word to either her new or her old boyfriend, was
crying quietly and blew snot into the night.

"Weltmeister?" Léon asked, a mixture of utter disbelief
and barely suppressed hate in his voice, and leaned closer
to Maier.

The Teacher grabbed hold of Léon's hair and pulled his
head up. "What's that? You know this guy? What did you
call him? I thought that was Vietnamese. Tell me."

Léon looked at his captor and grinned. "I've got
nothing to tell you and nothing to lose. You're gonna kill
me anyway."

The younger man turned his head so hard that the
Teacher was left standing with a fistful of hair. Léon

dropped to the ground. Furious, the old American soldier raised his gun.

Léon ignored his captor and continued to stare at Maier, a cruel smile on his deeply lined face. Maier could smell an end between them. Dust particles swirled in slow motion around the two men as death settled on whatever it was that connected them. The detective thought them beautiful, like the snowflakes that had dropped onto his childhood in Leipzig.

The Teacher turned to Maier, a sudden understanding in his eyes as he looked at the detective again.

"You are…"

The sound of the shot rang out as if from miles away. Léon continued to stare, his eyes glazed with deep guttural anger.

The Teacher fell into the circle of light with a heavy thud. His chest exploded the very same instant.

Kanitha screamed silently.

The next two shots took out the solar lights and everything went black.

For the third time, a sniper had found his mark right next to Maier.

Then something louder, much louder and much closer, blew him up and away.

REUNION HALL

"Young man, the first time I met you, you'd been beaten by ghosts. And now I find you bleeding to death in paradise and not a soul but you to tell the tale. Maier, I decided to save your life. Again. Because of our great friendship. You owe me. What is it the Americans always say? Big time."

Maier opened his eyes. Too bright. The world flashed as if armed with swords of light. He closed his eyes. He knew this voice. He could tell this voice from a thousand others. Sounded like a Hollywood bad guy. So much to think about. He'd been shot. He wriggled his toes. Both legs still there. What the hell had happened? Tattoos, ambush, Léon, Weltmeister. He was dead. He was definitely dead.

The likelihood of being resurrected by a gay Russian hit man was infinitesimally small. But there it was, that voice.

He sank away into unconsciousness.

"How long have I been here?"

The man wore a white coat and a face mask. He looked at Maier gravely but didn't answer. This time Maier was sure. He was alive. He was in a hospital, in Asia, and the man was a doctor. The white coat left the room and closed the door. A key turned in the lock.

A couple of drips were running into a catheter in his left hand. There were no electronic monitoring systems in the room, no blood pressure gauge, no heart rate monitor. He was probably still in Laos. The hand was heavily bandaged.

He looked down the bed. His feet, all toes included, stuck out from the bottom of a sheet that was too short and had been washed too many times. He pulled his legs up and pushed them back down and put his right hand between his legs. Everything was still there. He tried to wriggle his toes. They responded. He lifted his left arm. The tubes from the drip were short. His left hand looked too small.

Mikhail wore a loud shirt and a sweaty grin. The last time Maier had seen him had been months ago in the Cambodian jungle, in what now seemed another lifetime. Mikhail was a dangerous man, but he had saved Maier's life once. Twice? The huge Russian drank from a glass. That looked strange. Vodka. Neat. Maier could smell it. His sense of smell remained highly sensitive. The drink in the other man's hand had woken him up. He felt euphoric.

"Am I dead?"

Mikhail laughed and winked at the detective.

"You better hope that the relevant people out there believe you are, my dear. Otherwise, I suspect they will be in here very soon to finish the job. Maier, you're in a shitload of trouble. Just like last time we met. Welcome back. You're still handsome and you're wasted on those ladies."

Maier said nothing. He could feel a tear running from his left eye. He felt the tear intensely, like hot wax, as it made its way down his cheek. He wasn't sure why he was crying. It felt good. Every emotion that washed through him was magnified to enormous, obscene proportions. But why was the Russian in his room?

"Did you get me out of there?"

The Russian nodded. "It's OK, young man; the important bits are still there. I got you the best medical attention this part of the world has to offer."

"What's wrong with me?"

The Russian put his glass down, brushed his long, greasy gray hair from his puffed, red face and pulled a bottle from behind his chair. He refilled the glass and got up. He was as enormous and fat as Maier remembered him. A jolly giant, a specialist in murder and discretion. A rare breed. He handed the drink to the detective.

"No orange juice in here. That will have to wait. But you will need this, my friend."

Maier took a modest swig. His throat burnt. It was great.

"You want it straight?"

Maier felt dizzy. He nodded, worried his head would slip off his shoulders, and took another swig.

"Someone shot you. Close up. Not a very good shot and it came from the ground. He blew off the two smallest digits on your left hand and the bullet tore through your shoulder. No serious veins or bones hit. Shoulder is good, fingers are gone."

Maier raised his left hand again and stared at it.

"I arrived seconds after the attack by your tattooed holiday club. Daniels is dead."

"Who is Daniels?"

The Russian snorted in disbelief. "Come on, Maier, don't start playing with me. I have your life in my hands. Daniels, that one-legged macho CIA freak gone native. The leader of the tattoo gang. The guy who set you up. No great loss anyhow; he had too much body hair. Really not my type."

Maier nodded. Of course the Teacher had set them up.

"How long have I been here?"

"The attack happened a week ago. We kept you under, to make sure everyone thinks you're dead. We also need to wait and see if you would develop any serious infections from the surgery. I know you are capable of great mischief, Maier."

Maier laughed without wanting to.

"My hand?"

Mikhail shrugged.

"We did what we could. I couldn't medevac you. The job's not finished. It wouldn't have done much good, anyway. The fingers were gone, shredded. I had you sewn up, and you're getting a morphine shot twice a day. Tell me if the dope wears off. The doc says I can take you out of here in a couple of days. Minus your digits. You're coming back into the jungle with me."

Maier chuckled. The chance of meeting an assassin of Mikhail's caliber twice and living to tell the tale was slim. Happy as a clam, he took another sip and asked, "So, to what do I owe the honor this time?"

Mikhail raised the glass and grinned.

"You said you wanted it straight and I admire that. This story is big. You know nothing yet. This is your biggest case, Maier. Your pivotal moment."

"Did you shoot the Teacher? Daniels?"

"No, Maier, this is the thing. This is why I came out, so to speak. To save you, my good friend. Otherwise, you'd never have seen me. You know I'm the man in the shadows, bulky but invisible."

He threw his head back, roared with laughter and drained the glass.

"The only way to drink vodka."

Maier wasn't sure whether mixing vodka and morphine was a good idea. He doubted there was a name for it. But it was textbook treatment for a private eye who'd lost two fingers in a case he didn't understand. Then his mind, quite of its own accord, took the next step and he felt the hair on his arms stand up.

"So who shot the Teacher?"

"The same person that shot the old woman on the island and your boatman up in Muang Ngoi. That's three down. The same person who lured you to Laos. And who keeps shooting across your bow."

"You call killing innocents shooting across the bow? He shot May Lik in cold blood. She was the intended target. The murder of the boatman was another killing without reason, without motive."

The Russian grinned and winked at Maier. "The first killing was a kind of greeting. The second one saved you from your pursuers. The third saved your life. Someone is coming closer, Maier. Someone is coming for you."

"What, I have the devil on my trail?"

Mikhail snorted. "Ah, young man, your detecting faculties are obviously still intact."

His comment was laced with sarcasm, but Maier was too burnt out to counter the Russian's wit. He'd just lost two fingers. He didn't have a clue what was going on, and his girl had vanished. The morphine made him happy.

"What happened to Kanitha? Is she OK?"

Mikhail made an uncertain hand gesture.

"We're not sure, Maier, not sure. By the time I had secured the area, she and Léon were gone. Whether he took her or whether she went, we don't know."

"He was her boyfriend."

The Russian laughed. "So were you, Maier. What does it mean, I wonder? Just a girl a bit lost, or a shrewd operator with an agenda? So many players in this show, it's hard to see who belongs to which side. Or what each side actually signifies. Very hard to tell."

"What happened to the tattooed kids? The Free State of Mind?"

"Gone."

"What do you mean, gone? And how did you secure the area? How did you even come to be there?"

"In time, detective. We have more pressing things to discuss."

Maier sighed and lifted his left arm. The shoulder felt stiff, but it was functioning. He had problems looking at his hand. It was his, but it had changed. He could feel all five fingers but he could only see three of them. The case had gone to hell. He would call Sundermann and discuss his next move. His boss didn't like his employees getting maimed.

"Where am I, Mikhail?"

The older man got up and pulled the curtain from the only window in the room. With his right arm, Maier pushed himself up. The view was familiar. Temple roofs flashed in the distance like unobtainable jewels. A sliver of the Mekong was visible to the north. He was in Luang Prabang.

"We flew a doctor in from Vietnam. The older intelligence agent you saw at the camp was my friend and boss. He died from a shot to the head that was sloppily executed. It took him the whole night to go. The doctor came for him but he only managed to fix you."

"Can I make a phone call?"

The Russian laughed. "This isn't an American cop movie, Maier. You're not down at the precinct. You're in deep shit. Your life isn't worth your weight in borscht. Well, actually, your life is worth a lot to all the wrong people. We all love you for the connection you don't even know you have."

Maier was back at the prison camp and remembered the look in the eye of the Vietnamese agent just before the Teacher had executed him. It wasn't Maier he'd recognized when he'd looked at the detective. Léon too had stared at him in a similarly intense way, out of it, shocked to the bone.

"So let's start at the start. Weltmeister? Who is he and why do people mention his name when they see me?"

The Russian seemed to read his mind.

"This man is an enigma. A spy, an assassin. He has worked for everyone on all sides. No one knows who he is. Until now."

Maier felt uncomfortable in his own skin, like an old snake ready to shed.

"So who is Weltmeister?"

"Don't be slow on me, Maier. And you know what the wise men say. We all choose our parents. Your father is in town. And he's in a killing mood."

Maier passed out.

STICKY FINGERS

Maier woke in a different room. He was no longer in a hospital. The euphoria had gone. His shoulder felt stiff and his body hurt as if he'd been beaten with clubs. The catheter had been removed and his hand had been rebandaged. It still looked too small. Maier shivered when he looked at it. He would have adjustment problems for some time to come.

The world had carried on in his absence. The sky was blue, the winter sun pale, the air dry and full of life that he wanted to capture, consume, inhale. A dog barked in the distance, unseen. Another answered, even further removed from his current frame of operations. People were still loving and killing each other, also unseen.

The Buddha recommended that one ought not to worry about things one could not change. Maier worried anyhow. When one lost two digits, even the Buddha's advice found its limits. Perhaps he would be reborn with two good hands.

He got up. He stood. He felt a little dizzy, but no more so than in an average state of inebriation. The steel door was locked and probably tank-resistant. Definitely detective-resistant. The only thing he could hang himself with was the rough toilet paper. The only window was barred. The smaller window in the tiny bathroom was just large enough to fit a monkey. If they starved him long enough, he would be able to make a run for it. But Maier wasn't in a monkey mood.

The walls were painted government green and had started to flake. The view of the Mekong had been replaced by a view of paddy fields. A concrete wall topped by shards of glass, ugly as concrete walls can be, ringed the property he was locked up in.

One day, he would be able to turn the loss of his fingers into something positive. It would make him look more lived-in. It would impress the girls, or give him a villainous sheen when needed. He studied the bandage. He moved his hand. He felt a little pain, yet it burned to his very core. He could feel the missing fingers, as if the crippled hand were just a hallucination.

Life was ugly.

Except for a plastic bottle of water and the bed, the room was empty. No more vodka. After doing three desultory rounds and promising himself never to go to a zoo again, Maier lay back down and considered his non-existent options. A few moments of vapid meditation pulled him under, back to sleep.

"And how is our patient today?"

Mikhail entered the room with all the panache of an overweight torero, followed by a small man in a red Ferrari polo shirt. Collar up. Hair shaved back and sides. The Russian's companion, in his early sixties, looked familiar. The loud shirt which stretched across his stomach did nothing to dispel his military background. He wore a gun in a shoulder holster outside his shirt. No anorak in sight today. A flashy entrance for Mr Mookie, the dancing fool from the Insomniacs Club.

Behind the Laotian, a young woman in uniform tried to remain unseen. A bona fide member of the Lao PDR's heroic military. She was slim, dark-skinned and devastatingly beautiful.

"We're going to love you back to life, Maier," the Russian laughed.

The Laotian didn't laugh, but held out his hand and introduced himself in fluent German.

"I am your local case officer, Detective Maier. You can call me Mr Mookie. The man who was shot by Daniels, or the Teacher, as you knew him, was my brother-in-law. I am Laotian Intelligence. We work with the Vietnamese on resolving this issue, and I will bring you up to date with your investigation. Then you will help us. Failure to follow our instructions will result in your disposal. Our mutual friend Mikhail has been tasked with this mission in case you forfeit the trust we invest in you in the coming days. He will not show mercy, nor will he take your previous association into account. He will not torture you. We are not barbarians. But if you deceive us, keep us from our goal or lead us down blind alleys, you will lose a lot more than two fingers."

Maier shook the man's hand. His "case officer" still had his ten fingers, he noticed. The detective was very sensitive about other people's limbs, even the most insignificant and smallest. He wondered whether this feeling would ever pass.

Mr Mookie watched Maier attentively.

Mikhail looked out of the window, presumably at unseen dogs, leaving the playing field to his employer.

"Where am I?"

Mr Mookie ignored the question. The Laotian's finesse probably lay in interrogation. The Russian turned and brushed his gray hair from his face to throw the detective an unhealthy grin.

"You are in the Lao PDR, Maier. On a tourist visa, in case you want reminding. Jungle visa don't count in the real world. And you are up to your neck in shit. I mean real shit. Asian shit. Laotian shit. European shit. American shit. Shit that stretches from one side of the planet to the other. But mostly you are in Vietnamese shit."

Mikhail laughed so hard that Maier felt exhausted.

"What were you thinking? You took part in an assault on a Vietnamese intelligence unit. And you got caught. My clients don't take lightly to the murder of their operatives. Remember this when you consider your options in the coming days."

Maier didn't like being berated or lectured.

"These kids kidnapped me and Kanitha. Took us right off our boat. I did not know this tattoo cult was going to burn down the valley and kill everyone."

Mr Mookie smiled mildly, as if he'd just stepped off the dance floor.

"Of course you did, Maier. And as I said, we are not savages. We reacted with utmost pragmatism. We dragged Daniels back to the plantation and hung him right in the middle of his ganja plants. A deterrent."

"And what happened to Luong Pho Mai?"

"My assistant here – you may call her Miss Darany – shot the old monk. He was an unrepentant reactionary we should have finished off after the revolution. We were too soft. But not this time. The Free State of Mind no longer exists."

"What happened to those kids?"

Mikhail laughed. "Oh, Maier, always compassionate. You are the classic private eye, on the side of the downtrodden and the helpless, fighting the forces of darkness. Like in American movies. But this time you picked the wrong darkness, my dear."

The Russian slapped his huge hands on his thighs and looked like he was about to dance like a bear. This was turning into quite a party.

"The tattooed kids ran back south through the jungle and emerged in Muang Ngoi where the Lao police picked them up and charged them with overstaying their visas. They have been deported and blacklisted. Growing marijuana on an industrial scale is illegal in the Lao PDR. But the Laotians don't bear grudges. The government will take the plantation over for research purposes."

Mikhail left his words hanging in the ugly room.

Mr Mookie coughed and pulled a battered pack of cheap Laotian cigarettes from his pocket. He offered Maier a smoke.

"I have given up. Ask Mikhail. He will vouch for that."

"And for very little else, Maier."

"This is the good cop, bad cop routine? They have obviously introduced decadent western TV shows in Laos."

The door was open. The walls of the corridor outside were painted the same color as those of the room they were in. Maier had a longing to get up and walk out. As if Mikhail could read his mind, he stepped up to the bed.

"Tell my friend Mr Mookie why you are here. Please choose your words carefully. I do like you, you know. I mean, not in that way, of course, but still... we could have a future..."

Maier repeated his story, starting with his encounter with Julia Rendel in Hamburg. When he had finished, the room lapsed into silence.

Mr Mookie lit another cigarette. The room stank of cheap smoke.

Maier sensed that Mikhail and the Laotian were a tight team. They barely needed to make eye contact to exchange information.

Mikhail broke the silence first.

"You see Maier, this is way bigger than you think. We believe your story. Julia Rendel did hire you to find out about how her father was killed, but this is just a smokescreen. And behind the smokescreen is another smokescreen, and behind that smokescreen lie a number of truths. We're not here to get at the truth. We are merely interested in making it all stop. You understand?"

Maier shook his head.

"Your father was an intelligence agent, one of the best in business. He worked for TS2 towards the end of the American War. And now he has cropped up in Laos with something everyone wants. And believe me, a lot of people would like to get hold of him. The Laotians, our Vietnamese brothers, the Americans, all his old paymasters..."

His voice trailed off.

"My father? In Laos?"

Maier sat stunned on his bed and stared into the middle distance, assembling his new reality. He remembered that this was the second time the Russian had shocked him with the news of his father's alleged appearance. Even as he struggled to cope with the news, he knew the Russian was not telling him everything. He looked at Mikhail, but the hit man's eyes were neutral. Was this a message of some kind that was only meant for him?

Maier couldn't keep the bitterness from his voice. Whom were they kidding?

"You are playing games. This is all about a haul of gold from the Secret War, right? American drug money?"

The Russian laughed maniacally.

"Gold, Maier? Gold? Drugs? You don't think the Vietnamese government would send a top intelligence agent into the Laotian jungle because of gold and a few kilos of heroin that the Americans forgot to take with them? No, Maier, you weren't recruited for a treasure hunt. Get that out of your head! You were hired to help your father take revenge. He's calling the shots."

Mr Mookie flicked his burning cigarette butt into a corner of the room and leaned into the conversation.

"You didn't tell us you slept with Rendel at the Atlantic prior to her abduction."

"I'm not asking you who you're sleeping with. Or how old they are," Maier shot back.

The old Laotian smiled faintly. It didn't look good on him.

"We had a look at your email account. You received an email from the 1000 Elephant Trading Company a few days ago. If you want to see your Thai friend Kanitha again, you will have to meet up with them."

"She is Laotian."

Mr Mookie smiled sourly. "It remains to be seen exactly what she is. In the meantime, get moving."

"I don't know who is behind the 1000 Elephant Trading Company."

Mikhail laughed.

"You had a run-in with Charlie Bryson in Vientiane, didn't you?"

"The MIA guy at the Insomniacs Club? Sure, he is a creep."

"He's an American agent. A very good one. Don't be fooled by his brash character or his unhealthy complexion. He's looking for the same man we are looking for. Your father. He must not find him first. This is why you are now working for us."

Maier felt distraught but tried not to show it. It was all fine except the "father" bit. Why here, why now? Hadn't he long ago learned to live with his sense of mystery and loss?

"Who is my father? This Weltmeister everyone is scared of? And why is he in Laos at the same time as me? The chances of that are non-existent, given that I have never met him."

"Maier, he set you up. You're here because he is here. He wants to make some kind of deal. But we don't know with whom. Or perhaps he simply wants to make trouble, show off to his son. He always was a romantic."

Mr Mookie looked irritated. Maier must have looked doubtful.

"When did you first hear about Weltmeister?"

"I told you, I first heard this name at the camp the other day. From the man you say was your brother-in-law, moments before Daniels shot him. He stared at me as if he recognized me. So did Léon Sangster. And Daniels also got that weird look, right before he died. I had never met any of them before."

Mr Mookie answered, "We think he gave that name to himself. He has a high opinion of his abilities."

Maier shook his head.

"Can you prove any of this?"

The Laotian shrugged and looked the detective straight in the eye.

"Do we have to? I think the look my brother-in-law gave you prior to his murder should be evidence enough."

The Russian tried to defuse the escalating tension in the room and continued. "Weltmeister was last seen in Long Cheng, the secret US airbase, in 1976. We are sure he had changed his name and worked for Stasi at the time. We lost track of him after that. Decades of silence. Until now."

Mr Mookie calmed down and put on an almost paternalistic smile. "You know it's him, right?"

Maier nodded. Sections of this secret *mandala* were coming together, though he couldn't see any decodable patterns yet. An awful picture was emerging in his mind, its center blurred, its frayed edges coming into focus.

"So where is Julia? They wanted Léon Sangster in exchange for Julia."

Mikhail shrugged. "We aren't sure. We don't think that the 1000 Elephant Trading Company is holding her. I mean, they were holding her and then lost her. We have reports of a house being hit by some kind of a death squad, origin unknown, in Luang Prabang. Unheard of in Laos. Signature Weltmeister, if you ask me. The second email Bryson sent you didn't mention her. That only reaffirms our suspicions as to who freed her."

Maier looked sourly at the Russian. "So if it didn't tell me that they killed her and threw her down a mine shaft, what did the email say?"

Mikhail laughed, "Oh, Maier, young man. Don't get angry over everything or I'll hug you to death. It said that you must meet them if you wanted to see Kanitha again. We assume they have Léon as well. But he might not be a strong enough bait to draw Weltmeister out. You are. So you will meet them and find out what they want. And you meet your father."

Two women, connected to this case in entirely different ways, had been used to haul Maier in. Perhaps the kidnappings were mere distractions, tools to guide the detective towards the elusive Weltmeister.

Maier played his only trump card.

"So, what about the U48?"

The room fell silent. Mr Mookie turned to Mikhail, then back to Maier. He didn't speak for a long time, but simply watched the German detective, a look of intense concentration on his wizened face.

Maier left the question standing and continued. "What will I have to bargain with? I want to try and get Kanitha back. And we need to find Julia."

Mr Mookie laughed, softly clapping his small hands, turned to Mikhail and said, in German. "You were right. He really is the sentimental type."

He snorted derisively at the detective. "You will offer them your father. And yourself, of course. It's the only deal in town, Maier."

"They will kill me."

Mr Mookie countered gently, "Maier, you're getting there. The moment your father truly believes his son will die, he will show his hand. It's our only chance to get the U48. And Weltmeister. You wouldn't believe how much our Vietnamese friends want to get their hands on this man. And the Americans are no different. Trust us, this goes all the way up to the White House. And right now, the White House is concerned. Not just about planes flying into buildings. We spoke to the US ambassador in Vientiane a couple of days ago. I had a feeling he was waiting for my call. For the US, the Weltmeister affair is a diplomatic tsunami in the making, an ugly aftertaste of their Vietnam War. For us, it's merely a coming to terms with the past. If we apprehend Weltmeister, perhaps even honor him if necessary, Laos will be able to draw a line under the conflict, our American War. Trust me, Maier. If Weltmeister falls into American hands, he is dead. And Vietnam loses prestige. If we get to him first, anything is possible. Like it or not, you are embroiled in the biggest spy scandal since World War II."

Maier emphatically didn't trust anyone. He would not have believed Mr Mookie if the agent had told him that he was missing two fingers on his left hand. Maier wasn't in a trusting mood.

Mr Mookie waved for Miss Darany to step up to the bed.

"This is my cousin's wife. She is a mid-level intelligence agent. Someone who does dirty work. But she is not very bright. She helped facilitate the passage of the drugs from the cave to the Thai border to line her own pockets. She got too close to these tattooed kids. She cheated my cousin and she cheated her country. She doesn't speak German. She thinks her killing the monk has redeemed her somehow. She expects us to order her to sleep with you. Or to kill you. What do you think?"

"You will sacrifice your cousin's moral standing or mental health to keep an eye on me? There must be less-compromising options at your disposal."

The intelligence agent picked at his collar as if looking for dandruff. He became, quite suddenly, as remote as a cloud.

"I need to impress just one thing on you one more time. This is not a game. Your father is the most sought-after intelligence asset of the twentieth century. And we will have him. You will be the bait to draw him out. That is the only reason you're alive. And I will demonstrate the difference between life and death to you in the best way I can."

Maier nodded, trying his best to look agreeable.

"You are from Leipzig, Maier, aren't you?"

Looking agreeable wasn't enough.

Mr Mookie smiled faintly as if listening to a sad piece of music far, far away in his head.

"I studied there. Then I went back home and helped beat the Americans. You see, Maier, there was only one way to beat these white devils, to win the war. We had to be ruthless. We had to be cruel. We had to sacrifice that which we cherished most. We had to lose everything to win the war. We lost hundreds of thousands of our own people. Fathers, mothers, brothers, sisters, sons and daughters. And the Vietnamese, whom we have much to thank for, threw millions into a furnace to save their great nation."

Mr Mookie stepped back behind the young woman, who looked at Maier without expression. Her uncle said something in Laotian and she looked at the detective uncertainly, unable to grasp the situation.

Maier nodded gratefully, though he knew enough of people to feel sick. Sick of the world, sick of his job, sick of this room he couldn't escape from.

"We will use Miss Darany to impress our utmost seriousness on you. She is a spent force, anyway."

Mr Mookie pulled his gun. Before Maier had time to move out of the way, the Laotian agent shot his cousin's beautiful wife in the back of the head. The girl jerked violently forward and splattered on top of Maier, the spray of disintegrating facial tissue showering the detective. The bullet had whizzed past Maier into the bed's mattress. Mr Mookie threw the gun onto the bed next to Maier's good hand and pulled a small camera from his trouser pocket. He pressed the shutter to capture Maier amidst his bloodbath and grinned.

"You can't run, Maier; you've been framed and now you belong to me. We will meet again."

The old man laughed severely and left the room. Maier fought to wipe the girl's skin and bones off his face with his one good hand while trying to direct the projectile vomit that shot up his throat in the direction of the killer with the other.

PLAY ME A SONG OF DEATH

The Plain of Jars, a high, windswept plateau that stretched across the central region of northern Laos, looked like a giant's golf course. The scars of the American war were clearly visible. Almost perfectly circular bomb craters dotted the land in all directions. Tall grasses grew around the craters. There wasn't a single tree in sight. A cold wind blew across the rolling hills of northeastern Laos.

There were few towns and villages in the area. The old provincial capital of Xieng Khouang had been blasted to rubble. The region had taken its name from several collections of huge, roughly hewn megalithic stone jars, obscure remnants of a culture long lost from collective memory. The Americans had airlifted one of the jars back to the US, which was now displayed at CIA headquarters in Langley, Virginia. Scholars claimed the jars had been used as funeral containers. Others suggested they had been used to brew alcohol.

The jars reminded Maier of the stone virgin of Dölau, a menhir he'd visited with his mother when he'd been ten years old. As he scanned the hills around him, he clearly remembered a story of the stone his mother had told him: A woman had been shopping. When she'd been on her way home, it had started to rain. Her trail was full of muddy puddles, so she threw a loaf of bread on the ground and used it as a stepping stone to avoid getting her feet dirty. The gods were incensed about her squandering of fresh bread and turned her to stone the very same instant.

Maier assumed the Laotians had been more sensible and had really used the jars to brew local beer, not minding how dirty their feet got during the wet season.

The new capital, Phonsavan, was a dusty collection of shacks for the poor. The tumbledown township was interspersed with garish houses fronted by Roman-style pillars, painted in dirty pink or fluorescent green – the homes of officials, connected entrepreneurs or drug and gem barons. The fences that ran through town were constructed of CBU cases and other war scrap that had rained down on the plateau in the Sixties.

Maier and Mikhail checked into a couple of rooms in the dusty center of town. The hotel looked like a Swiss chalet and was decorated with war junk. Guided tours to crash sites of US jets and the final resting places of gutted Laotian tanks scattered around the province provided the main source of income on the Plain of Jars besides subsistence farming.

Maier spent a long time looking at himself in his room's mirror. His black eye had virtually faded. He kept his moustache at bay. His bandages were off. He raised his ruined hand to the mirror, touching the cold glass with his index finger. The short stumps tingled. He would never be a guitar player. Nor a typist. He didn't think the ladies would give him any credit for having lived dangerously.

Other than that, his situation was precarious and unsettling. He suddenly had a father. The last two women he'd slept with had been kidnapped. Or not. He was watched around the clock by a fat Russian hit man, half friend, half foe, all monster. Nothing was certain anymore. He missed Kanitha, her feisty attitude, her curiosity and her company. He had little to bargain with and no idea which side of the fence she was on. He'd never gone into a situation with a worse deck of cards. He felt old, used, unwanted, and he was crippled.

In Europe, they called this midlife crisis. In Asia, most people were happy to live to his age and had no time for periodic self-doubt. That in itself was a depressing thought.

At first light, Maier left the hotel alone and walked due east, unarmed, not a single ace up his sleeve. The most recent email from the 1000 Elephant Trading Company had stipulated he come alone. No tricks, no weapons.

He walked carefully and stuck to well-trodden paths. He felt sweat trickling down the back of his cotton shirt. The hills around looked safe enough, tranquil, but this was an illusion. Unexploded ordnance lurked everywhere under the shifting soils of the highlands. One false step could spell the end. At the close of every monsoon, locals got their feet blown off by bombs that had shifted during the rains. The weather was everything out here. It made and broke adversaries.

Maier knew the story well. From 1960, the US had secretly set out to dominate the Plain of Jars to create a buffer between the North Vietnamese and Thailand. A US secret army of montagnards – thirty thousand hill tribe soldiers trained by the CIA – had fought the communists each dry season, supported by bombers flown by Hmong pilots out of Long Cheng. But each year, they quickly lost their gains in the rains when the Pathet Lao pushed back with heavy artillery. The war washed back and forth like a sick, deadly tide. As the Sixties wound down and the summer of love went to hell in Southeast Asia, the US military wrested the war from the secret service. The ground war virtually abandoned, the US now bombed the country back into the stone age it had barely emerged from. The Plain of Jars, or PDJ, as the locals called it, became one of the most heavily bombed places on the planet.

The grass was knee-deep, and every time Maier lost track of the path, he retraced his steps. The going was slow. The dirty, leaking sky pushed down on him and the grassland, threatening to squash the hills and all that moved amongst them. Large raindrops splashed on his head.

When he reached the road, a black SUV sat waiting for him. A couple of white men armed with large-caliber scowls served as his welcoming committee. There was no need for introductions. Middle-aged suburban guys, tooled up and professional, most likely comfortably semi-retired with Asian wives and war loot in Florida, out for a short stretch of nostalgic hurrah and shit-kicking. One wore an MIA patch on his polo shirt. The other one wore a toupee that looked like it would blow off in a heavy gust of wind or turn into a mushroom if the skies opened.

They asked him politely to sit in the back of the four-wheel drive. One of the men sat next to him, bound his hands with double cuffs and put a bag over his head.

The other got in the front and started driving as if his life depended on it. That made Maier feel marginally better. They were being theatrical and he was being taken to a show. He wasn't sure whether he would be the main act or merely part of a supporting cast. Trapped in darkness and breathing stale cotton, he felt like he had all the time in the world.

Ten minutes later, the hood came off in the middle of nowhere. As Maier slowly opened his eyes to adjust to the dull daylight, he saw Charlie Bryson standing outside a typical thatch-roofed family home raised on stilts on the edge of a village. The American looked grim. Out of sorts, even. There would be no hugs this time.

The house stood surrounded by a low, broken fence. A high wooden gate yawned in front of the building like a gallows. The village spread across a low knoll, a great vantage point with a 360-degree panorama of rolling, almost featureless hills. The highlands of Saxony-Anhalt in autumn could not have looked more desolate.

Mikhail would have to keep his distance. There was no rock or tree cover and no way for anyone to creep up on their meeting. Not even a sniper, Maier feared.

"Well, merry Christmas, Maier. I thought we'd meet again. I made you right then in the Insomniacs Club. You're Julia Rendel's sniffer."

The American wore the uniform of his MIA outfit. He'd recently shaved his head, which gleamed like a lopsided bowling ball. He'd kept the walrus moustache. Neither the haircut nor the furry lip extension made him any more welcoming or agreeable than on their first encounter.

Maier stood with his hands bound and slowly stopped squinting into the pale light. He could see for miles.

Besides the village, a collection of fragile looking huts teetering on the edge of insignificance, there was no other sign of habitation. No shopping centers, theme parks, airports or other distractions. Except for the men around the house, the world was empty. A cool wind blew around them and kicked up dust beneath the hut. A family of chickens picked its way through life underneath the modest building. A bow-legged, slack-backed sow roamed the trail that led to the rest of the village, followed by a brood of mud-splattered piglets. Two more black SUVs stood parked near the hut. It was the perfect place for a hostage trade-off.

Maier had nothing to trade.

The old American walked around his de facto prisoner. The driver and guard leaned against the car he'd arrived in and smoked.

"I see you lost a couple of fingers on your left hand there, Maier. Laos getting to ya? Better be careful or there won't be anything left of you by the time the little cooperation I have in mind for us is through."

"Where is Kanitha?"

Bryson coughed and spat onto the ground next to Maier.

"Still into young girls, then? Well, she's around. Though she's traded you in for a slightly younger model. But you might get to see her alive before you expire. That depends on how we progress from here."

Bryson emphasized the first syllable of *progress*.

As Maier considered the hammy aspect of his predicament, the hair on his arms stood up again. He scanned the hills around the village. There was nothing to see but shifting monochrome grasses and pastel horizons.

But the electricity had changed. He knew what was likely to happen shortly. He knew that Bryson and his gang wouldn't get what they wanted. He knew he had nothing to worry about. He knew. For the first time in his life, he felt loved by a father, no matter how crazy this father might be, loved unconditionally, the way he had always wanted to love somebody. He also knew that this longing was deeply rooted in him and that reality never played out the way one imagined it. Never.

A BULLET FOR WELTMEISTER

Bryson must have picked up the change in the atmosphere. He barked at his enforcers. Three more armed men, younger and meaner, their eyes hidden behind wrap-around shades, emerged from the hut. They clung to automatic rifles and binoculars. They wore little earpieces and looked like past-their-sell-by-date B-movie actors on steroids. One of the men carried a guitar instead of a gun. Vince Laughton, the owner of the Insomniacs Club, dressed all in black, wearing a bulletproof vest and looking decidedly uncomfortable in this get-up, followed them. Maier doubted the rotund Canadian had any idea how ridiculous he looked.

Vince grinned at the detective with a sour expression filled with violence and sloth. "My grandfather was a pilot in World War II, Maier. He spent the war killing fucking Germans. Then he got shot down. Imagine how I feel about that."

This guy could spoil all the fun with the f-word, Maier thought.

"Your girlfriend is German, in case you hadn't noticed."

Vincent stepped up to Maier and hit him in the stomach. Maier dropped to the ground retching and watched the chicken, surprised the Canadian had it in him to resort to violence.

"My ex girlfriend since you fucked her in Hamburg. I don't take kindly to that kind of thing."

He moved in to hurt the detective, but Bryson restrained him, "Hey, hey, hey. Take it easy. We need this guy. He's the only asset worth anything in this godforsaken place."

Maier groaned and cursed his captors. Whatever they hoped was out there amongst the jars, now was the time.

Bryson bent down and laughed. "Well, you know, in the end I couldn't help myself. I mean you broke my man's nose in Hamburg. It cost money to fix that. So I told my friend Vince about Julia Rendel's unique recruitment drive. Vince, by the way, is an excellent help round here. He spotted you on the Nam Ou the other day. Eyes like a buzzard. Foul mouth. A real journalist. Good man to have around. Always thought Canadians were pale Mexicans wearing anoraks. Anyway, I told Vincent what it had taken to extract Julia. If you hadn't slept with your client, he would never have come over to us."

"So where is she?"

"I lost three good men over that bitch. At first, I thought you had sent these devils to free her, but now that I look at you, lying in the dust with fingers missing, that notion's clearly off the mark. We put her in a nice room in Luang Prabang, and then one morning last week, boom. Someone came in, killed my buddies, burned down half the building and disappeared without a trace. A real pro operation. Reminded me of the old days. Audacious, brutal, efficient. Nice. Couldn't have done it better myself. Which makes me think... it wasn't you. You smell a bit like a loser. So you tell me. Where is Julia Rendel?"

Maier couldn't help smiling.

"I hope it wasn't on the national register, Bryson. They take that kind of thing serious in Luang Prabang."

The American threw him a sick look but remained calm.

"The Vietnamese getting to you, Bryson?"

"This wasn't a Vietnamese operation. They could have just walked in with the local cops and taken her out. No, there's another operator out there, silent as a grave, heavy as a Dallas execution. I mean heavy."

He said nothing for a moment. Maier liked his comic turn of phrase. Bryson was growing on him.

"Well, I have a pretty good idea who it is. And so do you, I reckon."

Maier said nothing. Vince made moves towards Maier again, then thought better of it and angrily turned to the old American.

"Shut your fucking hole, Charlie. Let's get on with it. Let's string this creep up and see what happens. I wanna see some American justice done here."

Bryson straightened up and laughed.

"You really do have one filthy mouth on you, Vince. This isn't about justice. This is all about advantage. That's all. Let's not get all lofty here."

He waved to one of his goons, who disappeared promptly into the house. How many heavily armed Americans could one fit into a Laotian farmhouse?

"Fan out; keep your eyes peeled. I think we're getting close."

The old soldier didn't look worried. He took his time. He was dangerous. He nodded to the guitar player, who started playing a mournful country & western song. Charlie Bryson liked his killing spiced up with a spot of entertainment.

"We try to make our executions unforgettable experiences for everyone involved. It's all about projection, you know.

Everyone loves a spectacle. It's all Triumph of the Will, really. In that respect, the Nazis got it just right."

Maier had to concentrate not just on what this man had to say but on how he said it. His southern drawl stretched slowly towards the hills before it was whipped away by the breeze.

Bryson got into one of the SUVs and backed it up until it faced the hut's front gate. He jumped out and opened the back doors. The last row of seats had been replaced by a mounted machine gun. It looked ready to assault.

Maier sat up and looked at Bryson. "I know where the gold is, Charlie."

The American laughed. "So do we, Maier. Léon's on our side. Remember? You've managed to alienate just about everyone who counts in this little saga. No one likes you, Maier. Or rather, no one likes your old man."

The CIA man clapped his hands, and seconds later Léon and Kanitha emerged from the hut. It was hard to tell who was prisoner and who wasn't. Things were confused. The guitar player switched to a slow, torturous flamenco. The execution threatened to slide into the absurd before it got started. Triumph of the swill.

"You see, Maier, without a bit of theatrics, we aren't getting anywhere with this. If my hunch is right, Weltmeister is already in the building, so to speak. I mean, I got respect for the guy. And Léon told me you're his son. So we're gonna test the father-son bond, right here and now. We're in the anger business. The music might just bring him along to where we want him."

Kanitha looked at Maier wide-eyed. Léon kept her close by his side. There was no way to communicate, no way to connect. Vince came up behind Maier and pulled him back to his feet. Despite his small size, the Canadian was strong and propelled by furies that were born from his own insanities rather than the disappearance of his girlfriend. His round, clean-shaven face was twisted with enough anger to turn water into turpentine. His thin, unsmiling lips moved silently, perhaps reciting a mantra that spelled revenge. He had a rope in his hand and looked like a man who'd dressed up for a futuristic round of cowboys and Indians. With some people, it was hard to imagine they had ever had mothers. They seemed to have emerged into the world not from a woman, but from a hole in hell, birthplace of assholes.

"We gonna have ourselves a bit of old-fucking-fashioned Wild West fun here in the Wild East," he intoned with a football field's worth of glee surrounded by rusty barbed wire in his laconic manner.

He threw the noose around Maier's neck, tightened it and pulled the detective underneath the gate to the hut before throwing the rope across the gate's main beam and pulling it tight. It seemed unlikely, but he moved like a man who had hanged people before and had taken a fancy to the process.

One of Bryson's soldiers pushed Kanitha forward. She pushed right back, but the agent slapped her just hard enough to make her fall. He dragged her underneath the gate. Léon looked on, his withered face impassive. So much for love. Maier wondered what kind of reunion they'd had since they'd escaped from the Vietnamese camp in Muang Khua.

"Well, Maier, in this game, you got to have some patience. We have been trying to find Weltmeister for a quarter century. And now we're getting close. And a little sacrifice here and there to draw him out of the tall grass is entirely reasonable."

Bryson scanned the hills around the village again.

"The hills have eyes," he murmured, more to himself than anyone else.

"So we'll play a little game. A game of losers."

Two of Bryson's soldiers of fortune forced Kanitha to kneel down and motioned Maier to stand on her back. He didn't budge. They raised their guns. He took his shoes off. As gingerly as possible, he stepped on his partner in crime. She groaned with pain. The noose tightened around his neck a second time. If he slid off her back he was done for. Cold sweat soaked his shirt in seconds. The guitar went into crescendo. The player began to stomp one foot on the dusty ground. He wasn't bad.

Bryson looked satisfied and smiled down at Kanitha. "I know, I know, he's a big man. Far too big for such a delicate waif as yourself, little lady. Next time, choose your bedfellows more carefully."

He pulled a length of cotton string from his pocket, threw one end to the girl and ordered her to wrap it around her fist until it was taut.

"I'm telling you this because you're a Buddhist, and you'll get a next time."

He walked to the car, trailing string, and tied the other end to the machine gun's trigger. After some maneuvering, the gun's muzzle pointed at Maier's stomach and the string was taut. Bryson snapped the gun's safety off. Vincent positioned himself in front of Maier and stared up at the detective.

"If you fall, you hang. If she moves, you hang. If she pulls the thread, you get shot. If she lets it go slack, I will shoot her. It's failsafe. In a few minutes, the pain on her back will be unbearable, or you will lose your balance or she will let go of the string. So many possibilities. You better pray that Daddy is coming to bail you out."

Maier stared straight ahead across the hills into a bleak gunmetal sky. If he didn't move his head, he couldn't see a soul. The view was clear, all the way to heaven. He used the tension on the rope around his neck to lighten his weight on the girl's back, but it made little difference. He remembered Mikhail and Mr Mookie, assuring him that a deal could be struck with the Americans. Some deal. Outnumbered and outgunned. The rope cut into his throat, but there was nothing to say anyway.

Kanitha cried, "You're very heavy, Maier. Not sure how long..."

The men fanned out in a semicircle around the makeshift gallows. Maier swayed. His eyes blurred. He shoulder stung. The girl groaned. The guitar player started a new song. The wind picked up and he could make out tall grasses sway back and forth as if led by the somber chord progressions. The gunman with the six-string started to sing.

Well, I'm tired and so weary but I must go alone, Till the Lord comes and calls, calls me away, oh, yes.

His voice carried well. Maier, sorely tempted to give in to unreason, grasped the beauty in everything, even as Vincent leant in and feinted a kick to the detective's legs. He no longer cared about his torturer. All was forgiven. The game was up. Time rushed on with unlikely speed. He met Bryson's eye. The American didn't look happy. Perhaps he didn't enjoy executions. But that was all irrelevant now. The sky went time-lapse. The clouds opened and the sun broke through and lit the moment in an unearthly light.

And everything was good and blue. The abyss was near, and this time there would be no return. Maier remembered the kind of things one was said to remember in these last lucid moments – the sea, his mother, a long lost love, her breasts, his crippled hand.

There'll be no sadness, no sorrow, no trouble, trouble I see, There will be peace in the valley for me.

The wind picked up. Bryson's men moved in closer. They were keen to see Maier hang. These guys didn't want to miss a little death on the range. He swallowed hard. The guitar player strummed his last chord.

THE COMEDOWN

The first shot cut the rope. Maier dropped to the ground. He fell so quick, he didn't see the shooter emerge from the sliding door of one of the cars parked next to the house. As he fell, Kanitha pulled hard at the cotton string wrapped around her fist. The machine gun in the back of the SUV jerked hard to the left and started spitting bullets.

"Fuck," Vincent coughed as he took a hit in the throat and slammed into the dust next to Maier, leaking life and fear for all they were worth.

Bryson's men scattered, but the shooter from the car was fast and took out the two soldiers closest to Maier. The remaining men opened up in all directions.

Maier and Kanitha crawled away and hid behind the vehicle that held the automatic weapon. Maier slunk to the SUV's door. The Americans had their hands full and paid them no attention. The front seats were empty and the key stuck in the ignition. Maier jumped in and started the engine. The steering wheel was slippery in his sweat-soaked hands. As the girl jumped in next to him, he put his foot down and the heavy four-wheel drive jerked forward. He slammed the gear stick into second and hit the bumpy road on which he'd arrived, bound and blindfolded, an hour earlier. The mayhem receded quickly in the rear-view.

Léon popped up in front of the windshield. Maier almost pushed his foot through the floor of the car as he hit the brakes. He stalled the engine. A shot shattered the window and passed between him and the girl. The Hmong, a desperate grin on his face, was gone as quickly as he'd appeared, jumping into the tall grass to the side of the road at the last second.

Maier hesitated. The man they all claimed to be his father was somewhere behind them, killing people. He was very close. Maier had never met his father, a father who'd just saved his life. A man who could shock the world with his secrets, they had said. A man wanted by intelligence agencies across the planet. A father, everyone had been telling him, who had brought him into this case in the first place.

His father.

Father.

Dad.

Son.

"Let's go," Kanitha screamed, and shook him out of his stupor.

Maier restarted the engine and gunned the accelerator. The car howled and they raced forward, into the hills. After ten minutes of dust and potholes, they hit a larger road. Maier stopped the car and got out. He told Kanitha to wait and ran up a small outcrop the shape of an upturned soup bowl, a hundred meters off the road. At the top, he stood breathing heavily, trying to get a sense of himself, trying to get a grip. He was alive. Kanitha was alive. They'd escaped.

He could see most of the trail they'd come along. Smoke rose in the distance and he hoped his father had not burned down the entire village. No one had followed them.

Weltmeister had saved the day.

Kanitha shuffled up the hill, took his arm and leant into his side.

"You came for me. You saved my life."

Maier remained silent.

"I killed Vince," she added solemnly, her voice brittle with stress. He pressed her close for a moment, but he couldn't feel a thing. He had no words for her or anyone. He just stood for a while, catching his breath, listening to his heart trying to escape from his chest, scratching his neck where the rope had cut him. Kanitha pulled at his shirt and started descending the hill towards the car.

"Come on, Maier, I'm wasted; we need to get out of here. Miles to go before we sleep."

When they got back to the vehicle, Charlie Bryson stood waiting for them.

LAOS, SEPTEMBER 1973

FRIENDSHIP

Beginnings were easy. Dressed in black fatigues, his face darkened by paint, a black cotton skullcap on his head, Weltmeister slipped out of his hooch and made his way down to the runway. For a few hours each night, Long Cheng was silent, before supply planes and bombers started landing and taking off at the crack of dawn. For almost eight years, the secret US base had been the nerve center of the war in Laos. He was at the heart of things, a heart no one knew existed.

He'd picked a moonless night. His friends, Cronin, Taylor, Herr, Flitman and Daniels, would have passed out by now. He'd worked and drunk, killed and laughed with these guys for close to a decade. They'd shared good times and bad, both stateside and in Indochina's darkest jungles.

Nothing brought men closer together than the atrocities they committed in the name of God or country. They were tight. They were fighting the good fight. If they didn't look too closely at what they were doing, the professional justifications they were served by their handlers were sufficient to allow them to take pride in their work and to absolve them of the demons that arrived on the scene in the wake of rape and murder.

Weltmeister wasn't a drinker and he did look closely.

An owl sounded into the night, and Valentina's eyes, dark, almond-shaped, full of love and sorrow, washed over him briefly, piercing his heart deeper and more painfully than any bullet could. Bullets were easy; love was a killer. His mind played with the fringe of her short black hair, put his arms around her waist and remembered her sitting on top of him, moving gently like a Mediterranean tide, while he gripped her wide mother-hips and cried, eclipsed by the closest thing he knew to that feeling that bled across all the others. No one else had ever seen Weltmeister cry and no one ever would. It was near impossible to be a romantic and a pragmatist at the same time, but these were the cards he'd dealt himself. And he was about to play his last trump.

He was certain he would never see Valentina again. No one came back from the secret American prison in Cuba. They had him by the throat.

In war, everything and everyone eventually became expendable. Everyone became a lever in the pursuit of *Realpolitik*. And that included the love of America's most sophisticated assassin. He had a feeling for catastrophe. He had juggled it often enough, but now the different elements of control, loyalty, action and reaction had slipped from his hands. Weltmeister was on the way out. The darkest recesses of the US government had decided that its most prized asset was disposable.

The phone call from the Secretary had been personal and succinct. The secret bombing of Laotian villages would need more justification. One day soon, the querulous American public would want answers.

Weltmeister, a man rarely surprised, was taken aback by the loathing the Secretary expressed towards his countrymen's intelligence. The agency man had been in the game long enough to get a feel for when he was getting fucked. A word he didn't use often or lightly and only to himself.

Weltmeister was a private man.

He rechecked his gun, a German Luger, a 1969 reissue produced by Mauser in Oberndorf. He'd been given the old Nazi favorite by a black GI called Leroy in Danang a couple of years earlier. He liked the irony of Leroy's gesture as well as the weapon itself. He had killed with it before. The Luger was precisely that marriage of romanticism and pragmatism he so often missed in life. He screwed the silencer on.

He had disassembled the weapon several times during the night, fastidiously cleaned and oiled each part, put it back together, loaded, unloaded, reloaded. He'd tied a snub-nosed .38 Special to his left ankle, no silencer, noisy bang-bang death in its short barrel.

He didn't expect any challenges. He had killed many times before. But even in his world of far-out values, this was different. This job would propel him into a state of beyond he had glimpsed in the eyes of others, men and women he had dispatched himself. For the first time in his long and illustrious career as spy and "cleaner," he had run out of choices. He was about to do a great wrong. He would step up to the edge of the abyss and tip forward into the darkness from which one could only return with fever dreams, with reports on loathing and defeat. He was about to cross the threshold that separated the men from the monsters and the good folks from the motherfuckers. He would become an oblivion seeker, an outsider's outsider. Love could make a man lose everything, give up anything, do everything and anything. Love had a long breath and a short fuse.

He wiped the tears with the cloth his gun was wrapped in and started for the living quarters of the field agents. His mind turned to granite. Valentina's scent, her eyes, her shape, her essence slipped away. She became unreal, her perfume faded; her eyes retreated into the shadows, her words turned from song into memory. Today, he hated the metamorphosis. He hated getting into the killing state. But the sorrow of change turned quickly into a sense of liberation. Everything became easy in an instant. He was qualified. He knew how to do his job.

He was Weltmeister.

In complete silence, he made his way to the living quarters of the top CIA men who operated in Long Cheng.

An owl's hoot followed him through the narrow alleys of wooden huts that housed the Hmong rebels and their dependents. He passed the house of their leader, General Vang Pao, unseen by his guards and carefully approached the shacks used by the Americans.

The free-standing house of the Sangsters loomed ahead, the only building one might have called a home in Laos' second largest city. Why Jimmy kept his wife and children in one of the most dangerous places on Earth was beyond Weltmeister. He'd never liked the man, a staunch ideologist who hated communists to a point where they no longer counted as human. For a while, Sangster had paid a fistful of dollars to the Hmong soldiers for every set of enemy cars they brought back from the front. Then one day, he'd flown up to a remote Lima Site in the far north of the country and noticed that all the Hmong children who lived near the runway had had their ears cut off by their parents. Some get-rich-quick scheme. After that, he'd asked for heads. Weltmeister sighed into the silence. Everyone had their own reasons, obsessions and justifications for being in the spook business.

The low shack where the rest of the Americans slept was just ahead. He approached slowly, mindful of the shadows around him. He stopped in his tracks and crouched down into the soil as he caught a noise to his right, ever so obscure. A dog?

He sat, controlling his breath like a yogi, letting his eyes roam where there was nothing to be seen. A false alarm. He gripped the gun harder and checked the silencer one more time. He slid the safety off and waited. Nothing. And waited. He felt someone else breathing nearby, almost inaudibly. He could not exactly put his finger on the direction the faint sound came from. He tried to smell others in the darkness, but there was nothing. Perhaps he was overcautious.

It was time to go.

Weltmeister rose and moved quickly to the shack he had slept in countless times. The door stood ajar, as he'd hoped. Security was not an issue inside the dark heart of America's most secret base. These guys felt safe. He crossed the threshold unseen.

The bunks were occupied by the right men in the right state of inebriation. He knew them so well, he could tell them apart by the way they inhaled and exhaled in almost complete darkness. They were his friends. The room smelled of sweat and alcohol. He stepped into the center of the shack and thought of Valentina and how they had taken her and how he had run out of choices. It was the only way to go through with the unspeakable.

He moved between the two middle bunks and raised his gun. Weltmeister shot Cronin, the man closest to him, first and covered the weapon with a scarf to silence the slide action, then quickly put Flitman out and repeated the precautionary move. The third shot went into Herr's brain, just as Taylor, woken by the muffled gunfire and smell of cordite, raised his head and took a bullet in the throat. The medulla oblongata kill. Death came immediately.

Silence.

He was one man short of completing his assignment. Daniels was not in his bunk. He checked the bathroom. It was empty. The fifth man must have flown down to Vientiane for a debriefing or a spot of R&R. There was nothing to be done. His handlers had screwed up.

He had one more chore to fulfill. He would shoot himself in the shoulder and bury the gun in a hollow under the floor he had prepared the previous day. Weltmeister didn't worry about shooting himself. He knew how to inflict a horrific-looking but ultimately harmless wound which would divert attention from his involvement in an incident that was bound to rock the war establishment. No one would suspect an injured survivor. For a second, he grinned at his own audacity. The Secretary knew that Weltmeister was still the only man for the most difficult jobs. That's why he was being sacrificed.

He turned around and caught the eye of young Léon Sangster in the shack's window. The boy recoiled in fright and ran into the night.

Weltmeister had been seen. He wasn't sure whether the boy had managed to get a good look at him.

Ten minutes later, America's most secretive assassin, frequent visitor to the White House and treasurer of American dreams, crossed Skyline Ridge. He killed a young Hmong guard who, half asleep, stepped in his way, probably wondering what the commotion in the valley below was about the instant he died. Long Cheng had woken up. Léon must have alerted his parents. Troops fanned out beyond the runway. In the cold dawn of war, Weltmeister threw one more glance at America's secret city. Then he started walking east, towards Vietnam. He had lost his love and his country. It was time to lose himself. He would need to find another employer to stay alive. One day, perhaps, he would reclaim it all.

THE WHITE HOUSE

The *Weiße Haus an der Alster*, Hamburg's White House, a handsome late nineteenth-century building located in the Rotherbaum quarter of Germany's wealthiest city, had seen several illustrious owners. During the war, the sprawling property had served as the Nazis' city headquarters. Following Germany's defeat, the British squatted the grounds until the US purchased the Hamburg White House in 1950 and opened a consulate a year later.

Sundermann liked the striking edifice, though he hadn't come to admire the architecture. He'd never been inside the consulate, but there'd been no question of refusing a personal invitation. The consul's PA had informed the owner of Hamburg's most prestigious detective agency that the casual meeting would touch on one of his most troubled cases, Maier's gold saga in Laos.

Now he stood in front of the building, collecting his thoughts, arranging his very expensive tie and wiping his delicate rimless glasses on a fine cotton kerchief. Sundermann never rushed into things. He had his detectives to do that, on the ground and in the street. In the lofty social stratospheres the agency boss operated in, reticence, detachment and discretion were the most useful tools for survival. Of course he was being watched, and if he stood in front of the building long enough, security would come out and question him, no matter how much his Armani suit cost. America had just been attacked and the world was nervous. But he was ready. And on time.

As he approached the main gate, he could see that his visit was of some importance. A woman and a man dressed in business suits just slightly less snappy than his own were waiting.

It was time to get out of the miserable November rain.

"You see, we have a very delicate situation on hand here," the consul intoned while playing with her coffee cup. She was a rather large woman, a career diplomat from the Midwest who'd made it to a prestigious coastal school and done well. Sundermann guessed Pennsylvania, Boston, foreign shores. Hamburg was a good posting.

The man was a different customer, a hard face attached to a fighter's body gone to seed, a player who'd seen America's interests around the world rise and wane for decades. He had most likely put his boot in a few times to improve the country's prospects. He was completely bald and, like Sundermann, in his late fifties, perhaps a little older. The over-the-top walrus moustache should have made him look like a kind uncle. It didn't. He'd probably been handsome once.

The consul's name was Lieb, which she pronounced Liab, perhaps a subconscious move to distance herself from her German ancestry. First name Margaret. A bit nervous, compulsively flicking her shortish hair – dyed red – from her wide forehead with rather fat fingers.

She introduced the man as Bryson. No position, no job description.

Sundermann opened his file on the Laos case and scanned Maier's reports. He had all the pertinent information in his head, but he wanted to settle into the mood of the somber room and its occupants. No point rushing into anything with Ms Velvet Glove and Mr Rottweiler across the table bursting with expectations. He took in a rather heavy painting of settlers with high collars offering baubles to naked Native Americans before turning his attention back to his two disparate hosts.

"Detective Maier is off the case. He lost two fingers in a shoot-out. He also reported that you guys almost executed him in order to draw out a German double agent from the Cold War days who some people claim to be his father. A rather outlandish scenario. Should I get in touch with the authorities to inform them that the CIA kidnaps and tortures German citizens in third countries?"

The consul hid behind her files and said nothing. Bryson took control of the conversation, cutting right to the issue.

"You ever heard of an agent called Weltmeister, a German guy, a veteran with decades of experience in the field? A double agent, as it turned out."

Sundermann shrugged. "I have already heard all this from my own man, Maier. This story about a mythical US operative and an obscure file that you and the Vietnamese would like to get their fingers on is a little fantastical. Good for you if it turns out to be something of substance. The fact that this man might be of German origin is neither here nor there. And I don't see why you almost hung Maier from a village gate. And if indeed this man who you say is his father freed him and killed several of your men, then why would it be my business to influence my detective one way or another in relation to this situation? If your scenario is true, this is a rather personal affair."

Lieb raised her hands in a conciliatory manner. "This is all a misunderstanding. We've been on edge since the attacks on New York and the Pentagon. Our foreign policy is evolving faster than the Internet, and the executive branch is rewriting the way we deal with the rest of the world. America is at war, Mr Sundermann. And this meeting should serve in part as an explanation to your detective as well as to you. We would rather you didn't involve German authorities in this case. Trust me, apart from hunting down the terrorists who killed so many people on 9/11, the 'Weltmeister' case is the top foreign affairs priority at the White House this week."

She chuckled modestly into her double chin and continued. "And I don't mean our cozy little *Weiße Haus an der Alster*, I mean the real deal in DC. The President himself is looking at how we screwed up in Laos. Then and now, by the way. And we need to get things right before…"

Lieb didn't finish her sentence. Sundermann turned to Bryson.

"Maier told me it was you who personally set up his hanging. He reported that you used a female Thai journalist as his footstool for your makeshift gallows. Are you people out of your minds?"

Bryson grinned at the German without a hint of contrition. "Well, let's not ride our moral bicycles through the parking lot here. Your man is in Laos to find his father. I am in Laos to find his father. The Vietnamese have lost one of their top intelligence operators in the pursuit of his father. They lost soldiers. I've lost soldiers. I admit, it's all a bit *Alice in Wonderland* out there, and we did abuse privileges between friends. But if Weltmeister is not caught soon, we will have an international spy scandal on our hands that will put the Guillaume affair to shame. This man whom we thought dead for decades sits on information so compromising, it might lead to a very unfavorable rewriting of our recent history. It could lead to nasty political purges both in the US and in Vietnam at a sensitive time. A bilateral trade agreement between the US and Vietnam is about to come into force. I mean, this German used to be a guest in the White House, a trusted man, a good friend to our then Secretary of State. He turned and sold us out to the commies in 1973. And now he's back, and we think he wants to go public with our old laundry. We can't have that."

Sundermann laughed politely and made sure not to keep a hint of condescension from his voice, "You mean he fed Kissinger false intelligence? Are you serious?"

The Americans said nothing.

"Oh, well. Now you're breaking my heart. I am almost tempted to bring Maier back on the case just to expose a few old war crimes. But I guess that would be testing the great friendship between our nations?"

Sundermann caught himself and continued in a more conciliatory tone. "Consul, Mr Bryson, please, understand my irritation. There is a need to look at this affair with utmost sobriety. I run a respectable and well-connected business, not a fly-by-night outfit of divorce investigators and sleaze peddlers. My agency isn't interested in decades-old political crimes unless they become pertinent in current cases we have been asked to investigate. I answered your request for a meeting on a voluntary basis. And we have something called a *Rechtsstaat* in Germany at present. It means rule of law. I am sure you've heard of it."

Bryson was staring at the agency boss with barely suppressed anger, when Lieb interjected softly, "Let's not get all twisted up here. We're all friends in this room. What Mr Bryson would like to move towards here today is cooperation."

Sundermann countered, "Detective Maier is one of my best men. He gets outstanding results. And he is very seriously damaged at this point. He is off the case and no longer in Laos…"

Bryson interjected angrily, "Put him back on the case or we will make some calls and close your agency. And you can go on food stamps or whatever they call it here and kiss your nice suits goodbye."

The consul, wearing a pained expression, waved Bryson's threats away and added, "That would be a last resort."

Bryson snorted at the diplomat. "Last resort, my ass, Margaret Lieb. And listen, Sundermann, if we don't catch this Weltmeister guy, and if he publishes the contents of the U48, then some of our finest citizens will go to court and to jail, and our rapprochement with Vietnam will go down the toilet. Our influence in Southeast Asia will take a serious hit, and the man you describe as mythical will kill every single person who may be able to identify him. And that could include his son and, by association, yourself. If this particular scenario comes to pass, I swear to you, I will personally chop you up after he is finished with you."

Sundermann took off his glasses, pulled his kerchief from his breast pocket and started meticulously cleaning the lenses.

"This U48? What exactly is it?"

The consul exchanged glances with Bryson. Sundermann doubted that she knew anything of any real value about this affair. No more than she absolutely needed to. Intelligence was very compartmentalized in the US, and even apparently cooperating outfits often operated without any inkling of what their colleagues were up to in the same theater.

But Margaret Lieb answered, hesitantly, "A secret file containing information about some obscure but pertinent details of our involvement in Vietnam."

Sundermann looked at her impassively. "Surely there are countless files like that floating around. And this is all history."

Bryson cut in. "As we explained, the contents of this one are explosive. We believe Weltmeister is planning to sell to the highest bidder."

"Can you furnish me with evidence? Or is this a kind of Tonkin Bay maneuver to get my detective into a fray he doesn't belong in?" Sundermann quipped.

The two officials in front of him glanced at each other and remained silent.

Sundermann laughed politely. "You must have done something very stupid if this Weltmeister was one of your top agents and really went into business for himself. A little respect goes a long way, gentlemen."

Bryson countered, "Well, the only mistake we made was that we didn't kill this guy when we realized he was turning into a monster. But there's no point crying over spilled milk that has since turned to cheese. We are pragmatic people, Sundermann. We live very much in the here and now. We want Weltmeister and his file, and we will get both. We can't have our country's secrets on the open market."

The German smiled sardonically.

"Then you better pray that no one ever hacks into all these computers of yours. Imagine all the dirty laundry that would spill into the street. It would be on the wrong side of depressing."

Bryson nodded, "Well, it ain't our computers I am tasked with keeping secure. That'll be some other guy you should talk to."

Sundermann got up.

"Ms Lieb, Mr Bryson, it's been an interesting meeting. But these problems you have with your Weltmeister have little connection with the Sundermann Detective Agency. And they may not affect my case. Though I do see that they might. I will talk to Maier. Another file, as damaging as your U48, which outlines the threats uttered as part of this conversation as well as the details of your mock execution, is being created and will shortly make its way to representatives of the German government. And believe me, I am trusted in the corridors of power. You can flout international law in a small, developing country like Laos. You've done it before; you'll do it again. 9/11 will encourage guys like you, Bryson, to murder people you have no evidence against. Before you know it, you will get carte blanche from your president to kill with impunity. America will be disliked around the world and Germany may well be coerced into covering your asses. But today, the buck stops here."

He stopped for a moment to observe the CIA man stare into space defiantly. Mr Rottweiler was probably one of those public servants that couldn't be corrupted by money or by the enemy, but he was dangerous. He would always follow orders. He would never question his handlers.

"In the meantime, don't get so emotional. If you want cooperation, make a deal. Offer me something other than threats. If you want me to consider putting Maier on site, do me two favors."

Lieb opened her arms in a conciliatory gesture and looked at Sundermann questioningly. He was certain she had no idea about espionage, though she apparently felt safe as long as proceedings were wrapped in the language of diplomacy.

"I am looking for an operator, a freelancer, currently active in Laos. His name is Mikhail. Second name unknown. A Russian. Homosexual and extrovert. Extremely skilled. He is involved."

The consul looked dumbstruck, but Bryson betrayed no reaction at all.

"If you have a file on him, I want his file. I want more than his file. I want to meet Mikhail. If you help me get to the Russian, I will get Maier back on the case."

Bryson asked, his voice dripping with menace, "And what was the second favor?"

"Keep your fingers off my detective. Stop threatening me, my agency or my operatives. I am not a government official and I can't be strong-armed by a CIA assassin with a nice mug of coffee in his hand. In the event of another incident like the one on the Plain of Jars, this meeting along with the case file accumulated by my operative will be made available not just to German authorities but to the global media. Trust me, the sympathy the US have garnered from the attacks on the World Trade Center will evaporate in no time at all. It will crumble as soon as it becomes obvious that you are killing innocent people in poor countries. I thought you guys had packed that in after Vietnam."

The room fell silent. They sat facing each other, playing the games they had been assigned in life. Eventually, Bryson got up, walked across to the German and offered his hand.

"It's a deal. You get the Russian. He's not our man, but we have a line on him. We get Weltmeister. And we keep our hands off your sorry outfit. It's a price we're happy to pay. But we better be quick. And that includes Maier."

Sundermann knew instinctively that the agent's promises were almost worthless. He tried to meet the consul's eye, but Lieb preferred to stare at her carpet instead. These guys were not happy. Someone else was out there, wanting a piece of the man they called Weltmeister. Someone more ruthless than Bryson and his Vietnamese counterparts put together.

He got up and shook hands.

It was still raining as Sundermann stepped outside. A cold winter drizzle, with ambitions to turn into sleet, molested the city. He walked away from the consulate to the Außenalster, an entirely artificial body of water which looked a great deal more genuine in the dying afternoon light than the farewell expressions worn by the two Americans. These people always expected others to accept their sense of destiny. Everyone had a destiny. Even Detective Maier did.

The agency boss pulled his phone from his coat and dialed his operative's number. It was time to put his best man back to work. Getting their hands on Weltmeister before the Americans and Vietnamese or other contenders did would be one hell of a scoop for Sundermann. Getting the lowdown on the Russian would be a nice bonus. It was a win-win situation, as the Americans liked to say. And he was looking forward to a bit of sunshine.

THAILAND, JANUARY 2002

PARADISE

Maier lay in his hammock, counting the fingers on his left hand. He'd been counting for days. Christmas and New Year had come and gone, and he was still counting. He got to three fingers and two half fingers, then he started counting again.

The Thais had done a good job operating a second time, re-sculpting the stumps, into, well, stumps. Better stumps. Supreme stumps. The Thais were good at surgery. They had also crafted him two state-of-the-art metal prosthetics.

He could still feel the end of his fingers. Touching the cold metal was reassuring. There was still something there. For now the claws, as he called them, remained in the smart plastic box they'd come in.

He picked up a three day-old copy of the *Bangkok Post* that was fluttering around the porch of his bungalow. Crooked politicians, unfeasibly large kickbacks, murderous generals, and a beauty pageant for fat women filled the front page. A short article in the bottom right corner caught his eye.

Former US Secretary of State on unprecedented visit to Laos to advise on investment. Bilateral trade agreement soon.

Maier lingered on the story. It had to be a coincidence. Old American politicians always did trips to poor countries around the globe to level the way for US businesses into new markets. But Kissinger? Maier was surprised the grand old man of *Realpolitik* even got a visa from his old enemies. Obviously, the collective memory of the guys in the politburo was failing. The detective shrugged. This was all about wood, coffee and geopolitics. The Americans and Chinese were looking at expanding existing plantations on a massive scale. Local and international environmental organizations were protesting against the plans, which involved logging huge swathes of forest.

Kanitha had taken her skimpiest bikini for a walk down the beach and now ambled towards him from the waterline like a pocket-sized Ursula Andress. The Gulf of Thailand stretched like a lazy, luxurious blanket into the hazy distance of the tropical morning. To Maier, the girl was an expression of his limbo. He was off the case, his boss had seen to that, but Kanitha was part of the case. Every time he looked at her, the Laos quagmire came flooding back.

Sundermann had told him to write this one off. The client, Julia Rendel, had disappeared. Her fee had been spent. The gold had not been found. Everything pointed away from the loot, anyhow.

"Maier, there's a man coming down the beach, trying to take your attention away from me."

Maier raised himself out of the hammock quickly.

She grinned and threw a handful of sand in his direction. "Hey, relax, it isn't Weltmeister."

He shook his head. She was right. He wasn't himself. He was nervous.

A moment later, Sundermann, wiping his glasses, stepped onto the porch, carrying nothing but a small overnight bag.

"Morning, Maier. How are the fingers?"

Maier raised his hand. "Gone."

Kanitha had disappeared inside the hut. With his good hand, Maier handed his boss a bottle of water and motioned him to sit on the only chair the porch had to offer. Sundermann dropped the bag next to Maier and sat.

"What are you doing here?"

"Come to check up on you. The Sundermann Detective Agency is worried. And, by the looks of it, with good reason."

"I'll be OK."

"You'll be dead."

Maier raised his eyebrows.

"You know things I don't."

It was not a question.

The older German laughed gently, "Of course I do. I'm your boss. And I've come to save your life. You are back on the case."

Maier was impressed. He had envisaged time stretching into sunny infinity, a moderate retirement package and a beautiful woman to share his days, plenty of sunsets to mourn his fingers. Retirement, for the first time in his life, did not sound like a dirty word.

Out in the bay, two men were racing a jet skijet ski that sounded like a slowly approaching mechanical bee. Probably Russians, Maier thought.

"I answered an invitation to the White House on your behalf, Maier."

"I am that important?"

Sundermann took a swig from the bottle and put it on the porch's banister.

"The Hamburg White House."

Maier grinned. "Still, I feel honored. Were they pleased I did not try to kill their man Bryson in a fit of rage after he tried to execute me?"

"Bryson was present at the meeting. As was the rather ineffectual consul. A woman called Lieb. But they made their point. Unfortunately, the real White House is alarmed. We bit into a rather large fish this time, Maier, and it is make-or-break for me, too. Our reputation is on the line. Your life is on the line."

Kanitha stepped out onto the narrow porch, nodded at Sundermann and scanned the water.

"Those bloody Russians and their jet skis.jet skis. Last week they killed a kid off the beach in Phuket. The cops tried to blame it on sharks."

The two men in the bay made their vehicle jump and spin, slowly washing closer to shore. Maier watched them distractedly. They looked like Russians, all right: skinheads, bodybuilder figures, *Terminator* shades, big tattoos, no smiles, despite the stupid twirls they managed to execute on their ride. Maier had a better tattoo.

Sundermann switched to English.

"Bryson is on our side, Maier."

The detective laughed sourly.

"Of course he is. That's why I didn't kill him after we escaped the mayhem on the PDJ. I do admit, he's a weird one. More sophisticated than he looks. He tried to kill me in true American showbiz fashion and then begged to hitch a ride with us when we managed to escape. How weird is that?"

"That's why I am here. To fill you in. And to check up on whether you are ready for work."

Sundermann glanced at Kanitha.

"You look ready to me."

The girl threw him a dark look.

"I apologize, Kanitha. I'd like to offer you temporary employment. With the agency. We need all the help we can get. You have good contacts in the region. And you're in danger as much as anyone."

The girl stood looking at the older German as if trying to make up her mind whether to pull his hair out. But she said nothing and retreated into the bungalow again.

"So fill me in on our glorious new collaboration with the nice folks at the CIA."

Sundermann put his hand on Maier's shoulder. The detective shrank back involuntarily. He didn't know his boss was the paternal type. Maier couldn't remember Sundermann ever touching him.

"Open the bag."

Maier reached down from the hammock and unzipped the canvas holdall. A snub-nosed revolver lay on top of the agency boss' neatly folded shirts. A box of ammunition lay next to it.

"It's loaded. It's serious, Maier. Something could happen any time."

Maier sighed. "I don't like guns. And those shirts of yours probably cost more than your peashooter."

"Times change, Maier. We have to change with them or we go under. Weltmeister is coming and the world lives in fear of what will happen. He has plans. And he's your dad."

Maier almost felt sick as he listened to his boss' advice. Paradise was but a moment, and he could see it slipping though his remaining fingers like the fine sand on the beach in front of him. He wiped the sweat from his forehead.

"That remains to be seen. And the Viets and the Americans want to shut him down because he has a thirty year-old file up his backside. So what? He's not coming for me."

He pushed the bag away and sank back into the hammock.

Sundermann touched his shoulder a second time. "Maier, don't lie to yourself. I'd love to give you a month off, to get over the trauma, come to terms with the loss of your fingers, forget the case, enjoy your very enjoyable company, but it's not going to happen. Your father will make the world explode. He has scores to settle. Old, old injustices are about to be revenged. And he called you out here, to his side. To bear witness. Your father is the first messiah of the twenty-first century."

Maier snorted. One of the jet ski riders fell in the water and the infernal buzzing stopped as the vehicle slowed fifty meters off the beach.

"I guess I should shoot these two thugs out there first," Maier laughed. "Then we can deal with the messiah."

Sundermann got up and stood facing the sea. The first shot hit him in the shoulder and he tumbled backwards. Maier spun out of the hammock onto the porch. The man who'd fallen off the jet skijet ski stood waist-deep in the water and let off a second round from his semi-automatic, which ripped past Maier into the bungalow.

"Kanitha!"

The jet ski driver cranked up his engine and started accelerating towards the hut. A third shot ripped into the floor of the porch.

"Kanitha."

No answer.

Sundermann had slid into the sand in front of the hut, bleeding heavily. Maier grabbed the bag, pulled the revolver out and flicked off the safety.

He hated guns. But he took his time and aimed carefully.

He hit the man in the water square in the chest. The small gun almost jumped from his grip. Maier, shocked he'd found a target, rolled off the porch. Barely glancing at his boss, who was crawling behind the hut, the detective got up, brushed the sand off his chest and stepped into the light. He felt like lying in the sand and crying and never looking up into the sky again. But he was on his feet and started walking. The sun was behind him. Everything slowed down to the speed of sound and matter. Today, there would be no need for a sniper. Today, there was no longing for a father he had never known. Sundermann, he understood, was as close to family as he'd had in years. And Sundermann was down. Maier's will to live and fight back was very strong. His sacred tattoo burned into his back.

The jet ski ran out of water and slammed onto the beach, sliding towards the bungalow. The assassin jumped off in one fluid movement and sprinted towards Maier. The detective stood his ground and stared at what was coming with discontent. The world was on fire. He didn't need the CIA or the Laotians to tell him that. He didn't need to understand what was coming towards him right now. He raised his weapon with care and squeezed out a second shot. The jet ski pilot stumbled and fell. Maier felt tears running down his face. He didn't have the courage to turn. Had Kanitha been hit? Was Sundermann dead? He was too scared to check what was happening behind him. So he marched forward, towards his attacker.

The man was alive and grappling for something in his pants. Maier stepped between the killer and the sun and shot him in the arm. The bullet from the peashooter almost severed his limb. His assailant stopped grappling; a slim throwing knife tumbled into the sand. Beyond the jet ski, which lay on its side pissing oil into the sand like a dying horse suffering from a last moment of incontinence, the water had turned red. The second man was drowning, slowly turning this way and that, his life seeping into the crystal-clear surf.

It was over. Almost. Maier stepped around the man on the beach. The assassin was still alive.

"What were you assholes thinking? And who are you working for?"

Maier reveled in his moment. He knew he was at his very worst. He didn't care for answers. He knew that he'd never wanted to arrive at this point. He could see himself walking past villages as they went up in flames. He pointed the gun at the killer's head. There was no fear in the man's eyes, just a whisper of disbelief and hate.

"Go to hell, you fucking Kraut. We'll get you and your old man, dead or alive. This is just the beginning. And I'm not going to tell you anything."

Maier, in a daze, barely registered the man's American accent. Through his tears, he started laughing maniacally. He opened his eyes to let the man look inside.

"I don't want you to talk. I just want you to die. Don't fuck with the son of Weltmeister, my friend."

He pulled the trigger until the gun was empty. Times had changed. Oblivion-seekers ruled the land. Maier threw up into the sand next to the man he had just killed and passed out.

FATHER

Sitting in the Bangkok hospital's waiting room, Maier contemplated the benefits of technology. Helicopters were fine conveyances. The air ambulance that had plucked Sundermann from the beach had saved his boss' life after a passing boat of snorkelers had heard the shots and called the police.

The steel prosthetics the Thai doctors had given Maier were perfect tools to scratch his back with. Or someone else's back, for that matter.

But technology had its limits. Kanitha lay dead in the morgue a few floors below. Her parents, distraught, their lives smashed to pieces, their daughter lost to causes they could not comprehend nor cared for, had left. He hadn't even seen her after he'd collapsed next to his second victim. Bryson, gross Charlie Bryson, had broken the news, told him a headshot had disfigured her. Maier had no idea yet how Bryson had found out about the shooting and medevac.

He was both empty and nervous. He was in a different place, a dark corner, full of anger and resentment at the cards he'd been dealt. His batteries were depleted, the joy for life punched out of him. Not since he'd lost his best friend to a bomb in Cambodia four years earlier had Maier felt so lost, so utterly alone, so ridden with guilt and regret. Sundermann had instructed Maier to disappear and now lay sedated in ICU. Maier had ignored his order.

Bryson, who'd been at his side ever since the detective had gotten back to the Thai capital, forever wiping his bald plate and wittering on about security, only made it worse. Friend or foe, the man was a snake.

Sundermann would make it. The bullet had not hit any vital organs. Infection was unlikely. Thailand had good hospitals. Squadrons of nurses fussed around his boss, offering everything from new dressings to marriage proposals.

Kanitha had nothing to make. She would never smile again, never love again, never ridicule Maier for his hang-ups again. In time, her loss would turn into a wound. One day, the wound would close. Unless it got infected.

Maier almost wished for that infection. It would distract from his seething anger. It would slow the desire to murder a little.

The gunmen had not been identified. The local papers talked of a Russian hit on German holidaymakers, with an unidentified Laotian woman the only casualty. The kingdom was so used to acts of violence and backroom monkey business perpetrated by foreign gangsters that the police, once briefed by the US and German embassies, were busy brushing the affair under the table. Thailand's reputation as a safe destination for millions of international holidaymakers was on the line. The tropical fantasy of the world's most easy-going playground, a clever marketing ploy the country had nurtured ever since seven million Americans had washed through during the Vietnam War, had been shaken and stirred. In the coming days, the apparent freak incident on a relatively remote beach would be explained away in a couple of lackluster newspaper paragraphs, and no one would ask pertinent questions. Thailand's Teflon image rested on this kind of crisis management. The local media was easily malleable, routinely threatened and paid by the government. Ethical reporting was dangerous and consequently almost unheard of.

Only now did Maier contemplate the softness of her skin, her sharp wit, the quiet encouragement and manic energy with which Kanitha had infused their brief moments together. He'd never let her close. He'd thought her too young. He had not really trusted her. But he had not stopped her from becoming more involved in his case either. Whatever suspicions he had had about her motives, her death had neutralized them all. And now she was gone and his boss lay unconscious in intensive care, connected to countless tubes.

Distractedly, he ran his steel fingers along the metal arm of the chair he sat on, scraping off the hospital paint job. Bryson's phone rang. The American got up, nodded at the detective and walked off down the hall, barking into his device. Maier shuffled around in his seat. The corridor he sat in, in front of Sundermann's bed, lay deserted. All he could hear was the beeping of machines, of respirators keeping the seriously sick alive, and someone coughing desperately. It was around lunch and Maier assumed that most of the nurses were on their midday break. He was alone, for the first time since the attack on the beach.

"Maier, don't turn around."

The detective didn't recognize the voice. A German voice. Slight Saxony accent. Slightly overdone. He didn't know the voice, but he knew it for what it was. He started to turn but a heavy hand gripped his shoulder.

"You have to trust me on this one, Maier."

Maier relaxed back into his chair and stared straight ahead. The pressure on his shoulder diminished.

The man behind him chuckled. "So Ruth did not give you a first name? There must be one in your passport."

Maier had not spoken his first name in years. In his own world, in the construct he called life, he was just Maier.

"Ferdinand. But no one knows that."

A soft laugh rose from the other man. His voice had the subtle qualities of a good wine vintage, full-bodied, strong and aged.

"I will keep your secret. Our secret. It might come in handy."

"Who are you?"

"Ah, Maier, you know who I am. I am Weltmeister. And I need your help. What's been started must be finished."

"Why don't you want me to turn around?"

The man behind Maier said nothing for a moment. Then he cleared his throat and said quietly, "I am not ready."

Maier thought about it and replied, "There never is a good time."

"We have little time, good or bad, Ferdinand. Let's not waste it on essentials. We will have our moment. But first, we must… I must close down my legacy. History throws a long shadow sometimes extending across a man's lifetime. Mine is coming to an end. I am old. I am not as strong and efficient as I used to be. But neither is the opposition, however formidable it thinks it is."

"Did you bring me to Laos?"

"I did."

"So you used me in your damn schemes?"

"I did."

"And Julia was a set-up?"

"She was. She is."

Maier recoiled and the hand pressed down on his shoulder again. Someone nearby sighed and the detective stopped struggling.

"There's little time now for this, Ferdinand. Take it easy."

"Who is Julia Rendel?"

The voice behind him held its breath. The two men sat in near silence amongst the beeping machines.

"Julia is the daughter of Manfred Rendel, an old friend of mine whom I killed in Long Cheng in 1976. A useless man who was about to blow my cover."

Maier sat, waiting for more.

"And that's all you need to know about Julia right now."

Maier took note of the easy familiarity with which his father referred to his client. But he decided to stop pushing.

"Now there are others who want to expose me. I will kill them all. Every last one of them."

Maier twisted uncomfortably in his chair.

"So, it's because of you I lost two fingers, my boss is lying over there with a bullet in his chest, and my girl is downstairs in the morgue."

"We are all responsible for our actions, Ferdinand. You know the risks. Kanitha knew what she was getting into when she hooked up with Léon Sangster. She wasn't innocent and she didn't do it for love. Your boss is a wily operator who will come out of this as a winner. And so will you, your loss notwithstanding. But first…"

Maier brushed the hand off his shoulder. The touch electrified him, but he was unable to speak. Anger, sorrow and confusion raced through him.

The older man continued. "I have something that everyone wants. Information pertaining to the American War in Indochina which is as explosive today as it was then. Well, almost. Without it, I am dead. So I have kept it under wraps all these years. This information cost me dearly. I lost the woman I loved and I almost lost that which I now treasure most in this life, my anonymity. I thought it was all buried in the early Seventies, but people try digging it up again and again, for different reasons. The man who killed my wife, who betrayed me and the country I worked for, the man who made me change sides in the American War, is coming back. The two killers on the beach were his emissaries. They were like me, only younger and not as good. Otherwise, you'd also be dead."

Maier shook his head.

"But why did you abandon Ruth? You broke my mother."

He was suddenly overwhelmed by his father's presence. He no longer needed to turn around to see him. He just needed answers.

"All my life, anonymity has been my main weapon. And my passion. I loved your mother, but I was working as a US spy in Germany. She got pregnant, so as soon as you were born and I knew you were both healthy, I left her. I didn't even get to name you. My situation was too precarious. They would have gotten to her. They get to everyone a guy like me loves. They would have gotten to you, too. But over the years, the loneliness gets to everyone, even the best. So I got married to a girl called Valentina, long after you were born. And I went off to work, and one day she was no longer there and I never found out how they killed her. I did the right thing with your mother. If I had not left her, she would have been killed. Instead, Valentina was murdered."

"So you should have kept your hands off her, then," Maier retorted, but he realized in the same instant that he would have done the same. That his father was indeed his father.

"Sorry."

The man who called himself Weltmeister squeezed his shoulder once more, with less force. Maier reached out with his good hand and connected with old flesh. He tried to think of the gesture as comforting. He tried to feel something. For whom he was not sure.

"And now?"

"It started in Laos in 1973 and it will end in Laos. I'm not sure how it will end, but I hope, I really, really hope that we will be able to meet under better circumstances. It's my life's wish."

Maier tried for a long shot. "You are the sniper?"

"I am."

The detective inhaled deeply.

"Why did you shoot the old woman on the island? The boatman?"

The hand vanished from his shoulder. "I just wanted to see how persistent you are, whether you are up to it. Parents make mistakes, you know. And I am sorry. So very sorry."

"Sorry you shot those people?"

Weltmeister coughed into the empty corridor.

"Not really."

Maier had no answer.

"I've been wanting to talk to my son for years, so many years. I was always watching from a distance, far away, seeing you grow up and do well. You are everything I hoped you might become. But I was never crazy enough to contact you. Too dangerous. Until now."

"And it has become less dangerous?"

"No, it just became more urgent."

The two men sat in silence.

Eventually, Maier snapped out of his thoughts. "So, now what?"

The older man laughed, not happily. "Now I will set the world on fire. I will close my life's story. I will end the tyranny I have suffered under for the past thirty years, the tyranny of being a fugitive. I will release my dark side into the world and challenge my old masters. And I want you to help me."

Maier shrugged in defiance.

"How?"

The older man behind him chuckled. "You are reacting like a teenager angry with his old man, Ferdinand. I love it. Just trust me."

Maier didn't answer.

The hiss of an elevator door down the corridor made him turn his head. Bryson was running towards him, screaming, "Where is he?"

Maier turned but there was no one else. He was alone.

Weltmeister had left the building. And Maier had not even had a chance to ask what had happened to Julia.

He sighed. His father's words lingered.

PEACE IN THE VALLEY

"Of all places in Asia, why here? Why are we meeting here?"

Maier's mind loitered in an exotic semi-stupor. He was back at work. Early retirement hadn't worked out. It was hard to resist the Russian vodka and the freshly squeezed orange juice served by the painfully shy waitresses dressed in dark sarongs and shiny silk blouses who fussed around the group of middle-aged and jaded men. They sat on the shady balcony of the Phousi Hotel, one of the better addresses in town.

"The powers that be always meet in Luang Prabang. Historically, it's neutral ground. What's not to like?" Bryson replied lazily.

Sundermann, his arm in a sling, nursed a glass of expensive French wine. There'd been no shop talk. The conversation prattled on, tourism, bombs, economy, the impending visit of the former US Secretary of State. Maier kept his mouth shut. Nice stuff. No murder, no secret files, no explosive revelations. Like a couple of old friends.

They all needed to work together, Sundermann said. His boss sounded like a politician. Bryson was polite, careful not to antagonize the detective.

Maier didn't like working with others. Not even with people who'd tried to kill him. He started digging his steel fingers into the white plaster of the balcony wall and watched as young backpacking tourists in the street below tried to discover the delights of Laos for as little money as possible, all of them carrying hefty guidebooks in their hands. Columbus would never have found anything with one of those books. But at this very moment, as his eyes drifted back to Bryson, he envied these kids. They didn't even know what bastards existed out there, on the fringes, just a few meters away from them.

The locals were setting up a street market to help the visitors spend their money. As the sun dipped into the hills to the west, they put up their stalls at a snail's speed, happy in the certainty that money would come with very little effort. This was communist capitalism Laotian-style.

The two men he sat with exuded the charm of ancient reptiles about to devour the land beneath them. He wondered whether there was a sniper out there, training his sights on the balcony.

"Well, I know it's probably the last thing you expect from old Charlie Bryson, but I keep my promises, Sundermann. Of course, you guys know I'm not the sentimental type and I'm not looking for friends here, so just take it as good business practice."

The American got up and opened the door behind the small group.

"Surprise, surprise."

Mikhail, dressed in a loud shirt, Bermuda shorts and an unhinged grin partly obscured by strands of his long grayish-blond hair, stepped onto the balcony. A camera around his neck would have made him the archetypal budget-package tourist. Instead, he had a bottle in his hand.

"Ah, my friends, surrounded by lovely mamachtkas, guzzling high-quality vodka, waiting for the only real man with the only real game in town!"

Maier and Sundermann got up. The red-faced jolly giant opened his arms and embraced Maier. He was breathing heavily, as if he'd walked the four hundred kilometers up from Vientiane. He smelled, in equal parts, of expensive but carelessly chosen aftershave and pricey liqueur.

"Finally we meet under a good sky, my handsome German friend."

His bear hug done, the Russian proceeded to vigorously shake Sundermann's good hand.

Maier's boss gave the huge man an appraising look and grinned. "A great opportunity to meet the elusive Mikhail. It might be the only one, so I won't waste my time. Are you for hire?"

The Russian roared with laughter loud enough to make heads turn in the street below and waved for one of the waitresses.

"I might be, once we have resolved our current conundrum. How is it that the Americans say? I keep you posted," he added with a wink towards Bryson

"We say, fuck off, you commie fag," the bald American retorted, but only Mikhail laughed.

"Ha, I've never worked for you guys and I never

will. Americans are too uncertain. They always change direction when the going gets good. I blame the need for instant gratification. You are a young country. Immature. Not used enough to tragedy."

His next chuckle went straight into his glass, two thirds vodka, one third orange juice, with a few drops of mirth and anarchy to round off the flavor.

Bryson, Sundermann and Mikhail sat down. They were a little out of the ordinary, Maier thought, gazing at the odd team.

"You look like a bunch of heist vets."

This time, everyone laughed without smiling.

Bryson countered, "Well, I'm in, but this gotta be the worst place in the world to hit a bank. Biggest note is worth a couple of bucks. It's like eight thousand kip to the dollar. You'd have to bring a truck to move this monopoly money the commies trade in. But never mind; plenty of folks who start in the intelligence business go on to become gangsters."

"Ah, the Vietnamese would slap you, my American friend," the Russian interjected. "If there's any money in the banks here, it's probably theirs."

Sundermann struck his glass with a spoon and the lazy banter subsided. He turned to Mikhail.

"Are you still working for the Vietnamese?"

The huge man swallowed the last of his drink and waved for a refill.

He nodded severely. "You know how it is in this business. Never screw your client. I am here representing Laotian and Vietnamese intelligence in my usual private capacity. My current employer, the very magnificent Mr Mookie, sent me, and I have his trust. My old friend Maier had the rare honor to meet him and survive the encounter a couple weeks ago. Technically, Maier is working for us. But let's not snap spines here."

Mikhail laughed in Maier's direction. Everyone turned to the detective. Maier said nothing. He looked at his artificial fingers, then back at the men. What was happening to his life?

The Russian continued. "We are keen to make any deal to work with the CIA and your outfit on this, Sundermann, to find Weltmeister and talk him into coming in from the cold, so to speak, before the third party gets to him."

Maier shook his head. "And who might that third party be?"

Mikhail looked at the others.

No one answered.

Eventually, Bryson piped up. "We think the third party is American."

"The guys who attacked us on the beach in Thailand were Americans," Sundermann added.

Bryson looked to the street.

"These guys were not government issue. At least not officially so. We might have trained them but they were working in a private capacity. Highly specialized machine operators. Very nasty. I mean very efficient."

He turned to Maier. "You did very well, detective, and I'm sorry you lost your little girl in the crossfire. These guys usually clean up. And you stopped them. Congratulations."

"That does not make me feel better, Charlie."

The American looked away and opened another beer.

Maier picked up the thread. "Basically, everyone and his dog is after a man called Weltmeister who may or may not be my dad–"

Bryson cut him off. "Stop playing games, Maier; I know he was at the hospital in Bangkok. You talked to him. He's your old man."

Maier nodded and grinned at Bryson. "He told me he is sick of being hunted and that he is turning the tables. He told me he is going to set the world on fire."

Bryson jerked back, then checked his composure.

"Sure looks like that," he agreed.

Mikhail laughed. "Then we should help him do it. I doubt we can stop him. He's back because someone forced him to show his cards. None of us, and that includes you, his son, would ever have heard from him otherwise. It's a second coming."

Maier had to agree with Mikhail. Love and altruism weren't part of his father's motivation for his reappearance, no matter what he'd told him at the hospital. And yet the old man's acknowledgement of his mother felt right to him. Maier hoped his father had always watched from a distance, had always been there as a shadow, had kept tabs on his son growing up over days, weeks, months, seasons, years and decades, had supported him from within the system he used and abused with so little effort.

Bryson nodded. "I have some classified intel that's for our ears only. This comes all the way from the top, right out of the Oval Office. Weltmeister was a US agent who crossed over to the Vietnamese in the final days of the Vietnam War. He'd been an extremely loyal and reliable man, a brilliant field agent, a ruthless killer, an all-around full-blooded American, even if he was a Kraut. No Safety-First-Clive either. Took risks, did brilliant work. But in 1973, he turned. He murdered several CIA case officers in Long Cheng. Shortly after, we lost track of him. Along with the elusive file, the U48, which we are all after."

Mikhail raised his hand. "He did come over to the Vietnamese. But not because they turned him."

"So who did?" Maier interjected.

The Russian shrugged. "No idea what made him change sides. The killing of the American agents in Long Cheng was never made public, but under the table, the US used it as justification to intensify its bombing of a stretch of the Ho Chi Minh Trail that ran through Laos and Cambodia. I am guessing it served as a secret trump card in case the Long Cheng story was blown at the wrong time and public protests back home got out of hand."

Sundermann leaned forward and played with his glass. "It sounds to me as if his own people set him up. Made him kill those guys. Someone had leverage over him. And he got wind of it but did it anyway and escaped."

Bryson shook his head. "Well, we looked in our records, went through all the classified info within the agency. Nothing. It was an act of insanity. The men he killed were his buddies. He'd fought with them for years. That guy's a war monster."

Maier stayed silent. He didn't care to share his father's secrets and he felt no urge to convince Bryson of deeper truths. If the CIA man couldn't dig up what had happened, then there was a good chance his father's story of love and blackmail would be dismissed outright if anyone was ever taken to task for what had happened.

Mikhail continued. "He provided the Vietnamese with some excellent intel towards the end of the war. He was instrumental in the liberation, sorry, conquest of Long Cheng. He was as loyal and reliable as a Vietnamese agent. But they didn't trust him. They never understood why he'd done that killing and come over to them. They used him for two years – right until the end. A decision was made to dispose of him once the US had been driven out of Indochina. Somehow, he found out and had himself transferred to the Stasi. A year later, he was back in Long Cheng, killed his friend, the East German cultural attaché, and disappeared with a little gold and heroin, part of the stash the US had left behind. The stash that brought Maier to Laos. The Vietnamese never got that file."

"How do you know all this?"

The Russian smiled benevolently at Maier. "Mr Mookie is very close to the Vietnamese. In those days, he also worked closely with the East Germans. We have good intel on your father until 1976."

No one spoke for a while. The sun had dropped behind the hills and the temperature fell quickly.

Mikhail got up and waved for a refill.

"I have some good news. We found Léon Sangster and we are watching him, from a distance. It seems he has gone over to the third party. Last week, he was spotted in Vang Vieng, a small tourist town a couple hours north of Vientiane. He met several Americans there."

He glanced at Bryson. "They are yours?"

The American shook his head.

Maier shook his head. "It's pointless approaching them. They won't tell us a thing. The man I shot was laughing at me even as I pulled the trigger."

"Then we need to find Léon's weak point."

Maier laughed. "That's easy. He hates me almost as much as my father. I am the son of Weltmeister, the man who killed his sister. He will do anything to have it out with me. He had murder in his eyes when he recognized me at the Vietnamese jungle prison."

The Russian clapped his hands. "Great. We get Léon. Then we know about the third party. Mr Mookie has advised me to put a stop to any activities conducted by foreign mercenaries on Laotian soil."

Bryson waved the Russian's enthusiasm away, "Well, that doesn't tell us anything about Weltmeister's next steps."

Maier spoke quietly. "My father is angry, very, very angry. Someone forced him out of retirement, and he will not disappear until gets what he wants."

Maier felt exceedingly strange talking with so much certainty about family matters. Two fingers gone, one father gained. He wasn't sure what kind of deal that was.

FRONT PAGE NEWS

"I give you ten seconds to get lost."

Maier threw an empty glass at his boss, who quickly retreated from the detective's room. The editorial headline in the *Bangkok Post*, Thailand's most popular English-language newspaper, read *High-stakes spy game leaves trail of dead across Southeast Asia*.

Kanitha's parting shot was a good one and it hurt. The paper was three days old.

A high-stakes game of espionage stretching back forty years currently plays out across Laos and local authorities are suppressing a violent storm of cloak-and-dagger business raging right under their noses.

In mid-November, a former sex worker was shot at Ang Nam Ngum Lake, an hour north of Vientiane. A week later, a boatman on the Nam Ou River was killed on his vessel by a sniper. Shortly after, an eminent monk was beaten to death in his jungle cave. A few days later, local police retrieved the body of an old white man, apparently brutally executed by persons unknown in a large marijuana plantation north of Nong Kiaw. Also in November, a former Laotian prison camp reopened and closed amidst rumors of a bloodbath. Shortly after, three Americans, employees of an MIA program, and a Canadian journalist were found dead, buried in a bomb crater on the Plain of Jars. Just days later, a female Laotian intelligence officer was executed in a farmhouse near Luang Prabang.

My investigation has led me to some of the country's most remote corners. I met Vietnamese intelligence officers, American spies, Hmong rebels, and foreign private contractors, all of them hunting an elusive prize from the Cold War, the U48, a file, perhaps mythical, perhaps real, that is said to list all the double agents of the Vietnam War era as well as other sensitive US policy details of the time.

Laotian police steadfastly rule out any connection between these murders and deny the very existence of the file. No mention of espionage has been made in local papers. Is the Laotian government killing bad-news stories fearing the murders might affect tourist arrivals? Is the much-touted increasing transparency of the reclusive communist state on a backslide into a quickly developing political quagmire just as Henry Kissinger, former US Secretary of State and Nobel Peace prize winner, is about to visit the country? No US government representatives were available for comment in Vientiane.

The comment was followed by an editor's note.

Up-and-coming travel writer and journalist Kanitha Amatakun sent us this incredible story on the condition that it be published only if she were found dead.

On Thursday, Amatakun was killed in a bizarre and unresolved shoot-out on the island of Ko Chang in Trat Province, where she had been holidaying. Local witnesses say her bungalow was attacked by two armed men who arrived on a jet ski.jet ski.

Police in Trat have since claimed the assailants were Russian and that the bodies had been returned to their country. The Russian Embassy was not available for comment. A foreigner who had been staying with Amatakun has not been found.

Maier grabbed the vodka bottle, raised it to his mouth and tilted it back until he'd emptied it. Gasoline, he thought, and passed out into a dirty dream.

JULIA

"Good morning, Maier. Your looks haven't improved since we last met. And what happened to your hand?"

Maier was slowly getting used to the metal prosthetics and vaguely waved them in Julia Rendel's direction as she stepped into the room. He was quite lost for words. The sun, the hangover and the vodka orange he was nursing for breakfast made it hard to focus on his visitor. But he was relieved to see her alive and in one spectacular piece.

Julia appeared to have survived the past weeks in captivity well. One hell of a woman. Her hair was up in the unruly fashion he remembered. She wore practical but elegant clothes – a white, thin cotton blouse and low-slung, baggy beige pants, along with fashionable red soft leather slippers. Her high-maintenance hair extravaganza was accentuated by ethnically styled earrings and a tribal necklace of lapis lazuli big enough to serve as a generous dowry gift. There was not a hint of trauma in her eyes. She looked stunning, and Maier's thoughts briefly short-circuited back to the nights they'd spent together at the Atlantic. He got up and embraced her.

"What are you doing here, Julia? Where have you been?"

"I was kidnapped, remember? By people you now work with. And then other guys kidnapped me again. People you know nothing about. You're not on top of things, Maier," she snapped, and pulled away.

"I certainly wasn't working with the people who took you then, and I am a reluctant colleague now," he shot back.

She sat down on the room's only chair and lit a cigarette. Maier hated cigarette smoke. He made a show of opening the windows.

"No need to rub it in, Maier. I understand you're not pleased to see me."

He fell back onto his bed, exhausted by his attempt to clear the air between them. The fact that she wasn't shattered by her kidnapping unsettled him. He was happy for her. But she reminded him of his father.

"So who busted you from Charlie's clutches? And what did they want?"

"That's top secret, Maier. Let your imagination lead you, detective. But count yourself out. We know it wasn't you who rescued me. You just kill people, by all accounts."

"So do the people who freed you, I heard."

"You don't have that kind of clearance."

"You hired me to find your father's murderer, and now you withhold information. You're just another wily operator. You string me along and you blow up cars. And I was so stupid as to worry about you. What kind of working relationship do we have?"

"A cold one, Maier, a cold one," she retorted.

Maier ignored her jibe.

"And what makes you hang around?"

"Other people's greed and crimes, of course, Maier."

"Making the world a better place for all of us, are we?"

"Just for some of us. A select few, in fact."

She pulled a face and blew smoke in his direction before stubbing her cigarette out on the barrel of the gun he'd smuggled across the border from Thailand and left lying on his night table. A poor way to make a point.

He looked straight at her, a sour expression on his face. "Can't say I've found your gold just yet."

Julia grinned sheepishly and broke the eye contact. "It was never really about the gold. I would have thought you'd know that by now."

Maier said nothing and waved his metal claws at her again.

"Very handsome." She smiled, but he saw no sweetness in her eyes.

"So you are back for some tree-hugging?"

She shot him a look that would have wilted a cat and growled, "No need to be mean, Maier. I did hire you to find out who killed my father. The gold was just an incentive. And I loved our time at the Atlantic until those thugs came and dragged me away."

He supposed he was looking for a hint of vulnerability, but he could not detect any.

"Do you know who killed your father? Do I have to tell you?"

She shook her head, and her hair did something Maier liked despite his misgivings.

"I guess it was the same man who killed Vincent. You're not the only one who's learning painful lessons in Laos."

Maier left her answer standing in the room. He had no

intention to offer his former client information about his father. In a manner of speaking, Weltmeister had indeed killed the Canadian, although Kanitha had pulled the machine gun's trigger. Maier thought back to how Bryson had described Julia's liberation. It had been efficient and bloody.

"No, Vincent died because he tried to have me killed. Bryson told him about us. What a coward that guy was."

"Vincent was a calculated mistake."

Julia stared furiously into space, unwilling to say more.

"So why did you come back?"

"Kissinger is coming."

Maier raised his eyebrows and refrained from telling Julia that he already knew.

Kissinger was coming. There was so much secret undertow in the way she'd said it. They looked at each other and Maier had the feeling that they both knew they knew. Something. Julia broke his gaze and walked to the window.

Kanitha had mentioned that the former US Secretary of State was about to drop in for an unofficial visit in her final news story. Had she left him a message? The man who had ordered the carpet-bombing of Laos was returning to the scene of his misdeeds. Was there more to it than echoes of *Realpolitik*? What was the connection between the mayhem Maier had survived and the former US Secretary's visit? One look at Julia and he understood that the goalposts had shifted. The old diplomat's visit lay right at the heart of the schemes Julia was involved in.

"And?"

"Trees, Maier, are one of Laos' greatest assets. But they stand in the way of dam projects, road construction, mining and every other infrastructure project that the Chinese, the Americans, the World Bank, the Thais, the Vietnamese, the Asian Development Bank, and anyone else with cash and a profit motive have in mind. Don't get me wrong; we are not anti-development. But these projects only benefit foreign powers and local gangsters. Laos is coming out of its communist isolation, sniffing cash, and we're hoping to slow the damage this entails. TreeLine has a petition with three hundred thousand signatories, from Desmond Tutu to Paul the backpacker, calling for the enforcement of laws that already exist but are unfortunately never used. Laos has a good national park system, but logging and poaching go on anyhow."

The detective said nothing.

Julia continued. "Come on, Maier, don't be slow. Kissinger is coming to ink deals. To provide an unofficial counterweight to Chinese efforts in Laos. They can't send a US government delegation to a communist country. Not just yet. So they send Henry. He has connections everywhere and the war is long past."

Maier scratched the stubble on his chin with his thumbnail.

"There lies some deeper secret in this?"

"Could be just a story. But I suspect not. Time will tell. And we aren't really friends today, Maier, are we? So there's not much trust going around."

"Did you come here just to show off?"

She shook her head and pulled a long needle from her hair. It was a well-practiced gesture and an effective one. As she flashed him a winning smile, her hair cascaded down her back like a summer rain of precious jewels.

"No, Maier. I came to say sorry. I came to tell you

how sad I was when I heard the journalist you traveled with was killed. I am back to help you with your loss and depression, if you like. And you can help me with mine."

She looked around his messy room.

"And I came to tell you that I rented the suite. A more comfortable option than your current residence, Maier. Let's be friends."

He shook his head.

"I am quite happy here for the time being."

"No, you're not. You shot two men, executed one of them. You lost your girlfriend. And you know more about this case than anyone else, and yet you know almost nothing because you haven't put all the pieces together yet. I can help you do that. It will bring closure."

"Where did you hear I shot two men?"

"Oh, Maier, I'll let you figure that out. Come on, you're the detective. But in the meantime, scratch my back with those new fingers of yours. And I promise to scratch yours in ways you've never known."

She towered over him, offering him her hand. He saw a weird kind of love in her eyes, not a healthy one, to be sure. He saw she still had five fingers. And all the other bits were in place, too. She threw his clothes into his bag. She really had no clue who he was. As she brushed past him to reach for his jacket, he pulled her down towards him. He couldn't help it. He was Maier, private detective, survivor, veteran, killer. His father's son. In these moments, he hated it, all of it. All his monstrous selves.

"I was terribly worried about you, you know," she said under her breath. But Maier heard her remark clearly.

FLAME WAR

Vang Vieng might have been the world's most beautiful village. Surrounded by karst stone mountains that rose from paddy fields with primeval abandon, nestled along the banks of the swiftly moving Nam Song river, this modest collection of family homes, including a couple of banks and a dilapidated hospital, had an idyllic vibe. Farmers walked to and from their fields, local women fished *khai phun*, moss, from the fast-moving stream and threw it on the hot stones by the shore to dry, or set traps for freshwater prawns. Children caught lizards and rats in the rice paddy and carried them to the market. Stalls sold animals Maier didn't have names for. The surrounding villages were mostly Hmong, resettled by the government to discourage resistance.

Maier didn't care for the concessions that had been made to the dollar-strewing visitors. The backpackers were slowly overrunning Vang Vieng, attracted by the availability of cheap opium, hallucinogenic mushrooms, marijuana and alcohol. The entire community was about to turn into a university campus, without a university. Young Westerners floated in the river on inner tubes, beers and joints in hand, drowning frequently. The locals were friendly and a little overwhelmed. But the crowds of young travelers provided a modicum of cover for him. He checked into a cheap guesthouse by the main road and waited for dark.

"You shot off my damn fingers, Léon. I am very pissed off."

The Hmong jerked up from the low bench he sat on, but Maier waved him down with his snub-nosed revolver he pointed as discreetly as one could point a gun in a public place at the younger man.

"I will kill you," Léon hissed through his teeth, and looked around as if expecting the cavalry to ride to the rescue.

"You have already tried to kill me a couple of times, Léon. It's my turn today."

Mikhail's info had been good. The young Hmong had been easy to find. The café Maier had spotted his nemesis in stood right on the edge of Lima Site 409, one of the old airfields from America's Secret War. The former landing strip was currently utilized for less ambitious purposes – as a bus terminal and playground for local children.

"Fuck you, Maier. You haven't got a clue what's going on. You're out of your depth."

Léon moved again but Maier let his smile fade quickly as he pointed the gun straight at the other man's chest.

"We have to talk, Léon."

Léon's black eyes tried to burn a hole through Maier's heart, but the weapon in the detective's hand kept him from trying to rip it out.

"We're long past talking, Maier. Your family has brought nothing but death and destruction into my life. I recognized you immediately in Muang Khua. Like father, like son. You got your old man hiding in the bushes somewhere? Is that why you've suddenly developed balls enough to shoot people? I took you for a more passive kind of guy when I first saw you on your knees, about to be blown away by that stoned creep, Daniels."

"Daniels spoke very highly of you."

Léon pulled at his wispy white beard absent-mindedly, perhaps glad to hear a compliment, any kind of compliment, but he quickly turned sour again. It was easy to hate.

"Well, he's dead. And so is Kanitha, thanks to you. And so are you. You just don't know it yet. You are up against people so terrible, you can't even imagine."

Maier expected Léon to start foaming at the mouth. Reason had nothing to do with it. Most likely, it was the people Léon was working with now who had killed Kanitha. But he had to try and calm this man down. There was always something to be gained from people who did not have themselves under control – as long one stayed far enough away to avoid a physical confrontation and managed to push them in a useful direction. And in some ways, he liked Léon. Like himself, he was a child of subterfuge and secrets, quite unable to free himself from his past.

"You worked with Charlie Bryson until very recently, Léon. What happened?"

The younger man made an angry cutting gesture with the flat of his hand and grinned malevolently into the night.

"He went soft on me. He didn't even manage to kill you after getting you under the gallows. Just another sucker without a clear mission. They pass it from one generation to another. That's why the Americans lost the war. No clear mission, listening to the hippies back home while letting their soldiers get stoned in the jungle. Who's going to win a war like that?"

"That was a long time ago, Léon. History. All done. This is a new age. A former Secretary of State is coming to Laos next week."

He'd hit a nerve. Léon said nothing and stared at Maier, brooding. But he quickly found his sardonic wavelength again.

"The new age is going to eat you shortly, Maier."

He made motions to get up but Maier raised the gun again. Direct visual contact with the weapon was the only way to keep this guy in his seat.

Léon relaxed and grinned darkly. "You see Maier, in the end, we will win the war. Laos will not choose communism. The Chinese will overrun my country. Every time they offer the government an infrastructure project, they bring their own workers. And when it's all done, the workers stay. It's the new colonial capitalism. The Vietnamese have pockets of their military all over the place, trying to hang on to what they see as their sphere of influence. But the government is no longer going to accept this. The Vietnamese are on their way out. Trade relations with the US are the first step in our emancipation. Absorbing the Chinese is the second. Communism is going down."

"None of this has anything to do with us, Léon."

The man across the table laughed bitterly.

"Yes, you are right, detective. I don't really care about any of this. Your father killed his best buddies. I saw him do it. He betrayed my parents. He betrayed everything we believed in then. I saw him shoot my sister. He almost killed me. Of course I don't give a shit about anything else."

Maier understood the stateless, rootless man. His anger was genuine, lethal and in parts justified. The kind of history Léon wore like a suit of armor and a ball and chain would have turned anyone into a monster or a basket case.

But Maier was on his own learning curve when it came to loyalty, love and blood relations. He still had a father. A war criminal, a killer, a victim of circumstances, a prisoner to his vanity and love. A father he wanted to save.

Léon tied his long thinning hair into a pony tail and continued. "We all need closure, Maier. I was reasonably happy on my island with my dog. A year ago I met Kanitha, and sometimes she would come and stay. It wasn't much of a life, but it was something. Then you turn up and take it all away. I've tried to kill you twice. Now I leave it to the pros to take you out. But not today. We still need you to lure your father out of the woodwork."

"Then why did you try and kill me on the Plain of Jars after I got away from the hanging?"

"You were escaping with my girl. I have many reasons to kill you, Maier. But as I said, it makes more sense to keep you alive for the moment. And close."

"Then why did your current associates try to kill me on the beach in Thailand?"

"They weren't trying to kill you; they were trying to kidnap you. They didn't expect armed resistance, I guess. They killed Kanitha and shot your boss because you resisted."

Maier could see that the boy was thinking in circles, desperately trying to attach guilt to anyone but himself for the mess he was part of.

A great silence settled between the two men. Maier relaxed and quietly released the hammer of his gun. He had killed two men in self-defense. He was determined not to kill again. It wasn't part of his job description, nor his destiny. But he understood how one could get used to killing when it came to saving one's own life. One got used to it quickly.

As he faced Léon, he realized how they were both trapped in this story. Their personal investment was so substantial that neither would be able to walk away from whatever was coming at them, no matter how cruel and repulsive it might turn out to be. They were both checkmated. They had both lost their pawns and their queens. And the game had to be played to the end.

Léon laughed sadly. "It's funny, really. If you kill me, you won't be able to walk out of here tonight. If you let me go, I will come back with everything I have when the time is right and take you out. Bad cards, Maier, very bad cards. We'll win the war and kill the last of the secret warriors. And his son."

A gaggle of drunken British girls entered the café and ordered beer. They were young and loud and had no eyes for the conversation at the next table. Maier noticed the two who'd slipped in behind the girls too late. They sidled up behind the detective as Léon smiled triumphantly but without joy. The man to Maier's left wrested his gun from his hand and stuck it into the belt of his black jeans.

"You see, Maier. You're just never quite in the picture. The plans to catch your old man have been in motion ever since he first popped up again. Perhaps even longer. As soon as May Lik, my neighbor, was killed and I figured that it hadn't been the Viets who'd hit her, I knew something was afoot. When that idiot Daniels sprang me in Muang Khua, I made some phone calls. Charlie and his outfit became obsolete very quickly. They couldn't even hold on to the Rendel woman, Vincent's girl. Up in smoke, as they say. And now you are about to become obsolete. Your last mission in life is to serve as bait for your father."

Maier could not think of a way to reach out to this angry man, to contain his fury.

"I am not my father, Léon, and you should let go of your past," sounded lame even as he said it.

Léon grinned sourly. "Family runs deep in Hmong culture. It means so much more to us than it does for Westerners. It's our past and our future. My father died for his ideological beliefs, but my mother, she died because she loved her family, her children. And that's all that counts. We hit where it hurts most, detective. Your father's crimes are best avenged by taking you with us, Maier. At least it's a good start."

"I don't understand how you can hate someone you don't even know, Léon."

"You took my girl."

"She came voluntarily. And trust me, I wish she hadn't if it meant she was still alive."

"You killed her."

Maier shook his head and turned to the two men sitting next to him. "Your new friends, rogue killers, private mercenaries or whatever they say they are, killed her. Someone who isn't part of the unofficial official program of the Secret War killed her. Trust me, I was there."

The two men next to Maier shifted closer to him. They were neither upset nor nervous. For them it was just another job. The conversation didn't interest them. They were waiting on Léon's word to get on with it.

"Didn't make much difference, did it?"

He saw some doubt in Léon's eyes as they flicked from the detective to his two stone-faced guards. The man had been cheated of his life, had lost his family and his health to a war that had officially ended twenty-five years ago. A war that continued to rage through battle trenches in his mind, day after day. It was hard to get through.

"Look, Léon, we can resolve all this without further killings. At the end of the day, all parties involved in this affair want a peaceful outcome."

The Hmong brushed his hair from his face and grinned viciously. "Politician talk won't help, Maier."

Maier shook his head with irritation. "Which side are you on, Léon? Where is it going to go?"

"I'm on whichever side is out to squash you, Maier."

The detective held up his hand., "Listen to me. You loved Kanitha. I also liked her a great deal. She was a free spirit and she paid the ultimate price for following her hunches. She wanted the story. Your story, my story, whatever story was going in the wake of my father's reappearance. She understood the risks, and now she is gone and we should stop fighting. It's over. Let it go. Enjoy the time you have left; It isn't much even if you grow to a respectable age."

"Weltmeister shot my sister in the neck. He didn't hesitate. He shot her in the neck and she lies in a hole in Long Cheng to this day. Next to my mother and my father. My family hole, Maier. He promised me he would look after her, after he had already killed her. He's an animal and he needs to be put down. And you are part of him."

Léon rose from the table and threw a punch at Maier, who jerked back fast enough to dodge the swipe.

"Not here," the man on Maier's left hissed.

The drunken girls at the next table piped down and stared as the two heavies pulled Maier to his feet. Léon snapped angrily at them and they instantly turned back to their holiday debaucheries. Seconds later, his captors marched Maier across the cracked tarmac of the runway towards a waiting SUV. Where were his friends when he needed them? Mikhail and Bryson had persuaded him walk into the lion's den. Did they really want him to disappear with these two murderers? He looked across the runway, but there was no one else in sight. Léon stayed behind in the café. His depressed laugh followed Maier into the night.

The two men beside him held him in an iron grip. As they approached the car, the man to his right pulled the keys from his pocket. The vehicle, a black SUV with tinted windows, good enough for anyone's final journey, beeped as the electronic locks sprang open.

Then it exploded.

Maier was thrown onto his back by the blast. A part of the windscreen flew past him and smashed into the man to his right, instantly severing his right arm. The second abductor, peppered with glass and bleeding heavily, rose uncertainly, looked at his fallen colleague and stumbled into the night. The British girls at the café yelled in panic and spilled outside, clutching their drinks. One of them vomited in the light of a single solitary bulb above the café's front door. Another pointed her point-and-shoot camera at the carnage. The ground seemed to shake as bits of sport utility vehicle bounced off the tarmac. Maier lay still, too stunned to move, watching the fireworks.

A motorbike pulled up next to the detective. Julia, hair in disarray and eyes shining brightly, bent down towards him and smiled innocently, waving a mobile phone in the detective's direction.

"I just love technology. Saved the night, Maier. Saved your hide. Let's go."

He slowly got up and looked around. The tourists stood frozen and sober. A few Laotians peeled out of the night and carefully stepped onto the runway. No one moved towards the burning vehicle or the dying foreigner next to it. Léon, master of the great disappearing act, was gone. The injured operative stared madly and silently at Maier, gripping his gun in his left, too far gone to pull the trigger. He wasn't going to answer any questions. Maier waited until he'd lost consciousness and took his gun back.

"Find out anything interesting, detective?" she asked, her voice ripe with tense sarcasm.

"Family runs deep in Hmong culture, apparently."

She threw him an opaque look and answered, "That's a universal thing. Your aversion to the natural order of things proves you're dysfunctional."

"So is Léon, a bitter crisis of a man."

She shrugged, gunning the engine. "Léon Sangster is a victim, Maier. Dangerous when he has a gun pointed at you. We have to see that we don't become victims as well."

Maier sensed a dark undertone in her voice, so dark he quickly began to get over the flames rising from the shattered vehicle and the dead man on the ground in front of him. She'd put an emphasis on the we that he couldn't put his finger on, nor was he sure whether he cared for her certitude. The vehicle coughed and exploded again.

He walked away from the heat.

"You just made their hit list, I think."

She laughed bitterly and gunned the engine. "I was already on their hit list. These guys kidnapped me from Charlie and they weren't nice."

When he looked into her eyes, he knew she wasn't lying. He knew war was like this, messy, dirty, terrible, full of irredeemable moments that punched holes into people. He also knew that he'd never seen this woman like this before and that he had no idea who she really was. Something about her was so familiar, it frightened him. The detective, stunned but happy to be anywhere, jumped onto the bike.

As the old Lima Site burned, Vang Vieng receded behind them.

THE BIG MAN

Maier woke up at midday, pushed an empty vodka bottle off his bed and stared down into the street. Vientiane was hardly its sleepy, good-natured self today. Troops, armed and not nearly as bored as one might have expected, stood on street corners and in temple forecourts behind low piles of sandbags. Ancient diesel-spewing trucks packed with soldiers drove around town in a show of disheveled force. The government paper alluded to nothing, but Maier didn't expect revelations from the secretive communist leadership or its tightly controlled media. Hangover bearable. Brain intact. Breakfast first.

He had decided to be conspicuous upon his return to the Laotian capital. Carelessness had taken over. The game was almost up, anyhow.

He'd taken a room at the Lane Xang Hotel, a rather lived-in and tired survivor from the Sixties and once a haven of luxury, located on the riverfront. From his window, he could see a long stretch of the main road along the Mekong. An agricultural trade fair was being set up, nothing to get excited about unless you were a farmer in search of an imported tractor.

Julia had stayed the night and they had drunk together without trust or tenderness. She had told him nothing about herself or her plans or, for that matter, his father's designs. He was sure trees had little to do with whatever they were up to. She'd said nothing more about who her captors were nor how she had escaped or how she'd known he was meeting Léon in Vang Vieng.

When he'd regained consciousness, his former client had gone.

Bleary-eyed, he watched a helicopter sweep low over the riverfront, reminding Laotians that the politburo had nothing but their welfare in mind. Still, people raised their heads at this unusual spectacle. Airborne helicopters were a rarity in the impoverished nation by the Mekong.

Across the river, a balloon, bright yellow, the slogan of a fertilizer company emblazoned on its bulging skin, had risen into the sky, perhaps representing Thailand's free market contribution to the upcoming fair. The basket underneath the balloon was crammed with tourists.

Her perfume lingered like a curse. But it was not just Julia Rendel that Maier was worried about. An invisible hand, all five fingers intact, had settled over the Lao affair, picking at its innards like a starving vulture. Alliances around him were shifting quicker than the clouds that raced across the communist sky.

The knock on the door shook him out of his morning daze. He grabbed his gun and took a peek through the door viewer.

His father stared straight at him.

Maier dropped the security chain and pulled the door open.

"Ferdinand."

The old man quickly looked up and down the corridor and slipped past Maier into the room. Maier shut the door and dropped the gun to his side. They stood looking at each other. The two-dimensional silhouette that had followed the detective through his dreams had morphed into a real person.

"*Vater*."

Maier couldn't help but use the most formal title as he addressed his father properly for the first time.

"Call me Weltmeister. It's the only name I have left," the older man replied.

They embraced, awkwardly. Maier took a step back and continued to stare at the man he'd been dreaming of meeting all his life.

The man stared right back.

Maier Sr was a head smaller than his son. They shared the same broad shoulders, the same large hands and the same intensely curious green eyes. He must have been a handsome devil, all right. His face was deeply lined with life and sorrow, with victories and defeats. His hair might have been blond once; now it was gunmetal gray. He wore a white, short-sleeved shirt and gray slacks. As he came further into the room, he kicked off his simple black leather shoes the way any man who'd spent years in Asia would. Maier guessed him to be in his mid-seventies, though his body was that of a healthy man twenty years younger. Apart from the subtle charisma he exuded, he looked unremarkable, but Maier could tell straight away that his father's ordinariness was studied and refined to the point where he might pass through a crowd of dull people without anyone noticing him. Except for the eyes, of course.

"It's been a long time. I have only ever held you as a baby…"

The older man's voice faded with emotion.

Maier didn't know what to say. So many questions. So little time. As if his father could read his thoughts, he walked over to the unmade bed, pulled a gun from under his shirt, gently deposited it on the night table and sat down. As Maier deposited his own gun next to his father's, he realized that the distance between them was narrowing. Maier too had killed.

"What are you doing here?"

Weltmeister turned his head and beckoned his son.

"I am not sure. Trying to set a few things straight, I guess. I know it's late. Very late."

"Why did you never contact me?"

"I told you at the hospital. If I'd stayed with Ruth, she would have been killed. If I'd been too close to you while you were growing up, you might have been killed. Anonymity is the only way in this game."

"So, why do it? Why did you become a spy?"

Maier was acutely aware that his own choice of careers – that of journalist, war correspondent and private investigator – looked like a progression into eccentricity. Being an international spook was another ball game altogether.

Weltmeister sighed. "Fighting the Nazis, working for the resistance in Germany, it was the ultimate adventure for a young man, a near teenager, full of half-baked ideas of justice and values. When the war finished, espionage was all I knew. I was good at it; I loved the subterfuge, the honesty in the dishonesty, that quiet perversity in the subversive element. I came to love the privilege that spooks enjoy, the access to information, the being apart from the rest of humanity. I fell into it, completely. It absorbed me, like a fever."

He looked around the room and back at his son, his eyes shining with the memories of past conquests.

"I have been to all the front lines of all the wars of our time, Ferdinand. I have seen things most people can't even imagine. I have walked through firefights in Vietnam and cowered in caves in Laos while napalm peeled the skin off life itself a few meters away. I have seen B-52 bombers split mountains in half and pulverize entire civilizations. I have fallen into the abyss and climbed back out so many times, I can't remember. I only learned one lesson, son. The same one you're learning now. If you're going to do something, do it with gusto, or stay home, watch TV, and leave it to the professionals. If you let yourself fall down into the abyss, by your own volition, then be damned sure you come back with a story."

Maier tried hard to keep his resentment in check. He forced himself to take a step back from his anger, to absorb his father's words without reacting from the pit of his stomach. He forced himself to look.

The old man, the spook of spooks, looked his age. His years showed in the stoop of his back, the wrinkles in his huge hands, the slight sag of the skin on his lower arms. The most hunted man in Southeast Asia looked tired.

"It was a great life. For a long time, I was with the good guys. But after they took Valentina, after I killed those men in Long Cheng, I began to hate the world. And I no longer cared who I was working for. I became a gun for hire. You know, like in the Wild West."

Maier sat on the room's only chair, transfixed. Weltmeister lapsed into silence. Maier waited. But his father just sat there, trapped by memories.

The older man's heavy breathing filled Maier's world. The detective had no idea whether he should comfort his father or question him about his sanity. Neither of them knew how to deal with the moment. They both knew it was all they had, all they would ever have.

Weltmeister raised his wounded eyes to his son and tapped the side of his head.

"I am the U48. If I die, it's all gone. All that knowledge about the war. Including my orders to kill my best friends. Including the White House plans to nuke Laos."

Maier stared at his father in astonishment.

"Nukes?"

Weltmeister nodded. "The US contemplated dropping a nuclear bomb on the country as early as the Fifties. By the early Seventies, they were almost ready. They would have done it if the war in Vietnam hadn't turned against them. I have the file names and file numbers, all the right references to reams of classified material in my head. I know the names of all the officials involved, from the Secretary of State down."

"The same Secretary of State who is about to visit Laos?"

"The very same. We used to be close. I'd be the only person in the room who'd call him Heinz. It was Henry or Mr Secretary for everyone else. We had a special relationship."

In an instant, Maier understood his father, understood his reappearance, understood how the old man imagined the near future. As the detective was about to speak, his father raised his hand.

"Julia is your step-sister, Ferdinand. I adopted her. And I trained her in the arts of killing so that she'll always be able to look after herself. You see, after losing Valentina to the CIA, I couldn't risk having another relationship. I changed sides too many times; someone else would have gotten to me. But then, in the late Eighties, when I got out of the game, I was lonely. I still felt bad for killing Rendel. He was a sleazy bastard but we went way back. I went to university with him. His daughter needed help. Life is never the way you plan it. And she has grown into a formidable woman, as you know. I worked as a painter in London through the Eighties and Nineties. I no longer had anything do with the intelligence community, I thought. Julia's adoption was my atonement…"

He let the sentence drift away.

Maier was speechless. Almost.

"Does she know that I am your son?"

The older man shook his head.

"She knows on one level, of course. But she's in denial. I've tried, quite successfully, to keep some of the more fantastical events of my life from her. But not for much longer. I'll tell her soon that the family is bigger than she thought."

"Everyone else in the world has made the connection. She deserves to know. Now."

Weltmeister was silent.

"Why didn't you tell me at the hospital?"

The old man looked at his son, his eyes glazed and far away. "You'd just lost your girlfriend. Your boss was in ICU. We had to talk. But there wasn't time. It wasn't the right moment."

"You told me there never is a right moment."

Weltmeister made a conciliatory gesture.

"I am here now."

"You are here to kill the Secretary."

His father let the remark float between them for a moment before answering. "I am here to close the Weltmeister file. I want to see the man who killed Valentina. I want to look into his eyes. Time is short and we are getting old. We are almost the same age, the Secretary and I."

Maier shook his head and walked to the window.

"So where does that leave us?"

Weltmeister pulled a CD from his pocket. "The U48. The only copy. Everyone wants it. The US, the Vietnamese, the Secretary. It's yours. After I leave, you can do what you want with it. Sell it to the highest bidder and retire if you like. Make a deal with Mikhail. The Vietnamese probably deserve it the most."

"What do I deserve?"

"The money."

Maier felt himself getting angry.

"I make a living, Father. I don't need your money. Your shenanigans have cost me two fingers and a friend."

He stopped himself from giving in to the rising frustration and calmed down.

His father rose slowly and bent over to put his arms around his son. "I know, I know. So many mistakes. War and love don't lie together well. Family always pays the price."

Maier didn't resist, though he felt uncomfortable at his father's emotional touch. Julia his stepsister? Far out. Disquieting thoughts chased one another as he tried to pull all the different strands of his case together. Case as life, life as case, it was hard to keep it apart. Maier was being subsumed by his job.

"You already told me you sent Julia to recruit me."

The old man stepped away.

"I put the idea into her head. She was desperate to reconnect with her past, ever since her mother died a couple of years ago. She wanted to know more about her real father. At the same time, I found out that my anonymity was no longer watertight. Léon was telling stories, after being so quiet I didn't even know he had survived our encounter in Long Cheng in '76. With him back in the picture, I needed to act before they'd come after me again. I told her it would be best if she made efforts to find out what had happened to her father."

"Thereby condemning yourself? She will find out who killed her father sooner or later."

"Not unless you or Léon tell her."

"Or you," Maier snapped back.

The old man sank back onto the bed.

"It's incredible that anyone would care about all this Secret War business today."

Weltmeister shrugged. "Secret wars have a habit of continuing in secret. The Americans are desperate to come back into this part of the world. It's the same old game. The Great Game. It wasn't about ideology then and it isn't now. It's money. Power. Greed. Resources. Laos sits at the crossroads between China and Southeast Asia. Remember the domino theory? Kennedy said if Laos fell, the commies would overrun the world. That's how it all started. He lied about Lao neutrality in the early Sixties, claiming no Americans worked in Laos, while building up a secret US presence at the same time. All they really wanted was the oil in the South China Sea. The thinking hasn't evolved. If the U48 becomes public, the US will struggle to get a foot in the door. Trade agreements will be that much harder to sign, and Coca-Cola will face obstacles. America making a fast buck may take second place to China making two fast bucks."

Maier shook his head. "But the CIA is no longer after you. Charlie Bryson is on our side."

The old man laughed gently. "It's not that simple. Bryson and the agency are no longer in the loop. They have been instructed to hunt me down, so that the third force can quietly make diplomatic inroads against the Chinese and get rid of me quietly at the same time. The CIA screwed up in Laos in the Seventies. So, now it's done via secret diplomatic channels that the former Secretary of State has cultivated. He's the puppet master, and Bryson, the Vietnamese and Léon and his Hmong, they are all tools, distractions in a much larger game plan. The secret agents are not in on the secret this time around."

Maier stared into space, trying to distill the information his father threw at him piecemeal into a coherent narrative.

"Family, money, politics, ideology, old war stories, new capitalist realities all thrown together. Isn't it all a bit much for you?"

"The time machine is ruthless; even when bored, it throws you ahead and there is nothing to hold onto."

"All the more reason to retire, right?"

His father smiled sadly. "I tried to wash my hands of it when I went to the UK. I thought it was all over and that I was safe. I thought I had killed everyone who knew who I was and who might have had an interest in exposing me. I had a good life there, despite the food. The British like true eccentrics. I painted. I was quite good at it. I made money. I watched Julia grow up and came to feel that she was my daughter. Someone I could trust. Someone that made me miss my son a little less. So when my cover was about to be blown again, I sent her to you, in the hope that you'd be able to throw a spanner in the works."

He shuddered and continued, "And you have, of course."

"I threw two fingers in the works."

"I am very proud of you, Ferdinand."

"I will never get used to you calling me by my first name. No one calls me Ferdinand."

Weltmeister looked up at Maier. "You might miss it when I'm gone."

Maier let the thought go. His father had only just arrived. And nothing really added up.

"So what happens next?"

The old man pointed at the CD. "We should go and talk to the Vietnamese. They have more to lose than anyone if the Chinese or the Americans come into Laos in a big way. They might help."

"Help with what? Do you really think you can change the course of history?"

"I've done it before, Ferdinand," Weltmeister snapped, and got up.

Maier looked at his old man looming up above him, his squat shape an overbearing yet impermanent silhouette against the bright hotel windows. Hello and goodbye lay close together in this family.

Maier suddenly felt tired. So many people had died. The matrix his father had weaved for decades continued to expand, on and on. He reminded himself that Weltmeister's sway had reached all the way to the White House. The entire affair was epic. His father. His father was truly crazy.

"I have a line to Mikhail, the rep for the Vietnamese. It's a good idea to end this before more people get killed over lives and loves long gone. I can set up a meeting."

His father stepped out of the light, smiling. "I was sure you could do that, son."

ENLIGHTENMENT

Weltmeister and Maier left the car behind a shack by the side of the main road and walked through a dry rice paddy. The morning mist hung above the sluggish Mekong like a gray blanket. The water level was low. The monsoon floods had gone. The fields on the riverbanks were covered in dew. It was cold despite the first rays of milky sunlight that washed over the untainted landscape. Mornings in Asia had an ethereal quality. The crimes and defeats of the previous day had been forgotten. The hope for the coming day remained intact. Village girls wrapped in sarongs carried steel pots and bags of washing along the riverbank, giggling and shouting quietly as only girls in Laos would, their long raven-black hair trailing behind them, giving them the solidity of feys. A couple of buffaloes ambled across the fields on the opposite side, dark and solid shapes heading for the water's edge. No traffic noise, no loudspeakers, nothing but bird calls and the laughter of the girls penetrated through the mist and lent the scenery a dignity that was unlikely to survive the day. Laos could be that way, timeless, unhurried, busy with a quiet sensuality that was all its own.

A huge bird-like creature loomed out of the mist. A fierce stone garuda, some fifteen meters high, its wings spread wide, stared at them with an expression of overbearing authority. Maier had never seen a statue so impatient.

Mikhail had suggested meeting away from the capital at Xieng Khouang, an otherworldly collection of gigantic religious sculptures, constructed in the late Fifties and located in an overgrown park. The eccentric founder of this sacred medway, a self-proclaimed yogi, had combined elements of Buddhism and Hinduism to forge his own popular cult. When the communists took over, the yogi escaped across the Mekong to build another Buddha park in Thailand. His sculptures, some of them twenty meters high, lingered as ghostly reminders of more magical times.

Even at the very first light of day, several old women had already lined up along the broken fence around the property, selling freshly steamed *khao tom* – sticky rice mixed with black beans and banana, wrapped in banana leaf. With toothless smiles and hopeful eyes, they told Maier that the two men were the first visitors this morning. They showed no surprise or interest in the heavy black canvas bag that the older man carried.

Maier pointed an imaginary camera at them and clicked off a couple of shots. The snack sellers laughed at his antics and settled back behind their produce.

The two men drifted into the park. They passed a giant reclining Buddha, a fierce Shiva, and a garish Rahu which sat amidst countless human and animal shapes that rose out of the knee-high grass. Skeletons danced and frogs cowered, warriors mauled mythical creatures, and ladies bowed their heads in prayer. It was easy to become disoriented amongst the sculptures; many were virtually identical. As the sun rose, the lingering fog sustained the labyrinthine ambience. They reached a bulging pumpkin-shaped edifice that rose from dry grass in the center of the park. Weltmeister and Maier entered through a circular doorway and ascended three levels of narrow, damp stairs to the top of the construct. From here they had a perfect view over most of the area.

As they emerged onto the building's roof, Mikhail sat waiting for them.

"Good morning, my dear friends," he declared with his usual bonhomie, and stood to embrace Maier. He wore his lank gray hair in a ponytail. With the wraparound shades covering half his bright red face and his garish short-sleeved polyester shirt, he looked every bit the Russian hit man. He didn't seem to feel the cold. A revolver poked out of his khaki shorts.

He bowed politely to Weltmeister. "It's a great honor to meet you. We did our best to hunt you down. We even had a nice jungle hotel ready for you. And now here you are, free as a bird and on your own terms. My employers send utmost felicitations and are appreciative that you have agreed to this meeting. And I would like to add that your son is a handsome devil and the best detective active in the region today. You should be proud."

Weltmeister smiled politely and carefully scanned the park below them.

The Russian's smile vanished instantly. "There is a problem?"

Maier grinned. "This is the first time I've seen you surprised, Mikhail. What's up?"

Weltmeister sat on the curved roof and pulled his bag open. He waved Maier closer. The black canvas rucksack contained a sniper rifle.

He looked up at the Russian and lied effortlessly. "For once I trust the Vietnamese. More than they ever trusted me. The U48 is in my head. It's the only copy there is. I destroyed the file I took from Long Cheng in '76."

Mikhail waved the old man's comments away. "I will protect your life to the best of my abilities."

He observed Weltmeister with respect, his eyes alight with real curiosity. Maier didn't buy it. To him the Russian looked like a man asking the deranged inmate of a closed institution for the weather forecast. Everyone was lying.

"But why you have come back to Laos? You've been sitting on the file for twenty-five years. You might have taken it to your grave with you. Why did you come out, so to speak?"

Mikhail's comment was infused with high camp but turned into a whisper as he looked around the deserted park below.

Weltmeister shrugged. "Léon was making noises. The Americans are coming back into Laos. The former Secretary of State is on his way."

The Russian nodded. "He's the man who ordered you to assassinate your friends in Long Cheng? He caused you to cross over?"

Weltmeister didn't contradict Mikhail.

The Russian grinned. "So romantic. Maier's boss, Sundermann, guessed as much. Bryson wouldn't have it. He said he couldn't find any evidence."

"Secretaries of State don't leave evidence. They killed my woman."

"So macho. I like it. You're the last real man on planet Earth. Apart from your handsome son."

Weltmeister started to pull rifle parts from his bag.

Mikhail looked on with wide eyes. "I don't believe it; you use a Dragunov."

The German grinned. "I'm old-school. The gun is great. Only the sight is terrible, mounted to the left of the barrel's centerline and inaccurate. I took it off and put a Zeiss on the top. I can hit a leaf from a kilometer away."

He assembled the weapon with a few assured movements. The Russian was clearly impressed.

"You expect company?"

He brushed Mikhail's remarks away.

"Did you know they followed you?"

Mikhail shook his head and showed his teeth.

"Maier checked into one of Vientiane's largest hotels last night. The whole country knows you're in town. Do we have a deal?"

Weltmeister slotted the sight onto his gun and rested its bipod on the structure's stone roof. He offered the Russian his hand. "Integrity and anonymity are everything in this job. If we walk away from this, the Laotians and Vietnamese can have the file. I am definitely not giving it to these guys."

He pointed down to the ground. Some of the life-size statues moored in the park were shifting in the fog. Weltmeister waved Maier and the Russian to retreat back into the structure they sat on. With the assured agility of an old leopard, he climbed to the very top of the building and pointed his weapon at the advancing shapes below.

A howl of electronic feedback, the sound of a speaker cranking up, shattered the morning's quiet and instantly transported them into the here and now.

"Weltmeister and associates, you have five seconds to come down here. Otherwise, we will blast you into the seventh Buddhist hell and no one will ever hear of any one of you again."

Weltmeister called down to the Russian, "Did you bring backup?"

Mikhail shook his head. "I always work alone. Ask your son."

The man with the megaphone emerged from the dissipating fog and slowly approached the structure they sat in. It was Charlie Bryson.

Maier shouted to the American, "Hey, Charlie, you're on the wrong side of the road."

The CIA man laughed. "Maier, it don't matter which side of the road I'm going down or you're going down. It's our road, you see. Americans like to keep it simple."

"In that case, you're still on the wrong side," Weltmeister mumbled, and shook his left hand as if trying to readjust the position of his wristwatch. Bryson almost fell the same instant, the sonic whiplash of the shot bouncing around the concrete guardians a moment later.

Before the American had hit the ground, the old man lifted his rifle and started picking off the men below one by one. Several of the attackers shrank back. A second sniper shot them down. Automatic weapons fire echoed between the concrete structures. A couple of minutes later, it was all over. Julia Rendel emerged from the back of the reclining Buddha, carrying a rifle. She waved silently and disappeared.

They found five dead men below. Bryson had suffered a shot to his upper chest that had grazed his bulletproof vest, close to his armpit. He sat in the grass, pressing his fist into the wound to slow the bleeding.

"Julia left you alive so we might get some answers."

"Help me. Call backup; they will send a helicopter. Please."

Maier could see Bryson's eyelids flutter; the American would lose consciousness any second. Rivulets of sweat ran down his bald plate as his face turned green. Maier looked across to his father, who knelt down next to the CIA man.

"I can save your life, Bryson. Give me one good reason."

"These are not my men. They made me come here. My unit has been ordered to cooperate with a new outfit... the agency co-opted from within. Too much money involved to fight them."

Weltmeister shook his head. "I don't care about you changing sides whenever the wind changes. That's not news. Give me news. Now. Or I will take your fist away and your life will slide into this field. It's a beautiful day to die, Bryson."

The American shook with the increasing shock.

"What about Vientiane? The agricultural show? You guys are paying for that, no?"

Bryson managed a feeble nod. "A trap. Too many troops, Laotian police, Vietnamese intelligence, Léon and his guys, everything. Everyone waiting for Weltmeister. But they are all proxies for the Secretary. Get used to the new age of borderless diplomacy, to war without end."

"Weltmeister is just a story, Bryson; he doesn't really exist. You know that, don't you?"

"Always keep my word... this just business."

The old man opened his bag and pulled out a tourniquet. Maier sat the American up and they removed his jacket, wrapped the bandage around his chest and pulled it tight. Weltmeister fished a phone from Bryson's pocket.

"How long?"

The American whose complexion changed from green to gray to white and back every few seconds, smiled in the weird dislocated way badly injured men pumping adrenaline usually do.

"I have a son too, Weltmeister. I give you my word… please make the call. You'll have two minutes to get away. There's a boat moored at the bottom of the park."

Weltmeister passed the phone to Bryson and pulled a small first aid kit from his trouser pocket as the American auto-dialed. The old man popped the cap on a vial of morphine and filled a syringe. As the American's call connected, Weltmeister found a vein, stuck the needle in and rammed the plunger home.

"You're lucky that I once loved your country and that I have killed enough Americans in this life. You will make it. And if you do survive, they will punish you for letting me slip away. No winners in this game, Bryson," he said, got up and walked towards the river.

Maier and the Russian followed quickly. The boat lay ready. For once, Bryson had told the truth. Julia started the engine as they reached the riverbank. They jumped in and raced southeast.

Maier watched his father, who sat in the front of the boat, his eyes on the river. The old man's ability to show ruthlessness and compassion in the same instant was a thing of unsettling beauty. Maier, former conflict journalist, detective, a man with three fingers on his left hand and a magic tattoo on his back, was in slight shock and severe awe of his father. Yesterday he'd thought him almost demented. Now he seemed more lucid than anyone else around. He turned back to look at Julia. She wouldn't make eye contact but held the rudder with the determination of a warrior Amazon as she raced their vessel at full throttle away from the morning's killing fields.

Mikhail signaled for Julia to slow the boat. She cut the engine. Silence descended on the river. The Russian waved her to the eastern shore. The last of the long-tail boat's momentum propelled them against the low embankment. The welcoming party stood waiting, guns cocked. So was Weltmeister, his rifle pointing straight at Mr Mookie.

"Hey, take it easy; we're all friends here. No need for anyone to die now," the Russian hissed behind Maier.

The old Laotian soldier who wore a tight-fitting polo shirt embroidered with a Lamborghini logo underneath his anorak, laughed down at the travelers with false bonhomie.

"Good morning, Maier and family. I see you have already livened up this wonderful day with a little murder. No need to remind you that killing is not allowed while visiting the Lao PDR on a tourist visa."

Mr Mookie smiled at the travelers with barely disguised disdain, though he didn't dare make eye contact with Weltmeister. Maier got off the boat first, walked quickly up to his so-called case officer, pushed him hard with his right hand and unfurled the metal prosthetics on his left towards the Laotian's neck. Mr Mookie stumbled backwards into the wet grass. His men raised their weapons to Maier's head. The detective ignored them and put his boot on their superior's chest. His heart racing, he was barely able to contain the anger he felt towards his erstwhile captor. He bent down and scraped his steel prosthetics along the man's chin. His thoughts tumbled from his mouth.

"This is the new Maier. I no longer work for you. Neither does my father. We are not here to make deals and we are not scared."

The safeties of several rifles clicked off.

Weltmeister, standing in the boat, raised his voice towards the Laotian. "So much macho bullshit. You're completely outgunned and we will have you floating in the Mekong in thirty seconds if you don't drop your guns. My son will cut your throat from ear to ear before any of your boys pull the trigger. Half the American cavalry is right behind us. Visa or no visa, they will shoot it out with you lot just to have a conversation with me."

Julia, who'd kept the Russian covered, jumped off the boat like a cat, her rifle now pointing at the handful of soldiers, who looked to their fallen boss for orders. Mr Mookie nodded almost imperceptibly. Julia collected their weapons.

"Now," Weltmeister continued as he grabbed his bag, jumped onto solid ground and offered the prostrate Laotian his hand. "Let's make a deal."

Mr Mookie smiled thinly as the older man pulled him to his feet. The Laotian brushed the dust off his anorak and nodded softly. Weltmeister laughed along with him.

"Let's make a deal," the Laotian smiled. "Hand over the U48."

"Three million dollars."

The Laotian nodded without hesitation.

FAMILY AFFAIR

Just after dark, Mikhail and his Laotian paymasters dropped the Maier family off at the Lane Xang Hotel and drove away into the Vientiane night.

The hotel bar offered no foreign liqueur, but Julia had gone out into the night and procured several cans of too-sweet orange juice and a liter of Smirnoff. She'd rented the hotel's honeymoon suite, a tired affair with a huge bed covered in the most garish polyester spread south of the Chinese Wall. They sat and drank, their rifles propped up by the door, ready to go. There would be no more surprises.

Maier, halfway through his second glass, was the first to get back to the case.

"Why did you save Bryson's life?"

Weltmeister sighed.

"I don't like killing Americans."

Maier's look must have appeared doubtful at best.

His father continued. "It's a generational thing. I fought the Nazis. At the end of the war, the Americans were the good guys. They helped liberate Germany. My generation owes the US. The first banana I ever ate, the first orange

I ever tasted, all thanks to these foreigners who occupied
Germany after the war. And then in the Fifties and Sixties,
I worked with Americans. That's how I met Ruth. I went to
university in Leipzig and spied on people. Easy stuff after
working for the resistance in World War II. I mean, think
about it. Kissinger, a German, made it all the way to the
top of the government. I, another German, made it all the
way to the top of their secret service. I was judged by my
abilities and my loyalty, not by where I'd come from. It's
a psychological debt I could never quite repay, even after
I killed my friends in Long Cheng. Seeing Bryson bleed
to death in Xieng Khouang, my reaction was automatic."

He laughed dryly. "Don't get me wrong; it wasn't
informed by compassion for the man, only by my
sympathy, however misplaced and nostalgic, for what he
represented. It's a loyalty thing. At heart, I always wanted
to work for the Americans. I was not going to let this son
of a bitch die unless it put us in danger."

"He tried to kill us."

Weltmeister discarded Maier's remark with a curt hand
movement and stood up.

"You do make me think, son."

The room was suddenly dead silent. Julia stared at
the two men, her eyes drifting from one to another in
disbelief.

Coasting effortlessly around the bombshell he had just
dropped, Weltmeister looked at Maier appreciatively and
continued. "Your mother did a good enough job, you
know. Your heart's in the right place. You have standards.
That's nice. But understand this, Ferdinand: this century is
not one for the underdog. The rich will flex their muscles,
muscles like me, only younger and less inclined to

question their motives, to get what they want. Right now, they want market shares. And Laos is a market untapped. The Vietnamese have been logging here for decades and have barely made a dent. There is so much more to steal. Southeast Asia, Africa, South America, all new frontiers in a new economic war. They call this globalization in the West, but we are wolves in sheep's clothing, thieves in the night."

Maier cut in while keeping an eye on Julia, who was still struggling with the revelation that she had a stepbrother. "We can't stop it; we can't even slow it."

She was a hard cookie. She was already losing that hard-drive-full look in her eyes. She was busy adjusting to her new reality.

His father nodded and continued. "You are right. But for personal reasons, I feel obliged to leave a mark, to send a signal, perhaps to build a monument to commemorate the losses that underdogs suffer as a consequence of the endless pursuit of money. I was part of it for so long. I have killed so many people in the name of democracy, progress, liberation and wishful thinking. Always for others. To fuel the dreams of the wealthy. It comes easy to me; you saw that this morning. It comes easy to my daughter, too. I am as proud of her as I am of you. In fact, I am gloating in the presence of my wonderful children. A rare moment I have been longing for."

Julia, sitting bolt upright on the far side of the bed, nervously lit a cigarette and said nothing. She couldn't bring herself to look at the two men.

"Now, at the end of my life, if I have to kill more, I will kill more. Killing is not everything it's cracked up to be, son. It's actually quite easy if you have sufficient motivation. I've never lost any sleep over it. And I am so happy that you, Ferdinand, do not share the curse of feeling at ease with taking another man's life."

"You will kill the Secretary?"

"This is the second time you've asked me. I don't know what I will do. But whatever *we* do, we will have fun doing it, right?"

Maier and Julia looked at each other. Maier felt an immediate poignancy. Life could be heartbreaking. His father was a cold bastard alright, dropping the truth on Julia like this.

Weltmeister grinned. "I won't share the marital suite with my kids, so I'll leave you to it. The first international agriculture trade show starts tomorrow. I think we should all attend, don't you? Liven things up a bit. See if Mr Mookie sticks to his side of the bargain and brings three million dollars with him. I have no doubts he won't."

As the old man slid out of the door, Maier waved him to stop.

"Dad."

The master spy stepped back into the room.

"That's the first time you've called me that."

"What's your real name, your first name? I would really like to know."

The old man grinned and made moves to leave again.

"When this is all over, Ferdinand. I will tell you everything you want to know. Everything. We will have time. As long as I am a wanted man, the less you know, the higher your chances of survival. And mine."

FARMER'S LAMENT

Julia had gone when Maier woke up on the couch. He drank a liter of water and stood under a cold shower until he could take it no longer. She had taken her bags, including her rifle, and disappeared, the same way she had done in Luang Prabang. Only, this time she had left as a sister, not a lover. The inner world of Weltmeister was quite unhinged. His father was nuts, a crazy puppeteer, guiding people on invisible threads to furnish him with a narrative twisted to suit his jaded emotional palate.

Maier was the sole occupant of the honeymoon suite at the Lane Xang Hotel. A phone call to the lobby told him that his father had checked out. There was no plan he was in on. He had no idea where they'd gone. He opened the window and leaned on the sill. Turning back into the room, he noticed the cigarette packet Julia had left lying on the small Formica table by the bed. The only thing she'd left. He leaned back and picked it up. His little stepsister wasn't trying to get him to start smoking again. The packet contained a scrap of paper and a key.

Maier,

Go to the main branch of the Laotian State Bank and retrieve a suitcase with a million dollars from security box 6235. Check the cash and make sure it's packed in waterproof plastic. The agricultural fair will have a few stalls of NGOs working in Laos. Today, our father will give a short talk about the threat of unchecked development and the importance of the remaining forests in Southeast Asia. At 2.30pm sharp. Stall 1009. TreeLine. After the speech, we will all travel to Thailand together. Transport has been arranged. Be sure to be at the stall, with your gun, at 2.30pm sharp. Wear your passport, the U48, the money and other documents in watertight packaging underneath your clothes. We love you. I'm in shock. And I'm giddy.

Julia

Maier found a lighter, burned the paper and flushed the ashes down the toilet. He packed his bag and wrapped his passport and the CD his father had given him in plastic. He was annoyed with his father's parting shot. What a control freak, dropping the bomb about Maier on Julia while lecturing on global politics. He taped his package to his chest, put on a shirt, stuck the gun into his belt, slipped the metal prosthetics over his stumps and left the hotel.

The river road was packed with Laotians in from the countryside. The agricultural fair had been well advertised on local television. Countless farmers arrived on huge flatbed trailers pulled by motorbikes and stayed in cheap flophouses. Some slept in or underneath the trailers. It looked like half the country of six million had turned up in the capital. Most of the exhibits at the fair were beyond the budget of the average Laotian village, but that didn't stop people's curiosity. The lure of a capitalist dream and the better life associated with it was strong.

The former US Secretary of State and the Laotian Trade Minister were billed to take a brief walk around the stalls at 3pm.

Maier was early. The pale winter sun was high up in the sky, providing the warmth of a late spring day in central Europe. A bit too cold to go swimming, a bit too warm to die.

He walked along the river road until he'd hit the bank. He asked a girl behind the foreign exchange counter for the safety deposit boxes and she led him to the back of the room.

Box 6235 was empty.

Maier left the key in the lock and walked out of the bank and into the city, away from the river. The Laotians had not kept to their side of the bargain. What would Mikhail, who had brokered the deal, make of that?

Maier had thought it unlikely he'd be able to enter a bank, open a safe and walk away with a million US dollars in cash. He was sure his father expected the double-cross. The family reunion was stressing him out. Whatever happened today, Maier would do his best to look after his own skin. He no longer had a client, he no longer had a case and he had lost control of his destiny. It was all making him nervous. Everything had always gone so well for him. He would never be sure whether that was thanks to his father. The possibility that his life and career had been manipulated by outside forces, no matter how benign, now haunted him with the same persistence his father's silhouette had stalked him with in his dreams before their encounter.

He drank a coffee, black, no sugar, in a café by *That Dam*, a large moss-covered *stupa*, a mound containing Buddhist relics, a stone's throw from the US Embassy. There seemed to be no change in the security detail as Maier walked past the compound on his way back to the river. The former US Secretary must have been keeping a very low profile.

Clouds moved across the sun and Vientiane went a little monochrome, befitting its socialist decrepitude. Maier walked in a roundabout way, past police and troops. The closer he got to the Mekong, the more the streets filled up. The sedate traffic had been blocked off around the city center.

Once he hit the river road, he turned north and made his way down to the embankment. One day, the municipal authorities would concrete over the land between the road and the river, but for now this strip of brush, ravines, sandbanks and unruly lawns was where the locals set up small restaurants and bars, parked their long-tail boats, flew kites, promenaded or simply sat and watched the mighty Mekong flow by. As the water level declined, the land expanded and some enterprising urban farmers grew a quick round of cabbages on the nutrient-rich soil, before the next monsoon would submerge their temporary real estate.

The agricultural fair had been set up on a piece of uneven ground at street level. A metal fence appeared to run around the land on three sides. The fair was open towards the river. The fairground rose high above the water, a steep ravine tumbled down to the water's edge. No long-tail would be able to stop here. No sand banks. Deep, muddy brown water stretched towards Thailand.

A Ferris wheel stood near the ravine, its baskets dangling over the river. It was ancient, operated manually by young men who climbed the contraption like spiders and made the wheel turn by adding enough weight at the top. On the way back down, they had to jump. It looked like a tough life.

Maier entered the fair through one of three gates and made his way to the river's edge. Security was tight. The detective was swept along in the crowd. The gun bit into his stomach. At least he wouldn't forget it was there. The entrance was guarded by what must have been Laos' crack troops, tough-looking men in fitting uniforms, wearing boots, earpieces and brand-new weapons. There were only a few, but the artillery they had strapped on put the cops, some of whom carried Kalashnikovs, to shame. With this many people around, firing any of their large-caliber guns would create a bloodbath of epic proportions.

He watched a trio of teenagers wriggle out of their T-shirts as they stood on the edge of the ravine. A couple of camera-toting tourists, aliens from another world as far as the kids were concerned, had spotted them and were egging them on to jump. Maier watched the kids leap off with a loud whoop of joy. One of the tourists cursed in a language Maier didn't know because he'd missed the shot. As soon as the boys hit the water, they were washed downstream, arms flailing, living the dream.

He walked carefully around the entire fair and watched bug-eyed country people suck up farm porn – harvesters, tractors, trailers, silos, GM seeds, and toxically pink candy floss. Many of the punters carried plastic bags filled with *lao lao*, rice wine potent enough to drown a Mekong catfish. The roaming snack vendors sold sweet sticky rice with beans or boiled peanuts and did a roaring trade. The event was settling into happy chaos before the afternoon had started.

At 2pm, he noticed a change in the atmosphere. Police reinforcements arrived and the efficient-looking troopers who'd guarded the entrances now swarmed across the grounds, moving in pairs, mumbling into their mikes and headsets. It was all going James Bond. Maier hadn't spotted the other two members of his illustrious family yet, though he'd twice slunk past the TreeLine stall near the river. He returned to the main entrance, pulling a pair of cheap shades into his face. In a worn batik T-shirt and his vest, which helped hide the gun, he looked like any middle-aged hippie doing the *Lonely Planet*.

A couple of limos had somehow managed to get through the pedestrian chaos on the river road. A police escort was clearing the entrance, pushing the crowd in front of Maier. He could no longer see the cars. Why would a rich, influential seventy-eight year-old veteran of international politics come here, to this field by the Mekong, to be squashed by incompetent cops and farmers who had no idea who he was?

It was 2.25pm. They were more than half an hour early. Maier fell into the slipstream of the VIP commotion which flowed slowly through the fair, towards the river, but he couldn't get any closer to where he assumed the special guests were walking. He could see neither the US Secretary nor the Laotian minister.

He suddenly had the feeling that he was in danger and discreetly pulled his gun from his waistband, holding it with both hands stretched out and pointed to the ground. He stopped and shuddered, realizing that all the cops he'd seen were locals. No US government security, no huge, beefy foreign bodyguards. No advance troop of discreet spooks. It was all a con. There'd be no foreign guest of honor.

He abandoned the throng and turned towards the river. Straining his head above the crowd, he saw several soldiers bearing down on the area where the TreeLine stall stood.

"Maier."

Léon had a flick knife at the detective's midriff. He'd appeared like a flash out of the heaving crowd. Maier let the Hmong feel the steel of the gun.

"Léon."

"Maier."

They were both pulled along slowly in an unhealthy near-embrace. Léon wasn't drunk. He was cold and rational and no less angry than the last time the two men had met.

"I have the U48, Léon. Let's make a deal."

He retracted the blade of the knife.

"Now we're talking, Maier."

Maier lowered the gun to where he'd held it before. They were still moving towards the river.

Léon was slowing him down, trying to pull him out of the current of people they were being swept along in. Maier was sure he was floating towards a trap. A trap set for Weltmeister. And Léon was making things more complicated.

"I have the file, Léon. What do you think?"

The Hmong looked at Maier intensely as they walked on at a snail's speed.

"Your father shot my sister."

"I didn't even know I had a father until last week, Léon. Stop blaming the wrong people. Get on with your life."

"This file is worth a lot of money? A lot?"

Maier nodded and tried to sound convincing.

"The Vietnamese will pay top dollar for it, Léon. Take it and let it go. Money is better than revenge."

The son of another secret agent who'd grown up without his parents and without a country looked at Maier severely. The irony of the desperate expression in Léon Sangster's eyes wasn't lost on the detective. They were both refugees from madness.

They reached the TreeLine stall. Two pairs of soldiers were moving in from the sides. Music blasted from the nearby Ferris wheel that was just starting to move. His father stood inside the booth, watching the approaching police, his hands in the pockets of a thin cotton jacket. He wore shorts and looked comical. From his left, Maier saw Mr Mookie, a gun in his hand, pushing towards him. The old Laotian spotted the detective and Léon and started barking orders into a walkie-talkie. They reached the stall. Weltmeister looked faintly rushed, but he squeezed off a quick smile for Maier. The detective caught his father's next expression – a mixture of joy, concentration, love and murder that bubbled like lava – with pride and dismay.

Everything sped up. Mr Mookie now shouted out orders. Two uniformed soldiers pushed Léon to the ground and lunged for Maier. Mr Mookie raised his gun. He stood stock-still and took aim. Maier was hemmed in by farmers and soldiers. The Laotian agent was too close. Maier raised his hands and fell back.

Mr Mookie's face disappeared. It simply disappeared. Maier couldn't hear the shot above the din of the fair.

The killer must have used a silencer. The old intelligence man had dropped his gun and tumbled to the ground. The monster had just lost one of its heads. Another monster, more familiar and emotionally involving, had pulled the trigger. The family had spoken again.

Léon shouted, "Long Cheng, this time next week, we make a deal," and was gone, pulled away by uniforms. A couple of police were kneeling down next to Mr Mookie to stop him being trampled on. Few of the revelers had noticed what had happened.

The sun broke through the milky clouds. As Maier looked up, he saw Julia next to him drop her gun, silencer still attached, into a neoprene bag she wore across her shoulder. The cops missed it altogether. His father had trained her well. He had created another killer.

Maier pushed towards the TreeLine booth, his stepsister right behind him. He almost tripped over the prostrate Mr Mookie, guarded haphazardly by his men. He had no choice but to step over the dead man and squeezed between the two cops, who had no idea who he was. The stall was empty. Maier jumped across the table at the front of the cubicle, scattering brochures and documents. A blanket hung from the stall's ceiling. He pushed behind it.

Weltmeister handed him a diving mask.

"We have to be quick. This ruse will only work for so long. The money?"

Maier shook his head.

"Did you really think Mookie would pay up?" the detective asked, looking down at three sets of scuba jackets and tanks. A helicopter passed overhead. Julia pulled one of the scuba jackets up and heaved it onto her shoulder, silently watching the two men argue.

"Yin and yang. I wanted to switch Mookie off once and for all. Of course, they set a trap for us. Of course, there would be no money. The only reason they let us go on the river yesterday was because they believed my bluff of overwhelming American firepower coming up right behind us."

Weltmeister grinned from ear to ear. He lived for these moments. The close shave, the narrow escape, the ultimate gamble. He had been at the edge of this cliff so many times before. Had trusted his luck and jumped. He pointed at the helicopter.

"And we have yet to get away. It's going to be tight. But here is Plan B. Spread your arms and hold your breath and off we go."

Maier could suddenly see the essence of his father, the thing that made him tick.

He got angry. "So we are diving across to Thailand? That's the plan? You are seventy-five years old and you are diving to Thailand? You are crazy, Father."

The moment he said it, he realized that stating obvious truths was not going to get them anywhere.

His father shrugged. "Relax. It's been done before, son. A journalist kidnapped his Laotian girlfriend with scuba gear, from near here, back in 1978, after the Laotians didn't let her leave. There's even a Hollywood film about it."

"I can't believe you thought you could confront Kissinger in a mud field by the Mekong," Maier countered.

"I had my hopes. He was in Bangkok last night. Probably still is."

A shot rang out behind them. This time, the crowd panicked. More shots. The cops were firing in the air to stop people from stepping on their boss.

Maier was tempted to stay but he knew he'd be arrested. It was time to get out of Vientiane.

He put the mask on his head, stashed the gun in the pocket of his BCD, and lifted the heavy tank onto his back. He knew the drill. Though he'd never dived anywhere as murky as the Mekong.

Weltmeister had already strapped on the second tank. He showed Maier the two ends of a thin orange rope.

"As soon as we hit the water, we dive, connected by the rope. We all have a compass and swim due west. It doesn't matter how far downstream we drift before we hit the other side. We just need to get across."

Without another word, his father stepped to the edge of the ravine and jumped. Julia followed. She never looked back. Maier stood sweating with the tank on his back. He pulled the mask over his face and pushed the regulator in his mouth, tasting stale rubber. The blanket behind him was ripped down. He turned and faced several police with guns drawn, looking at him in astonishment.

Maier, seriously crowded by the authorities, bewildered by the antics of his family and without an idea in his head, did the sensible thing and jumped into the brown floods of the Mekong.

UNDERTOW

Weltmeister and Julia submerged. Maier took a quick look back at the fair and heard more shots. He released the air from his jacket and sank.

The water was a shock. Sight was normally the only useful sense below the surface. Not in the Mekong.

Nothing. He could see nothing. He had gone blind. He started equalizing as soon as he fell away from the water's surface. He picked up the depth and air gauge that was dangling from his jacket and held it right in front of his face. Visibility twenty centimeters. Depth, four meters, five meters. Bottle full, facing west. They moved in a dark brown shit storm.

He couldn't see anything of his father and Julia until she suddenly bumped into him. A second later, she was sucked back into the great brown nothing. He kept the compass right in front of his eyes and swam as hard as he could, tugging at the cord that connected him to his stepsister. He wasn't sure whether they would reach the shore before their tanks were empty. The current

291

got stronger the farther they got away from the Laotian capital. It was getting harder to move forward and he found himself breathing faster. Soon he would be hyperventilating, pushing used-up air back and forth in the tube between the tank and the regulator.

A boat passed overhead, its engine noise reduced to the whine of a dentist's drill.

The cord between Maier and Julia tightened and stretched downwards. Maier followed while trying to hold the depth gauge right in front of his left eye. It got darker. The water temperature dropped. Twelve meters. The light faded.

With barely a warning, he hit the bottom and moved forward in a murky twilight that flickered on and off like a faraway strobe. Far out, he thought. The boat came back, now barely audible, passing slowly overhead.

Maier hauled himself along the rope to Julia. The moment he bumped into her he saw that she was crawling along the river floor, holding on to rocks and plants to pull herself forward, kicking up silt that was swept away into the river current with slow-motion hurricane force. Maier almost choked into his regulator. Here he was with his new family on their first-ever holiday together. Scuba diving, no less. In the tropics. But this was the Maier reality, a far cry from the brochures. They were crawling along the muddy bottom of one of Asia's mightiest river like failing crabs, with half the Laotian capital's police in pursuit.

He pulled his air gauge close to his eye. He had about a third of his tank left. Somewhere ahead, it was getting brighter. They were now clawing their way along a barely noticeable incline. Maier clawed best with his metal fingers. He was sure of it. He took solace in it. The visibility improved slightly. The current slowed and garbage started to cover the river bottom – glass bottles, batteries, oil drums. Welcome to the free world. It was getting too dangerous to dig their way through the mud. They had to go up. He could see Julia, a meter away, crawling. His father, the mighty Weltmeister, the originator of their brilliant escape plan, was lost in the dust. Maier pulled the cord, hard. As Julia drifted into focus, he jerked his thumb upwards. She nodded.

It became easier to swim west as they slowly rose. The current seemed to pull them in the right direction. Maier surfaced. They were in a bend, about to be washed onto a sandbank. Forest reached from the waterline into the sky. Maier pulled Julia to the surface. They were in Thailand.

"Where's the old man?" he coughed. She held up her cord. It had been sheared off clean. Maier spat into the river. He wasn't surprised. Weltmeister had made alternative arrangements for his escape. There was some larger, overarching plan at play to which the kids weren't privy. Or perhaps it was just him who was left floating in the dark.

They drifted slowly to the nearest reach of sand and crawled onto solid ground. Maier felt like he'd done all the crawling he could ever have wished for. For a while, they lay side by side on the baking sand, drying, breathing, looking at the sky.

"Quite a creative way to leave a country."

She looked at him, her eyes both proud and troubled. "He is a great man in his own way."

"He shot two innocent people right next to me to

'warn' me. He is... He is a lot to take in."

She sat up with a quizzical look in her eyes, scanning the forest. For what?

"Would you give him up?"

Maier turned and pulled the gun from the scuba jacket. It was dry. He stuck it into the front of his pants and lay back down.

"No, I would not give him up. But I am not sure how healthy it is to be around him for any length of time."

"I've lived with him for years," she shot back, and lunged for the gun.

Maier didn't try to stop her. She pulled the slide back and clicked off the safety.

"And how difficult do you think it would be to be around you? You're his son," she spat.

She turned her head. Three men had slipped out of the jungle and walked towards them. Two of them were armed with assault rifles. The third man was Bryson, his arm in a sling. He walked slowly, dragging his feet.

"Well, this was supposed to be Plan B. Mr Mookie had the best crack team of cops in the country on the ground. And gets himself killed. By Ms Rendel here. We thought, just in case you do escape from Laos, we will have our people along the river. And now you're minus Papa. I mean, kids, we're just going in a circle here. One round after another. I'd love to just kill you and be done with it, but then I got that damn Weltmeister on my back. I love you guys."

Standing directly between Maier and the sun, Bryson droned down at the detective, a disembodied voice without much consequence. He wasn't making any decisions here. He was merely a messenger of bad tidings. He sounded weak. He had to be. Weltmeister had saved this guy from certain death just a week ago and now he was back in the game, without imagination or initiative.

Julia sneered at him. "I thought you had died in that field, Bryson. All on your own, slipping away with the thought of young girls but not getting any."

The two men behind Bryson were young Americans with finely chiseled cold faces. Professional killers. Secret murderers. The shadow front line. Every country had them.

Now Maier had them.

One of the men wrenched the neoprene bag off Julia's back. As he stepped into Maier's line of vision blocking the sun, the detective could see Bryson clearly. The American vet looked almost dead. His face gray, his moustache droopy like a dying bird, his eyes full of pain. Gray stubble on his head. He wasn't here by choice.

"Never a dull moment with you and Weltmeister," Maier said lamely to Julia.

She wouldn't look at him. They were both living through their father's narrative now. The feeling of having lost control of his destiny overcame Maier again.

One of the two heavies picked up the two bottles and masks and motioned Maier and Julia towards the jungle with his gun. The detective suddenly knew that he had arrived at that point again. The point of departure. It was his life and his death that were on the line here. Not his father's, but his own.

"In the end, we've all been had, friends," Bryson coughed, wheezing.

Maier turned and watched the soft afternoon rays of the sun break in broad golden strips through the trees onto the sandbank, lighting up the speck of earth like a stage. The second man had stayed behind with the old American. Maier saw Bryson go down on his knees facing the river. He didn't fall. He wasn't pushed. He just kind of crumpled slowly and with somber finality. They were just a few meters apart. The veteran didn't turn his head to Maier.

"How I wish my guitar player was with me," Bryson mumbled.

Maier remembered standing on Kanitha's shoulders under a gallows. But he couldn't feel anger right now.

Bryson was humming to himself. He consumed his last Asian sunset. His body heaved with sorrow. It looked so bloody dignified. The young American shadow soldier pulled the trigger. Bryson, American hero, expendable liability, fell face first into the sand. A couple of birds rose from the forest. That was all. But it was enough to take the men's attention off Julia for a moment.

She shot the man in front of her and turned quick enough to catch the executioner in the arm. The bullet propelled him into the sand next to his victim. Before he could sit up, she stood over him and pulled the trigger of Maier's gun again.

The silence that followed the shots was eerie, as if they were standing inside an empty cathedral, moments after the echoes of a child's handclap had faded. The three fallen bodies had kicked up fine dust that must have rained down from the canopies. For a moment, the light strips that fell across the sandbank became almost solid, a fine haze of gold and amber tones, a ladder to the heavens, or the bars of a jail; Maier wasn't sure what they reminded him of. He pulled his pants down and dug a spare clip out of the plastic pouch he had strapped around his leg and threw it to his sister.

She caught the clip and smiled sardonically. "You're becoming just like him, Maier. That's your destiny. To be like your father. It's something that happens to many men. You can't change it. All you can do is be aware of it. Especially when you live the more extreme aspects of his personality."

He shook his head. He had no urge to tell her or his father anything more. Maier was different. His father had always worked for a master, even killed for a master. He had always been a part in grander schemes. Maier on the other hand, was a lone wolf, a man in charge of his own destiny. He wasn't a killer.

"Let's head for Bangkok."

ABSOLUTE POWER

"Heinz."

"Sebastian."

So that was his father's name, Sebastian.

The sound was a little muffled, but with the help of a small cordless microphone Maier had fitted to the frame of a painting in the main corridor on the ground floor of Bangkok's Mandarin Oriental Hotel, he could hear what the men were saying.

The former US Secretary had emerged from a conference room, flanked by two bodyguards, and accompanied by a diminutive PA with pale skin and slicked-back hair. Maier understood immediately that all the stories his father had told him were true. These two men had once been close, he could see it in their body language. And Heinz, better known as Henry Kissinger, was a formidable presence; he filled the corridor with the easy aura of a Roman emperor.

Maier couldn't make out the young Asian woman's face from his discreet vantage point at a garden table, just outside the corridor his father had disappeared down two minutes earlier. She wore a short black skirt and had the poise of an angel. The kind of woman that looked right on the arm of an infinitely rich and influential man.

Hotel guests were busy coming and going around Maier, and the other tables in the hotel garden were all busy. For the moment he felt safe. Everything had been prepared.

Maier hadn't seen his father since emerging from the Mekong, watching Bryson perish and his stepsister kill two American agents. Since arriving back in the Thai capital, he had made all the arrangements Julia had asked him for. He had been tasked with creating an escape route from the Oriental following his father's meeting with the former Secretary of State. Beyond that, he had been left in the dark. But Julia had given him the feeling that he was almost part of the family and that they might all ride off into the sunset together. Deep down, he was certain it was all a sham. Maier knew little about family, and the situation reminded him of a spoilt love affair in which one party had lost the passion and the other was in denial. He would always be stressed with these two around. His loyalty would never be rewarded. And yet, the security, even affection of sorts, which the family appeared to offer was seductive. The temptation to throw his present life away and run off into the sunset with his father was strong. And he didn't even know whether his father would take him along. No one had asked him. For the first time in his life, Maier wished for simpler, irrevocably lost times.

Weltmeister wore a sharp, dark suit that looked like it had been tailored for him. An expensive pair of mirrored sunglasses hid his eyes, but as the two old men started sizing each other up he took them off and beamed at his nemesis. He had that same look on his face as at the fair in Laos. He was ready to jump off the cliff again. Everything had moved towards this moment. He had planned it all, right from the moment of Maier's recruitment.

"It's been years," Weltmeister said in German.

"Twenty-seven to be exact. And it's not a reunion I relish particularly, I can tell you that."

The former Secretary's voice, usually laden with diplomatic rhyme, carried a barely audible, darker, menacing tone. One devil challenging another.

"So what did you want to see me about? All this wahoo about the U48? Who cares about this today? The only pertinent fact that's not public knowledge is that we considered nuking Laos. We might have changed the situation in Vietnam that way. But that's history. This is 2002. The twenty-first century. The new dawn. Didn't you see the planes flying into the Twin Towers? Our brief encounter boils down to just one thing: What does an old relic like you want from an old relic like me?"

A couple of hotel guests walked past wrapped in beach towels. Recognizing the former US Secretary, they blushed and hurried on. The statesman's PA shifted her narrow back. Maier couldn't see her face through the glass, though there was something familiar about her.

Layers within layers within layers. Every reality in this game had alibis. The entire case was like an onion. You pulled one skin off to find another. And each one made you cry a little more.

Weltmeister said nothing and grinned. Lesser men might have been distracted by his intensely disturbing expression, but Heinz did not seem to mind. He droned on, like an archaic oracle.

"It was the war, you know. Wars need to be won. Go ask the Vietnamese if you don't believe me. They sacrificed millions to get us out of Indochina. And look at them now, poor, corrupt, hardly worth a thing. But their pride is intact. It means a lot to people. More than truth, more than reality. You knew the risks when you joined the outfit. You were our best man. We courted you. We trained you. You were the only sniper working for the agency that didn't have a military background. That's how special you were. But you got weak, fell in love, thought you could live like a normal person half the time and like a state-sponsored killer the other half. The moment that happened, you became a liability and an asset that could be exploited. Long Cheng was your downfall. Ours, too. We lost so much there."

"Is that why you didn't cross the border?"

Heinz did something to his face; perhaps it was his idea of a smile. Maier couldn't tell.

"I was never going to go to Laos. That was just a story put out by our embassy. It was part of my plan to bring Weltmeister out of the woodwork. It was me who found Léon and put it into his head that he could get his revenge. And it worked."

"A lot of people died in the process."

The former US Secretary shrugged.

"What was that old story about the omelet? If only you'd stayed in London painting your avant-garde crap, everything would have been fine, and I would not be standing here doing the secretarial shit with some guy I should have fired decades ago. But I guess you never managed to let go of that girl you loved. Germans are such bloody romantics."

The old diplomat's voice never wavered. He was becoming almost jovial and moved closer to the young

Asian woman by his side. The two bodyguards were rattling in their frames, pumping adrenalin, studying the threat in front of them. Weltmeister, the best-dressed man in Bangkok's most exclusive hotel, stood his ground and smiled that golden smile.

To Maier, old men either looked like war criminals or hippies. He supposed that the growing depository of the decisions one made during a long life slowly assembled into facial expressions, body language, wardrobe and sometimes aura.

"What's on your mind, Sebastian? You will strangle me in a hotel corridor in Bangkok? You couldn't have picked a more salubrious address for my passing? New York, perhaps, on the grounds of the UN? Or Angkor Wat? I'll be there on Monday. Life goes on. You know the game."

"I won't kill you, Heinz," Weltmeister said, switching to English. "I came unarmed. I just wanted to see you one more time before you die. And take the only thing you really care about."

The old American said nothing for a moment, and the two men lapsed into an odd silence. At the far end of the corridor, a young woman in a tight, long dress came clicking along on high heels, wrestling with a large shopping bag, cursing under her breath.

"Why did you have Valentina killed?"

"What, the girl we had taken to Cuba? When we realized that you had disappeared, we handed her over to the Cubans."

He paused, either for dramatic effect or in shock at the way he'd just said what he'd just said. The moment passed.

"When you popped up again this year, I took another

look at the file. She's alive, as far as we know. She lives in Santiago de Cuba. I suppose she must be in her fifties now. We have a phone number."

Maier could see his father's expression change. An unsound look came into his eyes. This look was the cliff about to be stepped off and left behind, with only the flimsiest of safety backups, the slightest of trumps up the proverbial sleeve. Weltmeister was ready to parachute with a cocktail umbrella.

The old diplomat sighed. His entire huge body seemed to heave for a moment. Then his posture was back to what passed for normal, full of self-confidence and bounce as he seamlessly transitioned into a different scenario.

"OK. I don't want to lie to you, Sebastian. You will not leave this hotel the way you came in. It's over for Weltmeister. We will take you and you will never be seen again. But you knew that before you came here, didn't you? And you have some incredible ace up your sleeve and will try and make a daring and honorable escape? Isn't this all about honor, Sebastian? Right?"

The former US Secretary's young PA stepped away from her boss and unzipped her handbag. As Maier rose, he could see her pull out a small gun. He spotted the tattoo on her back in the same instant. The five sacred strips on her skin, the narrow, lithe shoulders.

The jungle visa.

He tore the door to the corridor open.

"Kanitha."

She was alive. She had not died on the beach. Maier's mind was reeling. Everything came down like a monsoon shower, heavy, immediately and without mercy. He had been played. Played by his father. Played by Kanitha.

Played by everyone who counted in this case.

Kanitha looked at him as if at a stranger, raised the gun and fired. The shot was deafening in the narrow corridor. Maier hit the ground unscathed. Now he understood where this girl was coming from. His thoughts raced back to their first night together in Muang Ngoi and to all the lies that she had furnished him with ever since their very first meeting. Life could be so twisted. He had to admit to himself, very much against his will, that Kanitha had truly fooled him. And she had missed.

"Stop," Kissinger shouted. "Stop. Don't shoot. Not here."

His bodyguards lunged between the former US Secretary and the girl.

"We can't afford to have an incident here, of any kind, Mr Kissinger," one of his minders warned his employer, only to earn a withering look from the former statesman.

Kanitha turned towards Weltmeister.

The former Secretary of State, loser of several wars, winner of countless prizes and author of books recounting his triumphs, tried to stop her, but he was too old and it was too late. As he pushed past his minders and pulled at Kanitha's sleeve, the young woman in the long ballgown closed in on the group, dropped her shopping bag and pulled a wooden hairpin from a pile of unruly hair that now gave way to gravity and tumbled across her naked shoulders. In one swift movement, she plunged her beauty utensil into Kanitha's throat. The gun dropped to the ground. One of the minders kicked it away but made no attempt to grab the assailant. Julia was back and she was in a killing mood.

Kanitha collapsed, her eyes wide, retching for air. Without gracing anyone with so much as a look, Julia carried on walking, the click of her high heels fading like a weakening pulse as she moved away. Maier stayed close to the glass outside, looking in, in complete shock. Julia had told him there'd be no more killing unless absolutely necessary.

Weltmeister stood motionless, relaxed, offering his empty hands to the bodyguards. They stuck close to their boss.

The former Secretary knelt heavily next to Kanitha. His face was white, his savoir-vivre had given way to something he seemed unfamiliar with. He patted her hand like a dog, but she had already lost consciousness.

"Mr Kissinger," one of the security men said quietly. "It's time to go. We can't have a diplomatic incident involving a killing here. We will have this cleaned up for you in no time. But we must leave now."

He nodded, dazed, and got to his feet without their assistance.

"I want that woman dead."

His minders looked nonplussed. "We will leave now, Mr Kissinger, without delay. You will have to leave Miss Kanitha here. And we can't run round the hotel after the assailant. Another time, another place."

The former Secretary of State looked like he wanted his men dead too, but he pulled himself together and turned to Weltmeister.

"Yoga, you see," he said, squeezing out a savage smile for Weltmeister, "prepares you for anything."

With that he strode off in the direction of the lobby, his steps uncertain, flanked closely by his men, leaving Kanitha behind, lying on the cold, smudged marble floor. Maier pulled the door to the garden open and motioned his father outside. Julia was right behind him, her high heels in her hands, her long skirt hitched up to her knees. Maier pulled the door shut and locked it. For a moment he stood transfixed, looking through the glass at the dead young woman. What was this job all about? What was life about? Finding truths and watching people die? Getting to like people who never let empathy get in the way of their agendas? Falling for girls who bedded him one day and tried to kill him the next? Who died and came back to life and died again? Kanitha had been a great woman, so much energy, so much determination, so much subterfuge. Even now he found it hard to match her with the fading statesman he had just seen. And he found it much harder to accept, a second time, that she was gone.

"To the pier?" Julia asked urgently, pulling at his sleeve.

Weltmeister seemed to be in a world all his own. A beatific smile lingered on his face. He had stepped off the cliff but he hadn't hit the bottom yet. Perhaps he never would.

"No, to the lobby," Maier said.

Julia looked at him with skepticism, the way one doubted a child that claimed to be able to levitate.

"Half the US security forces in this city are going to be there in about two minutes."

"Exactly, and the other half will be on the river. And I am not going diving again. If we are lucky, they will be so busy looking for us that they will not see us. Trust me."

Julia looked at Weltmeister, expecting her stepfather to assert his authority, but he just shrugged like a happy drunk.

"I'm on holiday. I deserve it. I saw it in his eyes. Whoever said that revenge can't be sweet is a fool. I tell you it is, even when one revenges the unimaginable. Let's follow my son's game plan. He's not a fool."

Maier ignored his father's ambiguous proclamations and moved them along a garden path towards the hotel's main building. Someone shouted behind them, but he motioned them to keep walking.

As they passed the pool, the doors to the lobby flew open. Guests and staff rushed out into the sun, shrieking in panic. A young, heavy woman fell into the pool as they walked into the oncoming crowd. A child stood lost, wailing for her parents. It was pandemonium.

"Now is the right moment."

Maier took Julia's hand and pulled her along. They entered the lobby and plunged into chaos. Right in the center of the sumptuous first port of call of Bangkok's finest lodgings, two skinhead thugs, dressed in shorts, sleeveless shirts and expensive garish trainers, their arms bulging with crude tattoos, stood slugging each other on the now blood-spattered reception carpet. Twenty more men, all of them Russian and armed with cans of beer and angry red faces that invited no appeals to reason, screamed at each other, supporting one fighter or the other, occasionally lashing out at guests or staff who hadn't fled. The few people who remained in the lobby stood close to the walls or scrambled behind the reception counter, petrified. The atmosphere was electric. The simple, physical danger the men exuded was palpable. Any wrong move and someone would die. As Maier pulled his family gingerly through this tableau, the bedlam slowed down to a pinhole moment, and he had a feeling that the entire hotel lobby hovered on a precipice of a larger, more brutal unleashing of violence. Maier knew things unseen were happening.

He pushed Julia and his father past the fighters and towards the main hotel entrance. One of the thugs guarded the door. As Maier moved towards him, he stepped to the side and joined his friends closer to the action.

A bus had pulled up outside. A huge fat man wearing shorts and a Hawaiian shirt, sweating profusely, wiping his bright red face continuously, beckoned to them.

"All aboard; time for a round of sightseeing. I'm your tour guide."

Julia pulled a second pin from her hair.

Weltmeister shook his head and looked at Maier.

"Ferdinand."

"Sebastian."

"I did, of course, think of killing you too. If I wanted to be my usual one hundred percent, I would have taken you and Mikhail here out of the game. You know too much. But, as the former US Secretary said, it's all history, and who really cares. I got what I came for. I'm gone."

"Cuba is nice."

"Heinz was telling fibs. He was scared. He had his story ready. Even if they had given Valentina to the Cubans, she would have been a white female non-person amongst male police with no accountability. I don't go for this kind of hope. I'm romantic but not stupid."

Two motorbike taxis pulled up next to the bus. The riders were dressed in black and wore helmets, dark visors down, gloves, black leather shoes. The bikes had no plates.

"You think of everything."

His father clearly took Maier's remark as a compliment and grinned. "I will have to give the submarine I have waiting at the Oriental's pier the all-clear."

Maier stood lost for words. He was acutely aware of

the seconds slipping away. He stared intensely at his father. Julia smirked at him, and he didn't like it much. The old man stepped forward as if to hug Maier but then just grabbed his arm to lean closer. "Kill the Russian now and come with us. Prove yourself to me, son. Show some loyalty to the old man and we might take you along."

Maier gently pushed his father away and looked into his eyes. The man known as Weltmeister wore the same mocking expression on his face as Julia.

His father shrugged. "You're not made for the secret life, Maier. I did my best to get you up to Weltmeister level. But you'll never have that freedom of self that's called for in a true child of mine. Always remember, without me, you wouldn't be who you are; you wouldn't be anywhere."

Maier thought the old man's speech grandiose, absurd and, for want of a better word, depressing. He'd just pulled his family out of the frying pan, and they were threatening to kill him and called him soft. He looked across at the Russian. Mikhail stood sweating. He knew. His eyes flicked from the motorcycle drivers to Weltmeister and Julia and back. Maier could hear his heart beat away the seconds.

Julia pulled his father away. "Time to go; the cops are almost here."

A smile crossed Weltmeister's face as he looked at his son for the last time. Maier knew that it was not meant for him, but for his stepsister. She had internalized the same kind of freedom his father had gone for. Maier took a step back. It was all he could do. Julia and Weltmeister got on the bikes and shot off. His father never looked back.

Maier, dazed, boarded the Russian's bus. Mikhail

handed him a vodka orange, the juice fresh, the ice clinking in the glass.

He filled his own glass and looked at the detective thoughtfully. "It was very dicey out there. Your old man is dangerous. He's like a loaded gun. He was really thinking of getting rid of us there and then. You played it just right. Thank you, Maier."

He lifted his glass. "When this is over, we will have to have a drink together."

Seconds later, the police poured into Bangkok's finest hotel from all sides and herded all but the two lobby fighters back onto the bus.

THE BEGINNING

Maier lay in tall, dry grass just above the runway, pointing his binoculars at a cluster of wooden huts that spread like mushrooms along both sides of the tarmac. His heart was racing. Long Cheng, the legendary CIA airport, the nerve center of the agency's largest operation, lay just below. Despite the city's dilapidated state, the view and everything it implied were mind-blowing. An obscure but crucial moment in twentieth-century history had played itself out in this valley. And if one cared to look right into the dark heart of men and their games in this remote, subtropical and stunningly beautiful fleck on the planet, one might be able to spot the silhouette of a man walking straight ahead, while the world burned to either side of him. His father had been betrayed here, had killed his best friends and colleagues here, had thrown his humanity to the winds here. A man could only start his journey once he had arrived somewhere. Maier had arrived at the family shrine. He could not think of a better description for the place.

Sundermann's last call still bounced around his head.

"Your father planned brilliantly. He recruits his detective son to help him clean up his old ghosts and to find closure. I suppose one might say this is a plan twenty-five years in the making. Most people aren't able to think past the end of next week. A few, like your father, have very long memory. You should be proud that he entrusted you this mission. And he paid well. We can't complain. Except for the bullet."

His boss moaned in mock pain. "I won't come out to do field work again anytime soon. It's too dangerous. I will stick to politics. That kills you a lot slower. I have the utmost respect for operatives who live through these painful, difficult projects, come out virtually unscathed and go straight into another one. Laos has been a humbling lesson."

That was one way of looking at it. But Maier felt anything but unscathed. He felt used. He'd lost fingers and bits of mind out there. He'd killed two men. He'd been played by a wonderful girl who had died. He had a tattoo on his back. He'd gained a father who had barely a passing interest in his son and an assassin stepsister he'd slept with.

His boss' respect for his father's creative faculties outweighed the lack of any moral judgment on Sundermann's part on the deeds of Weltmeister.

"He has a brilliant mind. If he was a chess player, he'd be able to play ten masters at the same time and think five moves ahead in each game. He writes his own destiny, that man. Very few of us manage to do that. You're his son, and you are so much like him."

They'd both laughed at the cunning distraction Mikhail had pulled off at the Oriental Hotel.

"Look at it as time well spent with your family."

But Maier had his doubts about his life's new realities.

And while Sundermann's optimism was infectious, the detective was in two minds whether to honor his agreement with Léon. He knew his father would be there. He knew there'd be more killing.

His boss would have none of it.

"Finish the job, Maier. Go to Long Cheng, find out what happened to Julia Rendel's father. See if the gold is still around. Face off your father. Find some closure. I am sure he will find you there. Then we write our report and it's another case for the archives and you can go back to less emotionally searing work. Oh, and train the new guy. Bring him up to speed. Show him the ropes. And teach him some German; he will need it."

Maier had a habit of not contradicting his boss, but sometimes Sundermann was too much of a hard nut. Maier had silently nodded into the phone and, without saying another word, hung up, coming to a decision about the outstanding deal with Léon. He knew he couldn't save the Hmong but he had to try. Maier would have to outwit Weltmeister to stop the killing.

Long Cheng looked deserted. The landing strip was cracked and dotted with sprouting weeds. Crows circled ominously in front of the rocky cliffs at the end of the runway. The infamous CIA lair had collapsed in on itself. The wooden buildings were falling into the fertile soil. Papaya and banana sprouted everywhere. There was no electricity. A few more rainy seasons and only the runway would be left.

The road on which he'd traveled, on a dirt bike and mostly by night, had been atrocious. His back was killing him. Long Cheng wasn't about to be rediscovered by the world. *National Geographic* wanted nothing to do with it. But that didn't matter. For Maier, this was a pilgrimage. He needed to discover something essential about his father and perhaps himself. He hoped to learn something from visiting Weltmeister's moment of crisis. Just enough to make peace.

Maier was still wondering why the old man had come back, killed so many people, only to disappear again. Nothing was quite a secret anymore. The Internet had seen to that. Time had seen to that. Mobile phones, digital cameras, personal computers; the number of technological conveyances for our dreams and nightmares grew every day. Soon everyone would be a photographer, cameraman and storyteller. Everyone would be a spy. Everyone would be in the detection business. The increasing information overload made uncomfortable truths more available but less relevant, hardly evident in the tsunami of digital garbage that rolled across the world's virtual highways. Nothing was taboo and nothing quite mattered anymore. Everyone and his cat could be a superstar in the digital universe. A message was always just one amongst many. In a world like this, a man could barely be a man anymore. Hunters, their spears abandoned, their backs bent over computer terminals, their teeth blunted from eating processed garbage, were turning into geeks and nerds playing war games on their consoles, killing thousands while never experiencing the proximity of death. Soon, machines would rule the skies and take out undesirables and "enemies of the state." Hard times for true outlaws.

Perhaps Weltmeister had simply followed his ego for one last blast out in the open. Men with secrets had no audience unless they hung those secrets out to dry and basked in the attendant sunshine. But the coming-out corrupted them, their experiences became cheapened once shared, their mystery turned into the banality of the everyday exceptional. It had occurred to Maier that this might hardly matter to a seventy-five year-old man who enjoyed killing people.

Maier suppressed the anger he could feel rising in his chest. He relaxed and sucked up the view once more. He slowly got to his feet, stashed his binoculars and descended towards the base. He was unarmed. They knew he was coming. He was just a delivery boy. And one way or another, he would meet his father down there for the last time. It was all in Maier's script. He was taking charge of his destiny.

Maier stuck to the well-trodden trails on his way down to the airbase. Unexploded ordnance was likely to be buried around the war's covert nerve center. He walked carefully. He had brought the CD his father had given him. The U48. The very last copy of America's most secret military file from a war long gone.

"Guten Abend."

Just as Maier reached the first huts, Léon and a small band of Hmong soldiers appeared from a muddy alley. They looked like they'd been living out in the open for some time, unkempt and dressed in rags, all of them with the same unhealthy sheen that all men who rarely slept and ate poorly acquired. They stared at Maier in silence, the silence of people who never get good news. He wasn't sure whether he appeared as potential threat or savior to them.

Léon, a baseball cap hiding his long hair, a gun in his belt and his hand on it, looked at him sourly. "I can't believe you're dumb enough to come here. But then, I also knew you'd come. You want to make the world a better place. You want to die with honor. You want to undo what your father did. You're so German, Maier."

"I do not want to die at all. No one does. And I can't do anything about my father's crimes. What do you know about honor?"

"I saw a man without honor kill his friends when I was a teenager. I'll never forget it."

He nodded to his men. They searched Maier quickly and got moving, dropping right into the warren of small abandoned homes that stretched down to the runway.

"I met your father right here, twenty-five years ago. Just a year or so after the war had ended. He'd come with his friend, Rendel. And my sister Mona. We were walking down this same alley together."

"I'd like you to show me where he killed them."

Léon turned as he walked and grinned savagely. "Don't worry, Mr Detective; I will show you where Weltmeister murdered them."

"Aren't there any Laotian troops here?"

The leader of the rebel group spat onto the ground and muttered, "Nothing ever happens up here anymore. No plane has landed here for decades. The soldiers are scared of ghosts. By afternoon they all disappear to their little compound and leave the town to fall apart all by itself."

A feral, skinny dog lurked underneath the stairs of a stilted hut that leaned towards the earth at a sick angle. The mutt barked at them with cholera breath. Léon snarled back at the animal. It took no notice and continued barking. The other men walked in silence. Maier could smell the desperation on them. They had been abandoned by their erstwhile American paymasters. They were being manipulated by Hmong who had emigrated to the US and made a living by keeping the dream of a return to Laos alive in their communities. These rebels were too stubborn or entrapped by old politics to give up their hopeless fight against the Laotian government. They followed Léon in the hope that he would lead them to freedom. Maier had no hope for them.

They reached the runway. Léon motioned Maier to keep out of sight and off the tarmac, and they made their way to one of the concrete buildings along the airstrip. Apart from birdsong and the hound behind them, it was quiet. They entered through a shattered and boarded-up doorway. As soon as they stepped inside, Maier could smell dried blood. His hair stood on end and he knew that Léon had brought him to the right place. The wrong place. And he knew his father was here, too.

"My sister was lying there. She died almost instantly. I was hit in the chest. I didn't want to leave. I wanted to die, Maier. My soldiers took me out of here and saved my life."

The Hmong fighters stayed outside. Léon stood in the door of what must have been a master bedroom. Two metal bed frames stood in the center of the room, over a gaping hole in the floor.

Maier looked around.

"I have a feeling my father is here in the area somewhere. And that he wants to kill you."

The Hmong American grinned. "I know. That's why I asked you to come. What goes around comes around. Give me the U48."

Maier opened the pocket of his jacket and handed Léon the plastic case. Without a word, the rebel leader took his backpack off and pulled out a laptop.

"Léon, you are the last link to his past in Laos. He will kill you."

The Hmong shook his head.

"He has to get me first."

"Kanitha is dead."

Léon snapped around and looked at Maier with contempt.

"What do you mean, Kanitha is dead? Of course she's dead. Are you deluded, man? She was killed by those two CIA guys in Thailand."

"That's what I thought. But she wasn't hit during the beach attack. That's only what Bryson told me. The official story they put out and hoodwinked us with. I never saw the body. He made her disappear. She was a plant all along. When you started talking about CIA gold in Vientiane, Kissinger got wind of it. Suddenly Kanitha showed up, established herself as a travel journalist with a handful of stories under her belt and latched on to you. When she thought I'd be more effective at shaking Weltmeister out of the trees, she latched on to me. A sleeper. She was waiting for him. They were waiting for him. You brought them both out into the open."

The Hmong-American looked at Maier in disbelief.

"Yes, I remember now. She asked me about the gold. Several times. And I told her about Weltmeister killing my family."

Maier nodded, glad his face was hidden in the dark. Everything became clear, and he liked the version of the truth that was about to establish itself in his head. He was smiling.

"You were the bait they used to reel my father in. The US want a closer working relationship in Indochina and the U48 had to be tracked down, its originator silenced."

"When did she die?"

"Four days ago, in Bangkok. In a corridor of the Oriental Hotel. She pulled a gun when Weltmeister intercepted the former US Secretary on his way to his suite."

Deep lines formed on Léon's forehead, threatening to tear him apart.

"Who killed her?"

"Julia Rendel."

Léon rolled his eyes. The expression in his face softened. They both knew that a speck of trust had been established between them.

"Why?"

"She's Weltmeister's adopted daughter."

"He was trying to make amends after killing his friend, that sleazy East German cultural attaché, here all those years ago?"

The Hmong-American didn't expect an answer.

Maier continued carefully, "Kanitha pulled a gun on my father. Julia walked past in a ball dress and stabbed her with a hairpin. I think my father played through every possibility in this scenario a thousand times. It was his last assignment. In its own cruel way, it was beautiful, elegant, sophisticated. It all looked so effortless. They are really good at killing people."

"Who was Kanitha working for?"

"She was the former US Secretary's PA. And perhaps girlfriend. Kissinger looked beside himself when she died."

In the pale light of the laptop screen, Léon looked like a convalescing ghost. He was almost convinced.

"She lived with me, on and off, for almost a year."

Maier looked at this child of the war, this man trapped by his violent history, his voice full of sorrow and doubt.

Léon understood Maier's look and faltered. Maier could tell when a man had been beaten. The detective relaxed slightly. The truth could bring almost anyone down to the wire.

"I know. She told me. One day at a time. It sounds different now to the way she said it then."

Léon sat down heavily on the edge of one of the metal bed frames.

"She played us?"

Maier nodded.

"And your old man, he played us, too. The CD is a blank."

Maier carefully moved around the Hmong and looked at the laptop screen. Léon was right. Maier could not bring himself to feel surprised. He'd not bothered to check the CD himself. When it came to his father, he had very little faith, tempered by a faint longing that receded with every breath he took. Still, he knew that his sense of loss, loss of something he'd never experienced in the first place, would never completely go away.

"Another ruse, then. Weltmeister is here, Léon, and he wants to kill you. He will kill you. He told me in Bangkok that he was tempted to kill me too, just to bring the story to a neat conclusion."

The Hmong-American shut down his computer and replaced it in his backpack.

"I don't really care about the CD. That file. I don't need it. Look at this."

He pulled a powerful torch from his bag, switched it on and pointed it into the hole underneath the bed frames.

"In '76, after your father shot me, my men pulled me out. They also pulled out my sister and the German diplomat. Both were dead. We left them lying right here on the beds, and the troops that were chasing us never bothered to move them. Nor did they ever find out what was underneath."

Maier looked around the room. The bodies had gone.

"So the gold is still down there?"

Léon nodded. "I buried them later, years later. Just out the back. Couldn't carry them very far. They share the same grave."

He flashed the beam around and got down on his knees.

"The gold is still here. My parents are still down there, too. Over the years, I managed to come back twice. To pay my respects and get some gold for my soldiers. And only I know about it. No one else does. Except Weltmeister, of course."

He clambered down into the hole. Maier looked at him impatiently.

"Léon, you are in serious trouble. You cannot take the gold with you to where you are going if my father catches you here."

The Hmong looked up at Maier.

"How many people have you killed since coming to Laos, Maier?"

"I killed two men in Thailand. In self-defense."

"Of course, Maier. I forgot. Thanks for reminding me. You have a life to live yet."

Léon laughed bitterly.

"You could go and live in the States–"

Léon cut him off. "In a fucking trailer, with eight other Hmong families, with the men drunk and unemployed, and I gotta sit and listen to them beating their wives and kids every night because they can't assimilate into the American Dream. Come on, Maier, I'm not stupid. There's no place in the sun for the undereducated bastard children of America."

He disappeared out of sight and the room plunged into almost complete darkness. Maier walked to one of windows. The sun had already sunk behind the mountain ridges to the west. It would be dark soon. It could get very dark in Long Cheng. Time was short. Always short.

"You know, Maier, I'm not a hundred percent sure about you. You turn up and warn me about your old man coming to take me out. And I can't fathom whether you are part of his scheme. Or maybe the bait. Like I was bait. I mean, these guys don't care. Your father doesn't care. The former US Secretary doesn't care. I believe your story about Kanitha. It makes sense. Why else would she hang around with two old sacks like us?"

Maier didn't feel as humble about himself as the Hmong did. Kissinger was considerably more advanced in age than either of them. But he also had more money, charm, a good tailor and a better sense of humor.

The detective kept his mouth shut and let Léon talk.

"So the fact that she is dead tells me that the former Secretary, the man who ultimately caused all this shit, is in pain right now. The man who pulled the strings on everyone including Weltmeister got what was coming to him. And one day, he will deal with true Hmong justice in the court of the afterlife. Weltmeister, too."

Maier wasn't sure. If there was one person in the world who could escape such a Hmong court of the afterlife, it was Weltmeister.

As Léon dropped down into the hole beneath the floor again, Maier opened his bag and pulled out two small packages that Mikhail had given him. He quickly laid them in the darkest corner of the room. There was no furniture or rubbish to hide them under.

Maier returned to the hole in the center of the room just as Léon heaved a gold bar onto the floor. It made a dull thud and kicked up a small dust of cloud.

"There's quite a bit of heroin down here too, but lots of the bags have split open. A real mess. How long does that stuff keep?"

"Forget about the gold and the drugs, Léon. You can come back for it another time. Think of a way to get yourself out of here alive."

The Hmong laughed. "Oh, that's easy. I just go with whatever arrangement you have made for your getaway."

"There's no room."

Léon slapped a second bar of gold onto the floor in front of Maier.

"Oh yes, there is. I just hoped you'd be clever enough to save a space for yourself."

FLYING WITHOUT A LICENSE

Maier stepped out of the building. He carried two gold bars in his backpack. They were so heavy, he could barely stand. He wore Léon's clothes.

"Well, Maier. My men are gone. And I will leave presently on a conveyance of your choice. And I bet you anything, somewhere out there in the hills, a sniper is getting his scope in focus, even as we speak. You're not so bad, Maier. Once your father has shot you, I consider us even. Weltmeister will have his moment of loss just as the Secretary did. Just like I did."

The Hmong-American looked ridiculous in Maier's far-too-large hippie shirt and vest. Maier wasn't sure the ruse would work. Léon pulled his gun and motioned the detective onto the runway. He scanned the hills, but he couldn't see anything but monochrome forest. His heart was heavy. He wanted the killing to stop and his father to crawl back under the stone he had emerged from. He didn't want to die, nor did he particularly want Léon, just another victim of the Secret War, to die. They had a lot in common. Old wars couldn't be won in the minds of old men who'd fought decades earlier.

Maier, wearing Léon's army boots, kicked some gravel across the runway. The light was fading quickly. Soon, he would no longer be a realistic target, even for the best sharpshooter in the world. Léon disappeared back inside the building. Maier thought of dumping the gold and running for it, but he didn't rate his chances of escape too high. Best to stick to the original, haphazard scenario he had cooked up with the Russian.

A white bird rose from a tree on a slope to his right and drifted down towards the detective. Everything was about to come to an end.

Léon emerged from the building once again, carrying a gold bar, dropping it by the side of the runway. He barely looked at the detective and went back inside for more.

Maier truly hated the kind of decisions he would have to make in the next few minutes. No matter what he did, it would make him feel worse afterwards. He couldn't see the Russian yet, but he could feel the sniper's rifle on him, caressing his form, settling for the weakest point. He felt the hair on his arms stand up.

"Still alive, Maier?"

Léon laughed as he emerged, sweating profusely, with another gold bar. Maier looked at him, feeling sorry for himself. The Hmong-American pulled his gun, a quite unnecessary gesture.

"Come on, Maier; give the old man a chance before it gets dark. He's only got a few more minutes to get a clean shot."

Maier smiled beatifically, holding his breath.

"Otherwise, I might be tempted to do it when your pickup gets here," Léon added, and left to pull more gold from his family grave.

For a second, total silence hung over the valley. Maier

looked up to see the white bird circle cautiously in the darkening sky, high above his head.

Everything was so broken.

The shot went straight into his back and propelled him forward. He hit the ground and lay on his side, helpless. Pain shot through him from all sides. Part of him had exploded. Maybe it had. Maybe he had gone into shock. Maybe everything was totally irrelevant. The rifle's echo made the bird soar away across the nearest ridge. In the same instant, he could hear a faint but quickly approaching buzzing sound. The cavalry was on its way. A tear dropped from his left eye onto the warm tarmac.

Weltmeister had shot his son.

The buzzing of the microlight quickly grew louder. Maier couldn't move. He was looking straight at the entrance to the building that contained half the bad dreams of the CIA's Secret War. He could see Léon emerge from the hole in the ground and, with some difficulty, lift a gold bar. For a second, the two men looked at each other. Like soul brothers, Maier thought. Léon smiled. He stood up and carried the gold bar onto the tarmac. The bullet hit him the very second the building exploded. The explosives Maier had left in the room had done the trick.

Maier turned his head away from the billowing smoke that quickly spread towards him and down the runway. The buzzing sound turned into a mechanical scream. Flames licked around him as the microlight touched down and rolled past. His ride had arrived. Mikhail climbed out of the tiny aircraft and ran across to Maier.

"All OK?"

Maier nodded weakly. "The good times are killing me."

"That's because your father shot you in the back."

"He thought I was someone else."

"No, he didn't."

The Russian pulled the heavy backpack off the detective's back and ripped it open. The sniper's bullet had buried itself deep into one of the gold bars that Maier had been wearing in lieu of a Kevlar jacket.

"Don't go soft on me now. You want to live, right?"

Maier managed to sit up. He shook his head. There was nothing left of the final resting place of Léon Sangster, his parents, and the bad dreams of Indochina. The building had disappeared. The explosive Mikhail had given to Maier had buried the U48, the file that probably no longer existed. Léon lay where he'd fallen, his legs crossed at an odd angle. The bullet had caught him in the back of the head and made a mess of things. The small pile of gold bars that lay by the runway looked pathetic, but Mikhail scooped the first one up and loaded it onto the small plane.

"How many of these can we take if we want to take off?"

"Just one or two. It doesn't matter. We need to leave. Weltmeister may think you are dead, but he is a cautious guy, and seeing the building explode, he might hang around to see what happens next. I don't think he saw me coming in with the microlight, but you never know. Though it's getting too dark to keep shooting at us now."

The Russian shrugged and came back to help Maier up.

"You're in shock. You know what we will have to do?"

The detective nodded. With Mikhail's help, he limped to the small plane and climbed into the passenger seat. The Russian dumped one of the bars of gold on Maier's lap and handed him a headset. After Maier had put his seat belt on, Mikhail pressed a piece of steel wire into his hands that led out of the cockpit down the side of the aircraft.

"When I say now, you yank that wire hard. Then we go home."

"What is it?"

"You'll see; it's the proverbial string that pulls it all together and tears it all apart, Maier."

SILENCE IS MY HOBBY

"So how was that, sleeping with my son?"

"You're jealous?"

"There's no one to be jealous about."

"He was actually pretty decent, as lonely and proud men can be."

The man called Weltmeister grinned into the coming cool evening. He felt tired. He looked back across Skyline Ridge one more time. The fireball was gone, but a huge plume of smoke and dust still billowed across the valley. It was getting too dark to see whether there was any movement on the runway.

He looked at Julia. He was late. Twenty-five years late. He took her hand and pulled her up. A last look into the valley. There could not be any survivors. Even if Maier or Léon had not been killed by his shots or the explosion, the Laotian troops would finish them off.

They started walking towards their jeep. He sped up. He knew she didn't mind the spring in his step. She started jogging beside him, full of the years he no longer had.

"What about Maier? Was that really necessary?" she asked when they reached the bottom of the hill.

Weltmeister snorted. "He was my son. That was always a thorn in my side. Kind of a loose end."

"Aren't you overdoing it a bit?"

He snapped around to her then, a white flame in his eyes. Julia shrank back and kept her distance.

"Hundred percent. It's the only way. I have little time left and I want it for us. With Bryson, my Vietnamese handler, Mr Mookie, and Daniels dead, Léon and Maier were the only guys still alive who could identify me. I couldn't let them live. It's against my principles."

She laughed drily and hooked her arm under his.

"Anybody ever tell you that you think too much, Sebastian?"

He smiled, not a care in the world. "Just call me Weltmeister."

In their green fatigues, they soon melted into the surrounding brush, barely visible for another few seconds, then they were gone.

OPERATION MENU

Maier could hear Mikhail singing as they picked up speed and bumped along the runway like a demented rabbit on wheels. An old song from Mother Russia. It sounded mad. He was mad. The world was mad.

A bullet zipped past the glass cockpit. The microlight raced towards the karst stone formations at the end of the runway. Maier thought he could see shadows by the side of the tarmac. Laotian troops. The aircraft wobbled and left the ground, and Maier heard the Russian yank the stick with a sickening crunch to get the plane to rise and turn quickly into the coming night.

They were away. As they rose from the valley, the sun's last rays caressed the ridges in golden light. The former airbase below had already sunk into obscure darkness. Maier felt volatile in the tiny bouncing capsule, but it was a definite improvement to lying on the tarmac below.

"The shots that got you and Léon came from the east, so we'll buzz over there and take a look. They wouldn't have walked very far. We have about twenty minutes' worth of fuel, then we need to turn and make our way to Thailand." "You don't think we'll get scrambled by the Laotian air force?"

Mikhail laughed loud enough to almost shatter Maier's eardrums.

"Air force? There's a good reason why not a single plane has taken off from Long Cheng for twenty-five years. Their planes are all wrecked. We will have more to worry about when we cross into Thai airspace later."

Maier, glad to be putting some distance between himself and his family, wondered about the Russian's motivation to save him.

"What would you have done if things hadn't worked out and Mr Mookie had ordered you to kill me?"

The Russian chuckled into Maier's headset.

"I always finish the job and I never cheat the client, Maier. It's nothing personal, trust me. You are my favorite heterosexual friend. We're both from the East. I love you like my brother. In future, I will refuse any job that involves the assassination of Detective Maier. I promise. Anyhow, my client is dead and gone, and I don't care for Cold War secrets. I have my career to take care of."

They left the valley and flew over dense forest. The Russian brought the plane down low over the trees. Quite suddenly, Maier could make out a road beneath them.

It was almost too dark to make out anything moving down there, but Mikhail swooped lower and Maier spotted the headlights of the jeep before the Russian did. He held his breath. It was his father's getaway car. As they passed low, really low, he could see Julia open the door, lean out and fire her revolver at them. She looked beautiful, proud, and unhinged. She was his father's true child. He felt no jealousy.

"We will turn and come up behind them once more," Mikhail cackled into the headphones. He made a wide swoop upwards above the trees and turned the plane around. Five minutes later, they were back chasing the tail lights of Weltmeister's jeep.

"When I shout 'Go', you yank the cord, OK? It's not much, but it's also everything."

Maier nodded half-heartedly, to himself. The philosophical Russian dropped the plane, its engine buzzing like a sick hornet.

"Go."

They passed the jeep. Maier didn't touch the cord. He tried to turn, but all he could see was the bright flash of the exploding vehicle.

They flew on in near silence.

Mikhail shouted, "That was your chance to get even, to make peace with yourself. And you made me pull the damn cord. You left it to the professional."

The Russian roared with laughter.

Maier looked down at his two metal fingers. As his eyes drifted to the landscape below, the small aircraft banked, and the earth fell away from them in a flamboyant swoop. He inhaled deeply, suddenly thinking of the job done, of new beginnings, and of freshly squeezed orange juice and quality vodka. For a moment, he was free.

"This family holiday really took it out of me. I am tempted to celebrate. And to retire."

The Russian shouted, "No problem, my German friend; I will take your job."

ACKNOWLEDGMENTS

I first visited Laos in 2001, to research ideas for a documentary. I trekked with bush meat hunters, drifted through opium fields, and rode long tail boats along fantastically remote rivers. The markets were full of animals I had never seen (and bat doesn't taste good). With my wife Aroon and my brother Marc, I visited the Plain of Jars, a remote highland in the northeast of the country shaped like a giant's golf course, dotted in bomb craters, walked through villages built from American UXO (unexploded ordnance) – in this near silent land, a secret war had left deep traces. I kept hearing about the mythical US airstrip of Long Cheng, a secret former CIA base deep in the Laotian jungles north of the capital Vientiane.

Long Cheng served as the base of a covert military campaign against communist forces in Laos from the mid-60s to the early 70s and, for a while, was the world's busiest airport. Despite US President Kennedy's assurance that Laos was neutral and that no US forces were present in the country, the CIA recruited men from local minorities and trained an army of 30,000 mercenaries under the guidance of American field agents and Thai border police to fight the Pathet Lao. The population of Long Cheng, a city not connected to the rest of the country by road, swelled to some 50,000 people. At the same time, the CIA-owned airline Air America assisted local warlords and Laotian military with the purchase and transportation of opium, much of which was turned to heroin and sold to American soldiers in Vietnam. Most of the mercenaries recruited by the US, some as young as 14, were killed, and eventually the CIA abandoned its airbase and many of its local allies.

In the later stages of the war, the US dropped more bombs on Laos than the combined load of all munitions dropped on Europe and the Pacific theatre during World War II, making the country one of the most heavily bombed in the world. To this day, Laotians lose limbs and lives to unexploded ordnance which litters the countryside.

This story is the subject of the 2008 documentary *The Most Secret Place on Earth*, a European co-production for arte, WDR, NDR and Discovery Campus, directed by my brother Marc Eberle. Marc and I wrote the screenplay. The secret war also provides the historical framework for *The Man with the Golden Mind*.

I wrote and edited *The Man with the Golden Mind* at Z Hotel, Puri, India, at Les Manguiers in Kampot, Cambodia, and on Ko Panghan, Thailand.

Many thanks to my family, my wife Aroon Thaewchatturat, Marc Eberle, Hans Kemp, the Puri gang: Debu, Chico, Kaka, Lala, Bainah, Claire and Pulak, to everyone at the Z., to Harry and Liam, Fred Branfman, and Sousath Pethrasy (RIP).

Thanks to Mick Bradley for advice on weapons.

Thanks to Emlyn Rees for another wonderful edit, to Bryon Quertermous for pulling it all together, to Caroline Lambe for her wonderful promo efforts and to the team at Exhibit A.

Maier will return in *The Monsoon Ghost Image*